TOURQUAI

Also by Tim Davys

AMBERVILLE
LANCEHEIM

TOURQUAI

A NOVEL

TIM DAVYS

HARPER

An Imprint of HarperCollins*Publishers*
www.harpercollins.com

TOURQUAI. Copyright © 2011 by Tim Davys Corporation. All rights reserved. Printed in the United States of America. No part of this book may be used or reproduced in any manner whatsoever without written permission except in the case of brief quotations embodied in critical articles and reviews. For information, address HarperCollins Publishers, 10 East 53rd Street, New York, NY 10022.

HarperCollins books may be purchased for educational, business, or sales promotional use. For information, please write: Special Markets Department, HarperCollins Publishers, 10 East 53rd Street, New York, NY 10022.

First published in Swedish in 2009 by Albert Bonniers Förlag.

FIRST U.S. EDITION

Translated by Paul Norlen

Library of Congress Cataloging-in-Publication Data is available upon request.

ISBN: 978-0-06-179745-3

11 12 13 14 15   OV/RRD   10 9 8 7 6 5 4 3 2 1

TOURQUAI

PROLOGUE

The stuffed animal was shaking. Brief intervals of intense muscle spasms. Tears were running down its cheeks, or maybe it was sweat dripping from its forehead. The ground seemed to quake under its paws, and despite strenuous attempts, the stuffed animal found it impossible to focus its gaze on the tasteful wall-to-wall carpeting. The black squares against the blue ground were an elusive, frustrating target. Its head ached. Its brain was about to explode. There was a sound, high-pitched and shrill, that refused to stop. Its stomach was churning with nausea. And the stuffed animal hardly dared breathe—the Hated One was sitting only a few feet away.

How long had the stuffed animal stood hidden in the darkness? Eternities, it felt like. And what was waiting? What was expected? It was just barely possible to formulate these questions; the answers felt far away. And in this infinity of meditative futility—as the alcohol sank and rose in its body in an incomprehensible rhythm, and thoughts refused to make sense—suddenly the weapon was resting in its paw.

How did that happen? At that moment it was impossible to say, but there was a meaning. There was always a meaning, even if we didn't always see it, thought the stuffed animal. And again hatred welled up in its throat. Like a sour belch burning its palate. Wrath transformed its eyes to narrow slits and the nose wrinkled in a contorted expression of struggle. It could not be withstood, it was simply not possible.

Suddenly the darkness no longer shielded, suddenly the stuffed animal took a step forward. How did that happen? The weapon was raised, as if someone else were doing it. And in that moment time stood still, one moment away from an action that would irretrievably redefine a life. That soul would be darkened forever, and no forgiveness was possible. Yet there was no hesitation, no regret, not then. The stuffed animal did not want anything other than to separate the Hated One's head from his body. Regardless of the consequences, regardless of what this would mean.

"Swine."

That thought was screaming in its head just as the blow fell.

DAY ONE

1.1

The black plastic telephone that was on the desk when Larry Bloodhound took possession of the office many years ago had been exchanged for a modern version, a technical monstrosity that rang with high-pitched, aggressive signals. A digital display didn't make you a better cop, thought Larry. He refused to pick up the receiver; it wasn't often that anyone had anything interesting to say.

The superintendent sat rocking in the chair with his muddy paws on the desk. Confidential documents lay strewn across the desk. A rotting apple core was balanced on the computer keyboard, a half-eaten doughnut was stuffed into a pencil holder, and sticking up from the wastebasket was a half-empty package of ginger snaps. Throughout his adult life he had struggled with his weight. He liked food but didn't want to get fat. It was easy for him to gain a few pounds, but hard to get rid of them again. He tried rotation diets, weighed food on a little scale, and put his hope in low-calorie magazine meal plans, but the results were always the same. These self-inflicted reductions made him hungrier than ever, and that forced him to eat in secret. In the desk drawers, among papers next to the computer, inside seemingly thick binders, and behind many of the odd objects on the bookshelf half-eaten packages of crackers and cookies, candy, and chocolate were concealed. In the office, in the corner behind the door, hidden for more than a week now under a long scarf, there was also half a pizza, which his conscience wouldn't allow him to finish. Perhaps there was even an unfinished lunch in the mess somewhere. Saving and hiding food was an instinct that Bloodhound no longer thought about; everything got eaten up sooner or later.

The phone continued to ring.

Bloodhound was sitting in semidarkness—the blinds on the window overlooking the parking lot were pulled down—bored and staring at the computer screen, but all he saw was his own reflection. His dark brown cotton covering hung in bags from the cheeks and neck, the deep creases in his head were never smoothed out, and his long ears rested like epaulettes on his shoulders. Larry focused his gaze, observing the background image he had loaded into the computer. A faint smile was observable on his face. Cordelia. She was the apple of his eye. She was his only weakness. She was his caged bird, something as uncommon as a budgie. Not many stuffed animals in Mollisan Town had house pets—Bloodhound could not think of any offhand—and so he kept Cordelia a secret. He had many enemies, and in his profession it was best not to leave any openings.

For the fourth day in a row Larry Bloodhound had put on a wrinkled, white and blue striped shirt. The rings of sweat under his arms had worked their way into the cloth. His pistol holster sat loosely strapped across his chest. Larry did not use the recommended service weapon; instead he carried a large-bore revolver. Rumor had it that he shot with jacketed bullets. If that were true, he could blow a hole in a safe deposit vault if he fired the weapon.

The phone was still ringing.

"Even if I have a lot to learn, at least I understand this. If you pick up the phone, it stops ringing . . ."

Bloodhound heard the comment through the gap in the door. That had not been the intent. Falcon Ècu had been mumbling to himself, the words tumbling out of his beak without his wanting them to. It would be easier, of course, for Larry not to let on that he heard. Inspector Ècu's desk in the open office area was closest to Bloodhound's door on the fourth floor at the rue de Cadix police station. The WE squad had the entire floor, and Larry was the head of the department. He could sympathize with Falcon to a certain degree: Who wouldn't be irritated by the sharp ring tone? But at the same time, he couldn't let the comment pass unnoticed. Someone has to teach the newcomer some manners. With an exasperated grunt, Larry remembered that Anna Lynx, Falcon's experienced partner, had the morning off.

He reached for the receiver and brought it up under his ear.

"Bloodhound."

"Superintendent Bloodhound?"

"Yes?" growled the superintendent.

"Superintendent," said the voice, obviously affected, a he trying to sound like a she, "superintendent, a murder has been committed, and—"

"And what little asshole do I have the pleasure of speaking with?" Bloodhound asked nicely.

"That doesn't matter. The essential thing is that—"

"Which wretched little cripple with imitation leather paws is chirping on my telephone?"

"But, Superintendent," the voice objected, "the important thing is—"

"Now I'm hanging up, you crazy asshole," Bloodhound informed him and slammed down the phone.

With some weariness he got up, kicked over the waste basket to avoid being tempted by ginger snaps, and took a big step over it. He opened the office door and looked out over the department—his domain. The building on light brown rue de Cadix had originally been a hospital, with rows of sewing machines firmly bolted to the massive concrete floor. The original floor was still there, only partially covered by narrow, worn, black linoleum mats of varying lengths lying in all directions under the desks. The windows facing the street were tall, dirty, and permanently shut; the steel beams on which the floors of the building rested were black and massive, like thick tree trunks that disappeared up into the slightly psychotic system of exposed ventilation pipes and drainage barrels on the roof. The light fixtures hung low, placed over the desks to start with, but after a series of furniture rearrangements were now in an incomprehensibly asymmetric pattern. In this chaos there were approximately fifty-five workstations, fifteen more than what the unions had approved at one time, and when Bloodhound appeared in the doorway to his office, the sound of a collective inhalation was heard. It was not only the superintendent who had heard Falcon's unintentional complaint.

"What was that?" insisted Larry.

Inspector Ècu normally made a point of standing up for what he thought and believed, but he was no fool. Bloodhound's growling wheeze caused the falcon to close his beak and lower his gaze to the binder open before him. Falcon had been working at the station on rue de Cadix in the Tourquai section of Mollisan Town for less than a year. After having started his career with the GL squad at one of the smaller stations in Amberville, he had been relocated, at his own request, to WE in Tourquai after six months. Here he got the notorious Superintendent Larry Bloodhound for a boss.

"I heard something," Bloodhound said, "and it sounded just like when my grandma stuck her udder in the mangle. Or when my dad ate beans and soiled himself. But it came out of your beak, didn't it?"

Falcon glanced up. He looked terrified. The constant

murmur that ran through the office area had died out completely. Everyone was listening.

"Now, I picked up the phone." The superintendent nodded. "Exactly like you wanted. I picked up the damn phone. And to what use?"

Falcon was painfully aware that everyone around was listening.

"Mm," he managed to say.

"Every day they call," Bloodhound continued. "Sick monstrosities, factory defects, that's what they are. Confess and say they're sorry. And I have to listen."

"It was absolutely not my intention to . . . I didn't mean to . . ."

But Falcon's excuses were interrupted by the phone inside Bloodhound's office, which began to ring again. The superintendent stared at his inspector.

"If I want to know what you think about me," said Bloodhound in his friendliest voice, "I'm going to ask. 'Nice little falcon,' maybe I'll say, 'tell me what you think about me.'"

There was giggling now around the office. Falcon looked down again at his binder.

"Until then," Bloodhound barked, "you shut up!"

And with these words the superintendent returned to his office and grabbed the telephone.

"YES?"

It was the same disguised voice.

"Don't hang up!"

"Why the hell not?" the superintendent growled.

"Because it's true," said the voice. "A murder has been committed. A vulture is sitting in—"

Bloodhound hung up.

"That was an insistent little asshole," he muttered to himself, leaning across the desk to grab the apple fritter he had bought that morning, taken only one guilt-ridden bite of, and then hidden somewhere in the folder of "Ongoing Investigations."

It was getting close to lunch and Bloodhound felt the great hunger come creeping.

Larry Bloodhound had taken the long career route and patrolled the streets of northwest Tourquai for upward of a decade. By the end, he had stepped on every painted cobblestone so many times that he knew them all, and at the same time had thrown every petty pile-of-cloth criminal in jail so many times that he often mixed them up. Then it was no longer possible to resist the offer of a promotion, even though Bloodhound's contempt for "desk cops" was well founded and monumental. Nevertheless he let himself be appointed inspector, and later superintendent at WE. He promised himself not to decline into the sort of tired laziness—or bitter resignation—to which he had seen so many capable police officers capitulate. The temperament that made him famous was also his salvation; it kept him from becoming complacent.

Now he'd been at the office more than twice as long as he had patrolled, but it was still out on the streets where Larry felt most at home. The district was full of his ant tunnels, every doorway reminded him of a crime, every street corner of a mistake. Bloodhound considered it an honor to remain humble; only that way did you survive.

"Excuse me, Superintendent," said Falcon Ècu, rousing Bloodhound from his daydreams.

The inexperienced inspector had dared open the door to the superintendent's office, and now he was peeking in.

"What?"

"I beg your pardon terribly, Superintendent," Falcon repeated. "But . . ."

It was not Bloodhound who had picked Falcon Ècu. Anna Lynx had needed a new partner since the weasel moved to PAS in Amberville, and the personnel department brought in Ècu because he was next in line.

"I know it's not my concern . . . but we've received a tip, Superintendent," said Falcon.

His short plastic beak with the characteristic overbite was shiny and newly cleaned, a light blue shirt with an open collar contrasted with his pale pink neck and gray-speckled plumage.

"A tip?" the superintendent repeated mockingly.

"A murder has been committed. Supposedly we'll find the victim at his office. One Oswald Vulture. The company is called Nova Park. Vulture's the owner. They're located on the top floor of the Bourg Villette."

"Top floor?"

"Sixty-second floor."

"A vulture?" asked the superintendent.

"That's what the tipster said."

"The tipster," said the superintendent, "knew that it wouldn't work to shit in my ear and realized that there were others who would gladly accept it."

Falcon did not answer.

Bloodhound sighed but got up.

"Okay," he said. "Perseverance wins. I'll go along."

Superintendent Bloodhound drove. It was the first time he'd been alone with Falcon Ècu in the car; Anna Lynx had always been along otherwise, as a kind of diplomat and interpreter.

"Has she taken the whole day off?" he asked, without turning his head to meet Falcon's gaze.

"She might make it in this afternoon," Falcon replied. "Do you want me to call her, Superintendent? Because I can just—"

"No, no," Bloodhound growled. "I was just wondering."

They were driving in an unmarked Volga. It had the same engine as the painted police cars but was a discreet gray and without any distinctive markings at all. Which made it strangely conspicuous. The superintendent revved the engine at the red light, but then silence fell. He cheered himself up and made an attempt.

"I see," he growled. "I hear you'll be playing this afternoon?"

"It's just for fun," Falcon answered quickly. "That is, everyone plays so well. I just show up to . . . for the exercise. I've only been playing a few years. I can top my forehand nicely, but my slice isn't at all what I'd—"

"I don't know a thing about tennis," Bloodhound interrupted. "Looks like a sport for queers, if you ask me."

"I see," Falcon answered quietly. "No, tennis is actually a lot of fun, Superintendent, you should—"

Bloodhound belched. Concealed in this abysmal sound were odors from what he'd eaten that morning, including the oregano on the old pizza in the corner behind the door. Falcon fell silent; there was nothing more to say.

The traffic through Tourquai's business district was intense; it was Monday, right before lunch. The Boulevard had eight lanes, but in dense traffic no one cared about the lanes, not even when the drivers were crowded next to a police car. Bloodhound controlled himself and was content to hiss curses at his fellow drivers.

Oil black Boulevard de la Villette was bordered by skyscrapers unlike any others in Mollisan Town; central Tourquai was a pincushion of money and hubris. These towers of vanity were never renovated, they were simply torn down and rebuilt. With garages that branched out like roots deep under the asphalt of the streets, and on the roofs feelers in the form of blinking antennae and radio pylons that strove even higher up into the sky, the buildings formed a kind of living organism.

The superintendent did not feel at home this far south in the district. A different type of criminality occupied these towers. Here the battle between good and evil was fought out via computer keyboards, here the victor was the one who had the most expensive lawyers. Larry had no scruples, but the atmosphere made him uncomfortable.

For several years 365 Boulevard de la Villette had been Bourg Villette's address. The building was one of the most pretentious to go up during the latest building boom. It had sixty-some floors in a narrowing silhouette of dark, almost black, glass and gleaming steel; a projectile from the planet's interior.

In violation of any number of traffic laws, Superintendent Bloodhound parked on the sidewalk outside the main entrance. He took the short staircase up to the entry in a few bounds, and the glass doors—so large they really ought to be called glass walls—slid open without a sound. Ècu was one step behind.

Bloodhound had never been inside Bourg Villette before, and the sight of the lobby took him by surprise. It was as big as a bathhouse, with floors and walls clad in glistening black marble. The only piece of furniture was a reception counter, also of black marble, behind which sat an old frog dressed in some type of uniform. The frog looked up with surprise when the two police officers came in, as if he had been napping. Bloodhound identified himself.

"Nova Park?" he growled.

"The elevators in the last row," replied the frog, nodding toward the corridors with elevators. "Sixty-second floor."

There was a bowl of throat lozenges on the frog's counter, and Bloodhound took a moment to fill one of his jacket pockets before he signaled to Falcon to follow him to the elevators.

"This is rather impressive," Ècu whispered as they walked across the glassy floor. "All of it."

Even though they were alone, it felt natural to whisper.

"It's so pretentious it makes your mother look like a fine lady," Bloodhound growled.

Falcon decided not to start any more conversations with the superintendent for the time being.

Signs embossed with gilded numerals indicated that the elevators in the last row took visitors to floors forty through sixty-two.

"Hope no one's afraid of heights," Bloodhound muttered, pushing the button.

Personally he always had been.

Nova Park's reception was directly opposite the elevators on the sixty-second-floor landing. Neither Falcon nor Bloodhound had heard of the company before, and despite an attempt to get information during the brief car ride, they had not become much wiser. All they knew was that it was a financial company, but that was true for most of the operations in this part of the city.

The reception was soberly elegant: leather armchairs and dark red wall-to-wall carpeting, round cherrywood tables where there were financial magazines to read while you were waiting. But it was the view that took the visitors' breath away. Far below the floor-to-ceiling tinted windows lay south Tourquai, and you could see still farther than that, all the way down to Amberville.

"Amazing, isn't it?" said the receptionist, a young goat.

It was not meant as a courtesy; it was blatantly condescending. Bloodhound made an unfathomable grimace and again took out his police badge.

"Oswald Vulture," he growled, and his voice was harsher than usual.

"Have you made an appointment?" asked the goat, studiously avoiding looking at Bloodhound's extended badge.

"How fucking stupid do we look?" said Bloodhound.

The goat nodded, indicating the long corridor that started where the reception counter ended.

"Miss Cobra is in the office at the end of the corridor," he said.

The corridor must have been fifty feet long and was flanked by closed black doors with discreet name plates. There was a faint odor of lemon. The lighting was subdued, and the wall-to-wall carpet absorbed the sound of the police officers' steps. It was like walking through a dream. The door that formed the end of the corridor said "Emanuelle Cobra."

Without knocking, Bloodhound went in.

"Oswald Vulture?" he said.

The cobra sitting behind the desk gave them a wry smile.

"Do I look like an Oswald?" she asked with a hiss.

The office was yet another waiting room, a kind of drawing room, and the cobra was the most beautiful reptile Larry Bloodhound could recall ever seeing. Her eyes were large as a deer's, and instead of cloth she was made of black latex. The blouse she was wearing was white and almost transparent, and all of her glistened enticingly in the glow of the inset spotlights in the ceiling.

Bloodhound was distracted and did not answer, so Falcon felt obliged to say something.

"No," he said, "no, you absolutely do not look like an Oswald."

The cobra had an enchanting effect on Inspector Ècu; he was bewitched.

"Unfortunately, Vulture does not receive unannounced visitors," Emanuelle Cobra informed them, moistening the tip of her tail between her lips in a studied manner. "But I will happily schedule a time for you."

Falcon stood motionless, staring at this secretary as though she were one of Magnus's marvels. Larry Bloodhound sighed deeply—unclear really about what—and went over to the doors to Vulture's office with determined steps.

"Stop," said Cobra. "You can't—"

But Bloodhound's paw was already on the handle. Cobra

crawled away from the desk, Ècu followed the superintendent, and thus all three of them were standing at the door to Vulture's office when Bloodhound opened it.

The sight was macabre.

Behind an oversized desk, in a chair high enough to resemble a throne, sat Oswald Vulture, straight-backed. He was wearing a dark jacket with narrow white stripes, white shirt, and a wide, red silk tie. His wings were resting against the desk pad as if he were waiting for someone to set out food for him.

But where Oswald Vulture's head had been, only a few tufts of cotton were sticking up.

1.2

Emanuelle Cobra screamed.

A scream of terror and surprise. Then she turned around on the tip of her tail and fell into Falcon Ècu's wings. Impulsively he closed them around her.

"Shit your pants," Bloodhound growled to himself. "Shit your pants."

This was an expression of surprise.

The superintendent suddenly forgot the seductive cobra and the imposing office. His professional role absorbed him, experience took over, and he stepped heavily onto the dark blue wall-to-wall carpet. First impressions were important. He sniffed the room. He held his breath and observed the calm surrounding him. The lack of movement in the oversized office. The old-fashioned solemnity of the furnishings. Heavy curtain arrangements from floor to ceiling, two suits of armor between the windows, the crystal chandelier that seemed to sway freely from the double-high ceiling. The aroma of flowers and cleanser that concealed the hint of cigar smoke. The faint murmur of the air-conditioning.

Slowly Bloodhound approached the desk where the headless vulture was sitting.

"Are you calling?" he said to Falcon without turning around. "We need to cordon off the lobby down there and take all the witness statements up here. Tech Department, call directly to Derek. And forensics from place St.-Fargeau . . . but let's wait to inform Buck."

Jan Buck was the newly appointed captain at the police station on rue de Cadix, a career bureaucrat without experience in police work. He was not the first chief for whom Bloodhound felt deep contempt, and he would not be the last.

As he continued to survey the scene, it was the neatness that struck him, the overwhelming orderliness of the office.

"Pedantry, huh?" said the superintendent.

But Falcon was already on the phone, busy ordering up the personnel that Bloodhound had just asked for.

"Not even a shitty little booger on the carpet," Bloodhound mumbled to himself. "Not a speck of dust. If it were possible, you'd think the vulture himself had nicely and neatly cut his own head off . . ."

From the corner of his eye he saw the falcon move to the other side of the room.

"Don't touch a thing," the superintendent growled. "Not a thing."

"Absolutely not, Superintendent," Falcon replied. "I mean, that is . . . absolutely. I won't touch anything."

But Larry Bloodhound was in deep concentration and ignored the nervous inspector. The cobra had recovered and was back at her desk, sitting, in shock. Now Bloodhound had a few minutes to himself to see the entirety of the crime, try to sense the context. By this afternoon most everything in this elegant office would have been inspected and moved around. Connections and theories, times and motives would soon be established, an endless series of possibilities. It was then that Bloodhound must be able to return to these minutes, to this initial scene, undisturbed by knowledge, to avoid getting lost among the details.

"Shut your beak now, Falcon," the superintendent said calmly. "Now we're just going to look and remember."

The office was about three hundred square feet. The desk stood to the left of the window. The headless vulture sat with his back to the view. On the opposite wall was a sofa and a built-in bookcase.

Nothing suggested that any violence had occurred. Nothing even suggested that there had been a visitor here. A faint scent of cologne, true, but Bloodhound sensed that it was Vulture's own.

There was a door on the opposite side. Bloodhound went up to it, placed a handkerchief over the handle, and opened. The door led into a large bathroom with a hand basin and drying cabinet. The toilet was located next to a panorama window with almost the same view as from the reception desk. Bloodhound looked more closely at the window and determined that it could not be opened. Those were the building standards—all windows above the fortieth floor were permanently closed.

Larry Bloodhound stepped back into the office. In other words, there was only one way in to Vulture. The murderer must have come in through the door from the secretary's office, and he must have gone out through the same door.

Inspector Ècu was standing less than a yard from the desk, staring at the dead stuffed animal on the chair. It was the first time he had seen a headless animal, and he could not tear his gaze away from it. Not at all the loose-limbed piece of cloth he had expected. On the contrary, it was easy to imagine this vulture alive. Perhaps that was due to the headless vulture's sitting position, so upright and resolute.

"Don't touch a thing," Bloodhound reminded.

The superintendent went over to Vulture. The scent of cologne got stronger here; Bloodhound had been right when he assumed the aroma came from the victim.

"Forgive me for saying this," said Falcon, "but doesn't he look alive?"

It was as if Vulture were still sitting there, working, but without a head. Bloodhound grunted in agreement. The superintendent tried to imagine himself in the chair, sitting and working as Vulture must have been. Where would the center of gravity be, how would the shoulders be placed in relation to the trunk? `

Had the murder been committed somewhere else? With some effort Bloodhound got his large body down on all fours and inspected the victim's expensive black shoes. There were no signs of dragging, neither on the carpet nor on the shoes. And if someone had carried the body and tried to re-create a natural sitting position, how would that look? Not like this, the superintendent felt sure.

There were shaky letters written on the paper lying in front of Oswald Vulture on the desk pad. Bloodhound leaned over and read. A "C," an "M," and the word "ROD." The only way this could be interpreted was that the victim himself had written it. The pen that had presumably been used was still lying on the paper.

Was this a message, an attempt to expose the murderer? Or was it only chance, something Vulture was working on when he unexpectedly had his head removed?

Other than this piece of paper the desk was unnaturally tidy, Bloodhound thought. Pictures of the wife and son stood in two beautiful silver frames; there was something about the arrangement that bothered the superintendent, but he could not decide what it was. The computer sat to the left, a large screen on a futuristically designed stand, and alongside, to the right of the keyboard, a small laptop computer. Penholder and desk pad, but no plastic sleeves or folders with papers. Bloodhound did not open the drawers; better to let the animals from tech take care of that.

The cut itself, the decapitation, Bloodhound hardly gave a glance to. There were experts at forensics that could write a book based on this cut.

Voices were heard out in reception, and both Falcon and Bloodhound gave a start.

"Go out and meet them," the superintendent ordered.

Without a word Inspector Ècu took off, and the superintendent went slowly back toward the sofa. The bookcase was filled with books. On a wider shelf in line with the back of the couch were decorative objects. Glass sculptures that Bloodhound recognized, a few small goblets, a globe that seemed to be upside down: Mollisan Town below and the forest on the globe's northern half.

The lowest part of the bookcase consisted of closed cabinets. With some experience in similar offices, Bloodhound doubted whether there was anything in those cabinets. That, too, the Tech Department could find out. The superintendent could see for himself that the cushions on the couch and armchair indicated that someone had actually sat there today.

Then the room was full of animals.

The head of the Forensics Department at place St.-Fargeau, Theodore Tapir, came sauntering in along with his team.

"Larry!" he called happily. "None of yours are here? Where's Derek?"

Falcon appeared in the doorway.

"Derek and tech will be here in a few minutes," he reported. "And the building's cordoned off down by the elevators."

Derek Hare always arrived last at the crime scene. He was responsible for the Technical Department at rue de Cadix, and a test of wills had been going on between him and Tapir for many years. Sometimes it felt playful, other times the opposite.

"Shut up now, you long-nosed moth nest," Bloodhound

growled amiably at the forensic doctor, "and be a little helpful instead."

"I know what you intend to say," said Tapir. "Because you always say the same thing."

"Animal of science and mind reader at the same time," the superintendent called out. "Theodore, you never cease to amaze me."

"You want an approximate point in time to work with, don't you, Larry?" said Tapir. "You want me to say when this vulture lost his head before I've had time to find that out. And I'm going to say that you'll have to wait, that I have to do my job. And you're going to nag. And finally I'll give you an approximate time because I'll be tired of your nagging. I've gotten too old to argue with you."

"You've gotten old," Bloodhound growled, "exactly like me. But we do get a little wiser with the years, don't we? Ècu, let's turn this crime scene over to the pros."

And with that the superintendent left the room. Falcon followed closely behind him.

1.3

Superintendent Larry Bloodhound stopped at a Springer-gaast convenience store on the way out to Le Vezinot and bought a chocolate bar. It was a new kind, called Mammoth, because it was so large; dark chocolate around honey-rolled almonds and small bits of marshmallow. The fog was on its way into Mollisan Town. Bloodhound saw white veils forming over the clear blue horizon, and he leaned against the car and unwrapped the colorful paper. The aroma of chocolate filled his nose. The week before, he had finished a diet based on avoiding carbohydrates. For ten days he had followed—to the extent that it was reasonable at least—a carefully designed diet program that guaranteed weight loss of more than twenty pounds. Bloodhound didn't own a scale—he wasn't a masochist—but nonetheless he felt satisfied with the results. There was reason to celebrate a little today. With a Mammoth, to start with.

The superintendent had left Falcon Ècu on Boulevard de la Villette and was on his way out to Oswald Vulture's newly made widow. Talking with family members was something he had never learned to handle. He was not a savage. His manner was perhaps on the coarse side and he drooled a good deal when he was eating, but deep down he was a sensitive soul. The growling surface was only a façade, you might say. Meeting families crushed by sorrow, unexpectedly met by brutal violence, was an ordeal. And then, in their private moment of anxiety and emptiness, to get them to talk, to contribute something to the police investigation, was a balancing act that Bloodhound seldom managed very well.

Saliva mixed with chocolate was about to run down the corner of his mouth, and he dried it off with the sleeve of his jacket. The sleeve, he discovered, reeked of sausage, and he suddenly longed for a bratwurst. He ate up the last piece of chocolate and jumped into the car.

It was hardly surprising that the Vulture family lived in Le Vezinot. The prosperous western suburb, right at the edge of Tourquai, was the obvious choice for stuffed animals who wanted to show off their recently acquired fortunes. With every new generation of merchants and entrepreneurs, the houses grew larger and more elaborate. They were torn down and rebuilt, torn down and rebuilt, and nowadays nothing but short driveways remained of the yards behind the dense hedges that prevented animals from peeking in from the street.

Vulture and his wife lived in a villa that imitated a Tourquaian temple from the fifteenth century. Towers and pinnacles, narrow windows that resembled arrow slits in a fortress, and a kind of symbolic moat over which the superintendent passed on an arched stone bridge. It was not just tasteless, it was incomprehensible as well.

Bloodhound rang the doorbell, and the sound of a massive church bell was heard from inside the house. It took a minute or two before a reindeer dressed in livery opened and asked what he wanted.

"I'm here to see . . . uh . . . the widow," Bloodhound growled. "I believe that an Emanuelle Cobra called to let you know?"

For a moment the reindeer appeared to faint, but then he

opened the door. He led the superintendent through a bare hallway that smelled of stone and dampness. At the end of the hall they turned off to the right, entering a library where a fire was crackling in an open fireplace, even though it was the middle of the day. The superintendent sat down at a respectful distance from the dangerous sparks of the fire.

"Mrs. Flamingo will join you shortly," the reindeer said and left.

It took almost half an hour before the newly widowed bird condescended to appear.

During that time, Bloodhound was able to determine that none of the thousands of books on the lovely oak shelves had ever been opened, only the finest sorts of alcohol were in the bar cabinet (and all were nearly empty), and one of the five bridge trays he found in the drawer in the coffee table was set up so that the home pair would almost certainly make five diamonds or three no trumps. He didn't know which made him most depressed.

"I'm sorry," said Irina Flamingo as she made her entrance, "but I thought he meant you were sitting in the other library."

The superintendent growled something vaguely, held out his police badge to identify himself, and mumbled his condolences.

"Yes, now there's the money without the corresponding vulture," Flamingo replied cryptically, stumbling as she walked into the room but managing to avoid falling by sitting on the armchair across from the superintendent.

"Didn't you get anything to drink?" she added with dismay.

Bloodhound shook his head, and Irina raised her voice to call to the reindeer, who appeared in the doorway at once.

"Two cups of tea, please," she said. "Do you take milk, Superintendent?"

Bloodhound loathed tea but nodded anyway.

"No milk," he said. "But perhaps a cookie?"

The reindeer's expression did not indicate whether he even registered the suggestion. He left without a sound.

Irina Flamingo was like a caricature of a rich housewife in a successful male's first marriage. The flamingo's compact upper body was dressed in a white, broad jacket with big black buttons. This meant that she appeared rounder than she presumably was. Her pink legs had become somewhat crooked over the years. The long beak was painted in a bright red lipstick, and someone had recently plucked her eyebrows in a manner that made her resemble a bird of prey.

To top it off she was clearly inebriated. Whether it was from alcohol or sedatives was difficult to determine, but her fine-motor ability was not functioning, and the vacant smile she showed Bloodhound must have been unconscious.

The reindeer returned immediately with the teacups. Bloodhound did not see any cookies.

"Yes, I can already assure you here and now, Superintendent, that I intend to take measures," Flamingo said.

"Measures?"

"My attorney is connected. Established, yes? You understand?"

"Mrs. Flamingo," Bloodhound grunted amiably, "at this point you are not suspected of anything."

"That"—Flamingo sniffed condescendingly, filling her teacup with sugar—"I am aware of. No, dear Superintendent, this is not about him. This is about me. And I intend to sue the decapitated bird."

"Sue *whom*?"

"The bird. You know, the vulture."

She continued to fill her cup with sugar, whereupon the tea ran over the edge. This she did not notice.

"Your husband?" asked the superintendent. "But he's—"

"If all the money goes to that foundation for circus performers, then I will, excuse the expression, sue him," explained Flamingo. "There won't be any foundation here."

Bloodhound furrowed his brow and felt tired.

"Excuse me, now I really don't understand—"

"He's always threatened that. Instead of leaving the money to his dear, beloved family, he would let all of it go to a foundation for . . . circus acrobats."

"A foundation?"

"Have you ever heard anything so stupid?"

Now she discovered the overflowing cup in terror.

"But what kind of stupidity is this?" she asked, staring at the cup.

"Did your husband talk about his demise?" asked Bloodhound. "He wasn't old, but did he feel threatened in any way? Was there anyone who—"

"Stupidities," Flamingo repeated, but now with clear reference to the superintendent's line of reasoning. "He wasn't threatened by anyone. The only reason for that stupid circus idea was to annoy us. Take away our inheritance. Us. His own family."

"Do you mean that you won't get anything?"

"Practically speaking, nothing," she confirmed.

She sounded desperate now; it was as if the thought became more concrete when she said it out loud.

"Practically speaking?" asked the superintendent.

"All we have is what's in the bank. Twenty million or so."

"Twenty million?" Bloodhound exclaimed. "And you don't think that's anything?"

"The company is worth several hundred million," sighed Flamingo. "By comparison I get nothing. That crook-beaked swine."

"And this foundation," said Bloodhound. "Who will administer it?"

"I don't know a thing," Flamingo answered loudly. "I don't know a thing. I'm only a stupid home bird, aren't I? But I'm going to stop them—"

"Who, then?" asked the superintendent.

"Who, then?" repeated Flamingo, who apparently had lost her thread.

She poured the tea into an ashtray and started pouring more sugar in the teacup.

"Yes, Lord Magnus," Flamingo sighed as she filled the teacup with sugar, "what is one to do now?"

Bloodhound didn't know what she was talking about.

"With the body and that?" Irina Flamingo clarified. She suddenly decided that was enough sugar and set the cup aside. "Because I have an appointment at the manicurist later this afternoon, and tomorrow is my massage day. Can he stay at the office until Wednesday, do you think?"

The superintendent was about to answer but was interrupted.

"No, no," Flamingo cried out. "On Wednesday Guy is coming in the morning! And after a few rounds with Guy you're completely wiped out. He claims my backhand is getting better, but I haven't noticed it myself. Thursday. It will have to be Thursday. Can he stay at the office until Thursday? I don't think anyone will mind, they can just close the door, can't they?"

"The law is very clear on this point," Bloodhound explained amiably to the widow. "Stuffed animals without heads are not considered . . . dead. It happens fairly often that the heads are found again, and then they can be sewn back on. Simple as that. Some smarmy surgeon invoices the shit out of us and everything is back to normal. But we are . . . that is, not the police, but . . . the authorities are responsible for storing the headless body in a special warehouse."

"In a warehouse?" Flamingo asked, confused.

"It's the Chauffeurs who decide when life ends. We store the body in the warehouse until the Chauffeurs come and get it."

"And when is that?" the widow asked.

Superintendent Bloodhound refrained from the cruder ironies that popped into his head. Instead he replied, "One never knows, Mrs. Flamingo."

"But can't you call up the Chauffeurs? So that there's an end to this?"

"Don't give up," Bloodhound encouraged. "We have far from ruled out the possibility of finding his head, and—"

"Or can't you simply incinerate him?" the widow continued; it seemed as if she were talking with the books on the bookshelf. "Well, I don't know. Not that it matters, really, if he comes home again or not. We didn't see each other all that much."

"You and your husband?" the superintendent asked. "You didn't see each other very often?"

Unwillingly, Bloodhound began to realize that, true, this widow may be drugged, but sorry she was not. That felt sad, somehow. Larry had a romantic heart under his filthy shirts.

"No, no, not all that often," Flamingo repeated. "He was at the office, he lived at the other end of the house, and, well, he was an unpleasant animal, if I may say so myself. It was unpleasant to run into him, in the kitchen or in the garage, but . . . I suppose that's over with now."

Bloodhound nodded.

"May I offer you some tea?" Flamingo asked.

"I already have some, thanks," Bloodhound replied.

"What service!" Flamingo exclaimed with surprise. "Was there anything else you wanted to know, Superintendent?"

"Well," said Bloodhound, picking up his notebook. "Just a few formalities. Did your husband have any other family? Parents still living? Were there any siblings?"

"No siblings, no parents," Flamingo answered clearly. "But we have a cub. He's grown now, of course. Doesn't live at home. That was long ago."

"A cub . . . and you have informed him about . . . what happened?"

"I haven't got hold of him yet," Flamingo replied. "But he'll probably call back soon. He calls sometimes."

"And, can you . . ." Bloodhound began. "This is an unpleasant question, Mrs. Flamingo, but I have to ask it. Can you imagine anyone who would have wanted to kill your husband?"

Irina Flamingo giggled. "But, Superintendent, everyone knows that. No one liked Oswald. I can think of quite a few who wanted to kill him!"

1.4

He regretted it as soon as he opened the trunk and took out the socks. It was the sudden silence that made him realize something was wrong. He was in a windowless dressing room. Simple benches ran along the walls, and above the benches was a long row of hangers. The low ceiling and the closed-in smell of wet terry cloth made the room claustrophobic, and the light green paint on the walls had started to flake off. There were five of them, but there was room for just as many more. Nonetheless, Falcon Ècu was alone on his side of the room, and as he was pulling on the mauve socks, his colleagues on the other side could no longer control themselves.

"It's hellish," said a bear Falcon didn't know, "separating the white laundry sometimes."

Everyone laughed. Falcon smiled.

"You can laugh now," said Field Mouse Pedersen, "but when you see his mauve balls it's not going to be as funny."

And everyone laughed again, louder this time.

Field Mouse Pedersen was actually a friendly soul who, like Falcon, worked for Bloodhound at WE on rue de Cadix.

He had accompanied Falcon to Tourquai's Tennis Stadium straight from Nova Park and the scene of Oswald Vulture's murder. The stadium was in the northwest corner of the district, almost to the food industries. Twelve courts, a manager's office, a small pro shop, and an even smaller snack bar whose hours of operations no one had yet been able to figure out were housed in a dark green tent that appeared to be inflated to the breaking point; it would probably collapse like a punctured soufflé if a hole were made in the cloth. All the championships in that part of the city were played at the stadium, even though there were many other tennis courts around Tourquai. In accordance with tradition, the police rented the courts the entire first week of June. The dressing rooms were on the basement level.

Pedersen had not meant anything bad by his little joke, and Falcon did not take offense, either. On the other hand, he was now afraid to continue changing. His tennis shirt was in the trunk. It, too, was mauve, to match the socks. He realized that when he took out the shirt the jibes about the socks would sound like flattery.

"Is it so strange to want to look nice on the court?" he mumbled.

But so quietly that no one heard.

Falcon Ècu had joined the tennis club when he started at the station a year before, and more and more the club seemed like his only chance to approach his colleagues. On the tennis court his merits seemed to come into their own. He was a good loser; that was one of his better qualities. He played to win, he fought his way into a sweat, but he was technically inferior. So he quickly became a popular opponent; he was fun to beat. The club championship included all the police stations in Tourquai, and it had just begun. So far, it was a round-robin tournament, where everyone played everyone.

Falcon Ècu would not describe himself as a clothes snob, although he realized he might be perceived that way. He had grown up in simple circumstances, and it had always been important to keep himself clean and not shabby. If you could, why not choose a shirt that suited the pink color of your neck? Why not accentuate your natural straight posture by dressing in dark colors and vertical stripes? It was easier when he was a patrol officer, because a uniform suited him. As a detective he had to weigh his vanity against the ridicule he brought on himself. However, Falcon would never go to work in stained, stinking clothes like Larry Bloodhound. He realized that they joked with him when he sorted the pencils on his desk by size, and he had noticed that he was the only one who used disinfectant spray on the computer keyboard. But he did not intend to be ashamed that his clothes were ironed and clean.

With a sigh he took the mauve tennis shirt out of the trunk and pulled it over his head, while his colleagues on the other side of the dressing room burst into laughter.

Falcon Ècu was an animal who wanted too much.

How had that come about? He couldn't explain it. He wanted to help create a better society; he himself wanted to be a better animal. But despite valiant efforts, he didn't measure up. You have to start with yourself, he knew that. Therefore he followed the rules, the written and unwritten rules of life. He went to church on Sundays, he knew portions of the Proclamations by heart, and he lived as they taught. In his co-op association he was in charge of the laundry room and rose beds by turns, and yet he had time left over for his aging parents. He made friends, but for some reason these friendships never lasted very long. He was never stingy, and he gave the animals around him space and trust, and even showed his weaknesses, just as he had read that you should do.

Yet it didn't really work out.

Falcon didn't know why.

The laundry room was clean and tidy, the roses bloomed,

the deacon in the church blessed him, and none of his friends had anything bad to say, not even when he called them later and asked what he'd done wrong.

He had always wanted to be a police officer. For an animal like Ècu the choice was between the police profession and becoming a prosecutor. It was a choice between an intellectual life and a more physical one, and Falcon was better suited to the latter. He thought that within the police corps he would finally feel at home together with stuffed animals who shared his way of looking at life.

But it didn't turn out that way.

The hard-to-define awkwardness of which Falcon had always been aware created a distance between him and his colleagues. That had been the real reason he moved up to Tourquai and WE. Things had become impossible in Amberville, and he needed a second chance.

Unfortunately, though, things seemed to be going the same way with Larry Bloodhound.

But he was lucky to have Anna Lynx as his partner.

At first Anna seemed just as irritated as any other police officer with Falcon as a new partner. He no longer took it personally. No one wanted a new partner. The interplay between two colleagues was far too important for anyone to want to start with a newcomer. But Anna had showed her irritation in a different way than Falcon was used to. She had been frank. This had both shocked and disarmed him.

"C'mon, it might not be easy, but let's give it a try," she had said. "Who knows, it might work out."

Even then there had been something in her charisma that made him slightly better than he usually was. He could feel it clearly. And for the first time since he had started as a police officer, Falcon thought it might work out.

"It looks like it'll be you and me in the first match," Field

Mouse Pedersen said as they were on their way up the spiral staircase from the locker room.

"Oy," Falcon answered without turning around. "Well, then I'm lucky it's group play. I haven't recovered since the last time."

"No false modesty, Falcon. Besides, you had your racket restrung, didn't you?"

"It was necessary," Falcon answered quickly, blushing slightly. "It wasn't easy to—"

"But of course you should restring it," the field mouse interrupted. "Nothing to apologize about."

"Just so I don't have any excuses," Falcon explained.

They went out to the court together. Play was going on everywhere; the red foam rubber balls flew like missiles back and forth over the nets. Without wanting to, Falcon felt his competitive instinct awaken. He knew he didn't have a chance against Pedersen. The last time they played he won only two games in the second set. But Falcon knew exactly what he'd done wrong that time. If only he'd played more aggressively. If only he'd dared go to the net on Field Mouse's second serve.

"This is going to be a real battle," said Pedersen, taking the cover off his racket.

"This is going to be a warm-up for you," Falcon replied. "But I'll do my best."

"Just remember to bend your knees," said Pedersen.

But Falcon Ècu was not good at bending his knees, he was stiff and straight and had massive force in his wings. Deep inside he was thinking: If I top my forehand enough he won't be able to return. But out loud he said, "Who's going to serve?"

An hour and a half later Falcon Ècu was sitting with Anna Lynx, having a sports drink at one of the four tables at the Tennis Stadium snack bar. Anna had brought the sports drinks with her, as the snack bar was closed as usual.

"You really didn't need to come," said Falcon for the second or third time.

"C'mon, listen," Anna replied. "Todd is at a party, and we haven't had a decent murder to investigate for several months—I'm curious."

Pedersen had won by a score of 6–1, 6–0. Falcon said he lost the grip on his racket in the middle of the second set, but anyone could have seen that he threw it in desperation.

"Take it from the top, Falcon," Anna asked. "Although I don't really need to ask you to be thorough."

Falcon cleared his throat. He had received suitable taunts and then changed and left his colleagues out on the court. Many of them had another match later that evening; he would not be playing anymore today.

"You've heard about Vulture?" Falcon began.

"I talked with Larry," Anna confirmed. "I have a handle on the first part. But then you and Pedersen stayed behind at Nova Park and questioned the personnel?"

The snack bar was just to the right of the stadium exit. Two large potted palms marked off the area; the palm leaves hung down over four round metal tables and the chairs around them, small and rickety. Only Anna Lynx and Falcon were sitting there. From the food sack she had brought with her, Anna took out a prepackaged ham sandwich that looked positively inedible.

"Yes, it's a real mystery," Falcon nodded. "You won't be disappointed."

"Okay. And what do you mean by that?"

"Oswald Vulture's head has disappeared," said Falcon. "Someone cut it off. Outside Vulture's room on the sixty-second floor at Bourg de la Villette sits his secretary, Emanuelle Cobra. To get in to Vulture, you have to go through Cobra's office. And Cobra hadn't left her office all morning."

"C'mon, you don't need to be a genius to realize that it has to be Cobra who did it," Lynx stated.

"That's a very hasty conclusion," Falcon said. "Cobra was seriously shocked when we found her boss. I'm pretty sure the superintendent and I both had the same feeling. She wasn't pretending. She didn't know what had happened."

"Good-looking?"

"What?"

"Is she good-looking?" Anna repeated. "Cobra."

Falcon blushed.

"C'mon," said Anna, "anyone could fool you testosterone-ruled males."

"Since you already know who's guilty, perhaps there's no point in me continuing," said Falcon, deeply offended.

"Go on," Anna smiled. "Tell me everything you know."

"Well, when we talked with Cobra, we got a pretty good idea of the victim's morning. He arrived at work at the usual time, right after the Morning Rain, and behaved exactly as usual. He began the day by going over his calendar with his secretary. He had meetings all morning, and in the afternoon he planned to go to an auction where his wife was interested in a vase."

"C'mon, he lied about the vase."

"Yes, probably. There was no vase. Whatever. The first meeting in the morning he had with Leonard Earthworm. Earthworm is one of the partners and sits in the office closest to the elevators. But they had their meeting in Vulture's office. Earthworm stayed an hour, perhaps a little less. I talked with Earthworm, he told me about their conversation, though I can't say I understood that much. They were working on some big business contract."

"What does Nova Park do?" asked Anna.

"It's a financial company. They buy into companies they believe in, and then sell when they can make a profit. There are twelve stuffed animals in the office. Six partners and six assistants. Vulture's second meeting was with Oleg Earwig. Earwig is an inventor that Nova Park invested in many years ago, but evidently he didn't measure up. That's how it goes. You make five investments, and if one of them works out, then you're successful."

"Okay odds," commented Anna. "Don't think we can work with the same—"

"Oleg Earwig was the last one who saw Vulture alive. At least we assume so. Earwig was in Vulture's office for half an hour, maybe forty minutes. Half an hour after that, the superintendent and I opened the door and found Vulture headless."

"Did your little cutie talk with Vulture after the meeting with the inventor?" Anna asked.

"Cobra is a little vague on that point . . ." Falcon replied hesitantly, finishing the last of the sports drink. "Maybe, but she's not sure."

"Hm. Do you want the ham sandwich?"

Falcon looked with disgust at the prepackaged sandwich and shook his head. Anna picked it up and unwrapped the plastic. When she got in the car to drive up to the Tennis Stadium the breeze had not yet reached the city, but now twilight was falling quickly over Mollisan Town and she was hungry.

"Sorry," she said, "but I didn't have time to eat anything."

"We talked our way through the whole office," Falcon continued, "but I don't think anything leaped out that . . . here comes Field Mouse."

Falcon pointed with the tip of his wing.

Field Mouse Pedersen had played another match but was now changed and on his way home. Anna Lynx called to him, and he joined the two partners.

"Do you agree, Field Mouse?" Anna asked after Falcon had summarized what he had told to that point. "Nothing interesting to report?"

"They work extremely independently and are isolated up there," said Field Mouse. "Everyone seems to sit in their offices, reading papers and making a call or two . . . No one heard or saw anything."

"It could possibly be that electrician," said Falcon.

"What electrician?" asked Anna.

"It was the goat in reception who said there'd been an electrician who came and went several times during the morning," Falcon clarified. "But I don't know . . . we have to question the goat again. He didn't seem exactly reliable."

"No, he didn't," agreed Field Mouse. "Someone has to talk with the goat in reception again."

"And the head?" asked Anna.

"Don't know," Field Mouse Pedersen replied. "But both Hare's and Tapir's teams were still there when Falcon and I came here. And one more thing. Everyone described Vulture the same way. As a hard and merciless business executive."

"That's right," Falcon sighed. "I don't recall who said it, but when I asked who would want to kill Oswald Vulture, someone answered, 'Who wouldn't want to kill Oswald Vulture?' There will be no lack of stuffed animals with a motive."

1.5

The yellowish glow of the lanterns revealed salmon pink Avenue Michelle Duboir. The street lay broad and shameless before Emanuelle Cobra. She got off the bus one stop early, simply to have the satisfaction of personally slithering the final blocks. She loved this part of Michelle Duboir, between orange-colored rue Leblanc and yellow North Avenue. Along the sidewalks the city had planted small but proudly blossoming cherry trees. They cast long shadows across cars that had finally found their places for the night. The occasional stuffed animal was en route home after yet another day of seeming significance or obvious meaninglessness; for Emanuelle Cobra, Monday, the third of June, had been bewildering. And it was not over yet. But what remained was the high point of the month, and not even the decapitated Vulture or the embarrassed police inspector who had questioned her that morning could cause Cobra to despair today.

For those who remain, life goes on, she thought. Life goes on, but in new clothes.

She had on a long coat from Carél and a high-heeled red

shoe from Dot that was strapped over the tip of her tail. It was obvious that reptiles wore out clothes faster; with all that scraping against the stone and asphalt of the sidewalks it was unavoidable. She knew that the others also appreciated the first Monday of the month, but for Cobra this bonus was considerably more valuable than for stuffed animals who walked on two or four legs.

She reached the gateway on Avenue Michelle Duboir just as she heard the Evening Storm's first ominous whispering. As usual the gate stood open, and she crawled in through the arch and across the cobblestones of the dark, gloomy inner courtyard. She knocked with her head, waiting for the electronic lock to open, and then pulled open the door. The stairs down to the basement were like one long, winding promise.

She was the first.

"Terrible," said Jasmine Squirrel, who came to meet her at the door. "Simply terrible."

"What are you talking about?"

Cobra did not want to converse. She did not even look at Squirrel. The clothes were hanging in long rows on racks in the middle of the floor in the well-lit room. There were two makeshift dressing rooms, little more than curtains hanging over spanned steel wires, but usually no one tried on the clothes anyway.

"No, but . . . Emanuelle, you have to pull yourself together now. I'm talking about your Oswald Vulture."

"Oh, yes. Sure."

"What did the police say?" asked Squirrel.

"The police? They . . . asked their questions. Is that a Luigi Barcotta?"

Cobra nodded toward a white dress with ruffles and shoulder straps. It would absolutely not suit her. Jasmine nodded in boredom, and her long, luxuriant tail billowed expectantly behind her.

"Correct. Barcotta. I thought we should try him for a few months. I've never been truly converted, but—"

"Vulture was a swine," Cobra stated. She wanted only to wriggle over to the rack of Barcotta garments before anyone else arrived. "I didn't even miss him at lunch. There are lots of swine, so I don't intend to make a big deal out of Vulture, and it's clear that it was . . . horrid. But life goes on. And if you're going to cut someone's head off, Oswald Vulture was not a bad choice."

"And you said that to the police?" Squirrel mumbled ironically.

"Now I must go over and look," said Cobra.

Jasmine Squirrel nodded, and Emanuelle was over by the clothes racks in a matter of seconds. Squirrel went back and sat down at a little table where she had her papers. She did not need to give any instructions. Cobra knew the rules. She could get clothes for ten thousand. Not a cent more. Every month they returned, the females who were part of the secretarial pool, and picked out new clothes. The company had tried other limitations: a certain number of garments, a certain number of a certain kind of garment, but all such variations led to arguments and jealousy. Easier to put price tags on everything, and let the females keep track of the amounts themselves. Besides, this had proved to elevate the experience.

Doesn't she even wonder what will happen now? thought Jasmine Squirrel as she looked over at Cobra, who was completely engrossed by the new Barcotta collection. In principle, thought Squirrel, Cobra has lost her job. Doesn't she understand that? But there was no worry in the black latex body squeezing into a red sleeveless top and hurrying over to the mirrors to see how she looked.

Carefree, thought Jasmine Squirrel. Or hopeless in the full sense of the word.

1.6

Superintendent Larry Bloodhound took a short detour past his office. There he threw together a suitable number of papers to stuff into his briefcase, accidentally spilled a half-full can of cola over the keyboard that he never used anyway, and left for the day. Determinedly he made his way to the stairs. He kept his gaze straight in front of him. If he glanced to either side and let himself be drawn into a conversation, it would mean another hour or two at the station. He was well acquainted with all the ongoing investigations, likewise all the underlying conflicts that arose over time among the inspectors. Despite his reputation and his broadly applied harshness, he was an excellent head of WE. He solved problems wherever they arose and he was accessible even when he was busy. Larry had never thought it was hard being a boss; it was a lot harder to be a police superintendent. He dug in his jacket pocket and found a few raisins, which he ate up as he hurried down the stairs. He was on his way to Chez Jacques; he could already taste the cold beer.

The police department in Mollisan Town was set up according to a simple structure. The police authorities were classi-
fied, for budgetary purposes, under the Ministry of Finance.
Commander Gaardsmyg was not, however, subordinate to
the head of the ministry but instead reported directly to the
mayor. There was a certain amount of administrative coordination among the organizations, but for the most part the
Ministry of Finance and the police existed side by side. In the
free elections that took place in Mollisan Town every fourth
year, the stuffed animals had the opportunity to elect a new
commander. Partly due to the media's focus on the mayoral
election, which for practical reasons took place the same day,
the election of the commander often ended up in the backwa-
ter of the debates. Six years ago there had been a couple of
strong candidates, but Gaardsmyg won at the finish line. On
the other hand, the last election two years ago turned out to
be a landslide. Gaardsmyg was not a media animal; he kept a
low profile, which distinguished him from his predecessors. It
was hard to find anyone who spoke badly of Gaardsmyg, and
he was said to have an excellent relationship with Mayor Sara
Lion.

Commander Gaardsmyg had four majors under him. They
were each responsible for one of the city's districts—Amberville, Lanceheim, Tourquai, and Yok—and were also heads
of the largest police stations in the districts. These animals
were not politically appointed, and, at the moment, none of
the four had any political ambitions. They were police officers, experienced and hardened, and had come up through
the ranks. By keeping careerists away from the major posts,
Gaardsmyg minimized the number of potential rivals leading
up to the next term of office.

The police chiefs at the smaller stations, like the one on rue
de Cadix, were called Captains, and Jan Buck was a typical
representative of this position. Though one of the foremost
members of his graduating class at the Police Academy, sur-

prisingly police work itself was never something that interested Buck. Larry Bloodhound's young chief was interested in
success, and evidence of success. He had sufficient self-insight
to choose a career in the public sector, and he bragged about
his short memory as a guarantee for future ruthlessness. Buck
was more concerned that the columns in the monthly reports
were correctly color-coded than that his superintendents—the
heads of the station's three divisions, WE, GL, and PAS—had
sufficient resources.

Buck was not planning to remain at rue de Cadix. This
police station was not ranked low, but many were higher up
on the list.

"It'll be better when he's gone," one of the inspectors might
speculate.

"There'll be a new Buck," Larry Bloodhound would reply.
"I'll be damned if they don't build that sort at the Academy."

This resulted in laughter and sighs in equal proportion. Because it was true.

All the police stations in Mollisan Town had their counterpart
to Chez Jacques, to which Larry Bloodhound was directing
his steps this late Monday. The bar was on the same block as
the station, and was a place to wind down after work. The
majority of the customers were police officers. This created a
special atmosphere, a pleasant feeling of mutual understanding that pervaded the place.

A narrow corridor with an opening to the cloakroom on
the right side led to the restaurant. In the room facing rue de
Cadix there were fifteen or so small tables and a long counter
along the outer wall. Toward the courtyard there was another
room, smaller and darker, but it was preferable not to sit there
because the stench of sour cigars clung tight to your fabric as
soon as you sat down. The old-fashioned fans whirling slowly
above swirled the cigarette smoke, and the jukebox all the way

back by the toilets was loaded with fifties classics. A saxophone that wailed, a cautious whisk against a large cymbal, fingers clambering up and down the long neck of a bass.

From out on the street Larry Bloodhound saw that Philip Mouse was already sitting at their usual window table, waiting. Bloodhound smiled. Philip Mouse was one of the city's few private detectives, and the reason he hung out at police bars in the afternoon was obvious. He was fishing for information and maintaining his network. Larry and Philip had found a kind of friendship over the years. True, it started and ended inside Chez Jacques, but those were the rules of the game.

Larry pulled off his jacket but refrained from leaving it in the cloakroom. He draped it over his arm and made his way over to the table where Philip was sitting.

"Mouse," he growled, nodding.

He set his jacket over Philip's white trench coat, which was already on the empty, third chair at the table, and sat down.

"Larry," Philip said. "A rough day? Looks like it. Do you know you've spilled something on your shirt?"

Larry looked down at his large-checked shirt and could see that Mouse was completely correct. Could it be the Mammoth chocolate? But then he remembered.

"It's from yesterday," he said. "A rat that threw up when we picked him up at the Star."

"You're joking? But, Larry, that's so disgusting that—"

"But it doesn't smell like anything," Bloodhound defended himself. "Smell it."

He held out his stained shirt toward the detective, who turned away with distaste.

"Now you're joking," he decided.

A waitress came with the superintendent's cold dark ale, but Bloodhound shook his head.

"Not for me, Doris," he said. "This mountain of fat is going to be a package of muscle. This is serious now. Do you have a light beer?"

Doris concealed her smile and went to get Bloodhound's order.

Mouse lit a cigarette. He brought his paw to the brim of his hat and adjusted it imperceptibly.

"Heard you found a headless vulture," said Mouse.

Neither of them was big on small talk. Better to sit silently, each with a beer, than to discuss imaginary climate changes. In Mollisan Town the weather was reliable; the rain and the winds drew in over the town with absolute regularity. But in all ages the stuffed animals still discussed the tiny, tiny shifts they thought they could observe.

"Finance vulture," Larry replied. "The type that not only shits money, it's a case of diarrhea. Presumably a real swine, otherwise they never get that rich. Going to need a bouncer for the suspects."

Philip nodded.

"It's usually that way. There's a limit on how long the heirs can wait for their money."

"Hmm. I'm hoping for a fool. It's always easier then. There are a few possibilities among the vulture's business acquaintances," said Larry.

"Certainly a good idea to start there," Philip nodded.

"Have a feeling it'll either be solved tomorrow or else it's going to be like shitting out an iron on an empty stomach," said Larry, draining his mug.

"Hope for the former," Mouse replied. "Another?"

He made a gesture toward Larry's empty glass, and the dog nodded.

Philip got up, took the few steps over to the bar, and ordered two beers. He not only worked as a private detective, he also dressed like one. He wasn't always comfortable in the hat, suit, and suspenders, but it was a matter of meeting his future clients' expectations. If you went to a private detective to get help, you didn't want to find a security guard in a homemade uniform. While Mouse was waiting, he took the opportunity to exchange a few words with the animals from GL who were standing at the bar. Mouse knew everyone.

Larry looked out the window. The light brown street was empty. The sky was still blue, but the sun was on its way down. He suddenly felt that he missed Cordelia, the budgie waiting for him in her large, gilded cage. One more, he decided, then he would go home.

"And you?" he asked when Philip returned. "Are you getting anywhere?"

"Not yet," Philip replied, unconsciously lowering his voice.

"Got stuck?"

"The walrus is still paying," said Mouse, shrugging his shoulders. "I've been at it long enough to know that success is only about the bank balance."

"How was it, you were supposed to get hold of some joker who . . . ?"

"I'm not going to find him," Mouse maintained. "But my very well-known client, unfortunately I can't utter his name, still believes in me. And so I'm going to send the next invoice, too."

They drank in silence.

"I was thinking of making it an early one this evening," said Larry.

"Me, too," Philip agreed. "Daisy gets furious otherwise."

Daisy Hippopotamus was Philip's patient assistant, his secretary, and partner in one. The reason that she put up with inconvenient work hours, a fluctuating monthly salary, and not always pleasant treatment was a mystery.

"By the way, did you hear that Surayid, that pile of shit, was arrested tonight?" said Larry, changing the subject.

Philip nodded.

"Caught red-handed, if I understand correctly?"

"With his claws in the jelly jar. In front of witnesses. A fool."

"A pro disguised as an amateur?"

"So chock-full of shit and pills, it was a marvel he could even move."

"What the hell . . ."

"They should have brought him in months ago."

"There's no prosecutor in Mollisan Town who would—"

"I know, I know," Larry growled. "That's just shit. They tiptoe around a hundred rotten stuffed animals up here in Tourquai that they really ought to just pound the shit out of—"

"Maybe not a *hundred*," Philip objected.

"Up yours!" Larry barked. "At *least* a hundred! And instead of picking them up and driving them right out to King's Cross, they set traps for them. Gather evidence. It's pathetic."

"I know you think that," said Philip diplomatically.

"What the hell," Larry repeated.

He raised the mug and emptied it. Set it down on the table with a thud and got up. Took his jacket, used it to dry his mouth before he put it on, and raised his paw in farewell.

"Now I'm leaving," he said. "Otherwise I'll stay too long."

The superintendent left Chez Jacques well before the Evening Storm and decided to walk home. He didn't live very far away, on licorice black Impasse Laisse. He knew he shouldn't, but couldn't restrain himself, and urinated against the entryway to the abandoned building on turquoise rue de Gobelins. If a patrol car came past, they would stop him. But maybe, thought Larry, it was no catastrophe anyway. Maybe pissing on the sidewalk was just what his colleagues expected of him?

"Yoohoo, I'm home!" he called as he stepped inside the door.

It was ridiculous. Cordelia was a budgie who could neither talk nor think. Although she ate, slept, and sang for him, she was not a stuffed animal; she used her wings to fly. She shared his solitude and his anxiety, and she was his best friend. That was without a doubt worth a few friendly words.

The superintendent wriggled out of his jacket, which fell down on the pile of old mail and foul-smelling shoes and socks, and with a few long strides he was in the living room and up at her golden cage. On her perch sat the very small, green bird. She was chirping merrily.

"And I'm happy to see you, too," Bloodhound replied.

He sat down on the couch alongside the cage. Late one night Larry had carried the armchair that was on the other side of the table into the bathroom and placed it in front of the drying cabinet. Then he sat in front of the open door to dry off. There had never been any reason to carry the armchair back in.

Larry's living area was sixty square feet, which meant that almost everything was within reach. The kitchen nook stood unused—food could be bought already prepared—but he counted the refrigerator as his most important piece of furniture. The bed was a mattress lying right on the floor. Often he moved it as close to Cordelia's cage as possible at night.

From the inside pocket of his jacket the superintendent now took out a small mirror, no larger than a playing card. Then he took the pistol out of the holster and set it next to him on the couch. From the holster he fished out a carefully folded-up envelope. He opened it and methodically sprinkled the cocaine on the small mirror. With the envelope he made sure the edges of the white stripe were straight, and with a slender straw that he stored in the same pocket as the mirror he snorted the powder through his nose.

The whole procedure took no more than a minute.

Bloodhound sat on the couch, leaned his head back, and closed his eyes. He collected himself while the cocaine raced around in his system like runaway helium balloons in a clear blue sky. Cordelia sang. She had never sung so beautifully, he thought. Then he remembered that he'd had that thought before.

IGOR PANDA 1

The gates slowly parted and Igor Panda put the car gently in gear. His wide, new Volga Deluxe purred like a mature cat under the hood, and Igor enjoyed the feel of the car's power through the clutch and gears. The black finish glistened in the sun, and the tinted black glass he ordered for all the windows gave the car an ominous appearance. Now he carefully maneuvered between the gate posts. He had never been here before, but the dozen or so mansions down by Swarwick Park all looked the same, a long driveway ending in a yard that some landscape architect had planned down to the smallest detail.

Panda whistled as he came over a small rise and saw where he was heading. The white house with columns and balconies outdid the others in ostentation.

The Morning Weather had just swept in over the city, the sun was shining from a clear blue sky, and the Volga's wide tires crunched along the gravel drive. In the middle of the yard a fountain had been set up, a rearing bronze horse that sprayed water from its ears.

Igor Panda was dressed like a gangster, in a narrow, double-breasted striped suit, shiny shoes, and big, black sunglasses. He had on a white shirt and black tie. For a moment he considered retrieving the package from the trunk but decided to leave it.

The old lady would have to show the money first.

He got out of the car and walked up toward the house. Just before he got there, the outside door opened and a zebra looked out. The animal had red and green stripes, and Igor Panda knew it was the buyer herself who stood in the doorway, Zebra von den Schenken-Hanken.

"Do you have it with you?" she asked before Panda was even across the threshold.

He did not answer but instead entered von den Schenken-Hanken's hallway with dignity. There was a shining marble floor, tall white plaster statues on pedestals in the background, and behind them rectangular, barred windows facing the courtyard.

"Do you?" asked the zebra.

"Do you have the money, do you?" asked Igor Panda, childishly imitating the zebra's tone of voice.

Von den Schenken-Hanken stared at the panda in surprise and nodded.

"I have the money," she answered awkwardly.

"Show me."

"Now? But I don't usually—" she started.

"We've never done business together before," said Panda brusquely. "And Esperanza-Santiago is not like other artists."

"No, no, I just . . ." said the zebra without finishing the sentence.

She was an elderly stuffed animal with threadbare cloth around her nose. Panda didn't care about that.

"Come along into the dining room," she said, leading the way.

On the dining room table, a piece of furniture worthy of a

knight's hall, was a brand-new, black attaché case, exactly as Igor Panda had instructed.

"Two and a half million," said the zebra as she opened the case's combination lock.

"And another half million after delivery," said Panda.

"What?"

The good-natured zebra seriously believed she had heard wrong. They had already agreed on the price. Two and a half million. Zebra von den Schenken-Hanken had never paid that much for a painting, although she had been collecting art most of her adult life.

"The price has recently gone up on Esperanza-Santiago's smaller oils," Panda explained.

"But—but—didn't we have an agreement?"

"The market rules," said Igor Panda indifferently. "It's not something either of us can do anything about."

Dismayed, the little zebra sat down on one of the dining room chairs and threw out her hooves.

"But," she repeated, "didn't we have an agreement?"

Panda looked coldly at the colorful zebra and shrugged his shoulders.

"Then I think we have nothing more to say to each other."

He turned around and started to leave.

This was not the first time he had played this scene. Based on what the collector seemed able to pay, he often raised the price at the last moment. When a passionate art lover was so close to getting something as valuable as a genuine Hummingbird Esperanza-Santiago, they seldom backed out. Judging by von den Schenken-Hanken's house, it ought to be possible to squeeze out another half million.

But when she didn't call him back, even though he was almost to the hallway, he started to doubt. Perhaps he'd overdone it?

Well, there were others to turn to.

"Mr. Panda, wait, Mr. Panda! I was just so . . . surprised."

Igor took a few more ominous steps before he stopped. Slowly he turned around, hesitantly coming back toward the dining room.

"I don't need the additional payment before . . . the day after tomorrow," he said thoughtfully.

"No. I mean, yes, that sounds . . . okay," said Zebra von den Schenken-Hanken. "And you have the painting with you?"

"I'll get it if we're agreed on the extra half million," he said.

Zebra nodded. In her eyes there was the desire that Panda often saw in these rich animals, a kind of veiled glow, a mixture of self-satisfaction and emptiness.

"So we're in agreement?" Igor repeated. "Half a million, the day after tomorrow? I'll pick up the money here the same way as today, and at the same time?"

"If it has to be that way," the zebra conceded. "Would you be so kind as to get the painting now?"

Igor turned and with rapid steps went out to the car.

Fifteen minutes later Igor Panda left von den Schenken-Hanken's stately property in Swarwick Park. The sun was still shining, and now it was easy for him to appreciate it. The attaché case with the money was on the seat beside him, ten years' salary for an ordinary working animal in Mollisan Town, and when Panda reached South Avenue he pressed the gas pedal to the floor. The black car accelerated, and the panda was pushed back into the seat.

He could not hold back a wry smile.

Of all the artists currently active in the city, none could compare with Hummingbird Esperanza-Santiago. It was not obvious that Esperanza-Santiago was superior to her colleagues in genius, feeling, and technique—but the price of her paintings was sky-high above everyone else. The reason was that she hardly painted anymore. While building up her reputation and gaining recognition, she had produced up to four or five canvases per year. Then self-criticism put a stop to her creative flow. Nowadays Igor Panda had to be happy if Esperanza-Santiago completed even a single painting a year. And, he asserted, neither she nor he could live like that.

Igor sneaked a glance at the attaché case.

He smiled again.

"I don't give a damn how you live," he said out loud. "It worked out for me anyway."

A little farther on he caught sight of a police car and reduced his speed.

DAY TWO

2.1

Anna Lynx woke up with a pounding headache. She didn't open her eyes, she didn't budge. Red wine. She could feel the taste of it on her tongue, and she realized that was why it felt like a tiny chimpanzee had crawled in through her ear and was now hammering right against her temple. Cow Hellwig. Anna squinted carefully, as she slowly twisted her head. The bedroom was still blessedly dark, and there, beside her in the bed, was her friend Cow Hellwig, sleeping.

Her anger returned. Cow must not return home. Must not be allowed to return home! Then Anna felt the impotence come creeping back. She was a police officer. But she could do nothing. She had spent half the night trying to get Cow to agree to divorce her husband. The very thought that she would go back to that . . . Anna didn't even want to think his name. No, it was not abuse. But it was everything but. The position of females in Mollisan Town had not changed in the last hundred years, she thought. Not really. Even if the oppression had become more sophisticated.

There was a knock at the bedroom door. Hard, angry knocks.

Anna Lynx got up out of bed.

"Coming!"

"Mama, we've overslept!" Todd howled.

He stormed into the room, ignoring the stench of red wine and the sleeping cow on the bed. He was her crocodile cub, her darling, her green cuddle toy. Todd's dad was another story. Being a single mother was Anna's own decision, and she had never regretted it.

"We're going to be late," Todd cried.

"C'mon, no, it—"

"*Again*," he whined. "We're going to be late *again*."

Anna staggered over to the bedroom window and pulled up the shade. Outside it was already starting to get cloudy.

"Have you brushed your teeth?"

"No."

"Off you go and do that," she ordered. "Now!"

Todd left the bedroom in tears, just as the cow woke up.

"What's going on? Oy. My head."

Anna ran around the bed, looking for her clothes. She found her slacks and tried to jump into them while shaking the rolled-up bedspread to see if her blouse was inside.

"Simon!" Cow Hellwig exclaimed. "Lord Magnus, he must be beside himself. I've been away all night."

"Don't call him," said Anna Lynx, just as she discovered her blouse under the nightstand.

"You're out of your mind. Of course I have to call. Immediately."

"Don't call him. He's completely—"

"I'm hungry!" Todd called, again standing in the bedroom, tooth-brushing finished. "I won't get any food. You won't have time to make breakfast!"

"I'll have time!" Anna shouted, to drown out the cub's crying.

A moment later Cow Hellwig lifted the telephone receiver on the nightstand. Anna threw herself to the floor and yanked the phone jack from the wall.

It was then that she thought of it. In the midst of this chaos she was struck by an insight. Since yesterday the thought had been gliding around in the unfathomable passages of her brain, and now it let itself be put into words. It was a particularly poorly chosen occasion. The cow was yelling, Todd was crying, and she was lying half-dressed on the floor, with a hangover, and with a telephone cord in her paw.

The tipster.

If Vulture was still in possession of his head when Oleg Earwig left the office, and if Falcon and Bloodhound arrived half an hour later, how and when had the tipster been able to phone in the tip? If the tipster was not the secretary herself, then it must have been the murderer. Who else could have known? But why would the murderer alert the police?

"What are you doing?" shrieked Cow.

"I want porridge!" shrieked Todd.

"Anna, now you're being childish. Plug in the phone."

"C'mon, we were in agreement," Anna shouted. "Your husband is a dictator. A repressor. A fascist pimp."

"Fascist pimp?" Cow repeated and could not keep from giggling. "You're out of your mind, Anna."

"You can stay here, until you find something else."

Todd increased the volume a few notches, and it became impossible to drown him out. Anna took the phone with her under her arm and scooted the cub out to the kitchen to make breakfast.

But Todd continued to be willful. He didn't want to wear his blue shirt and he wept large tears when there was no more of his papaya-and-mango-flavored cereal. Anna fought on. Cow came into the kitchen about the same time as Anna capitulated, ironed a yellow shirt instead, and let Todd have chocolate milk, even though it was against her principles. It was impossible to talk about equality and patriarchal structures at this time. To get Todd's jacket on, Anna had to promise to take him to Circus Balthazar. There were posters up all over the city, and she had said no for a whole week.

"Stay here awhile, girlfriend," Anna called to Cow from out in the hall. "You can crash with us as long as you want, no problemo."

"Anna, my friend," Cow called back, "I'll call you this evening."

Of course it would be possible to find out exactly when the tipster called, Anna thought, seriously late, as she ran with her crocodile cub in paw down the stairs to the entryway. All incoming calls were logged.

Despite a dubious parking location yesterday evening she hadn't got a ticket, and, relieved, she pressed Todd into the backseat. On the way to the day care she called Charlie at the Technical Department at rue de Cadix. He was the best at tracing ones and zeros through copper and fiber cables. She gave him the approximate time. She theorized that the same subscriber called twice on Bloodhound's extension and once on Falcon's. She wasn't sure of that, but that was what Falcon had told her. With such a tight target range it was easier to get results. She knew how they worked. First the district was established, then the block was narrowed down, and finally, possibly, the specific telephone could be determined. If it were possible to uncover someone's direct line at Nova Park, the inspectors' work would be considerably simpler. Anna was certain that the tipster was at the office. Anything else seemed impossible, considering the tight time frame.

Charlie promised to get back to her as soon as he had something.

With screeching tires a few minutes later Anna stopped outside Todd's day care. The rain was already falling from the dark sky, and she would be forced to run across the street into the entry with Todd in her arms. The teachers abhorred wet cubs in the morning, but what could she do? It was not the first time she had brought him late, and it wouldn't be the last.

2.2

The meeting had already begun when Anna Lynx threw open the door and burst into the room. She was still feeling stressed after having been scolded by the preschool teachers and leaving a crying Todd with the other cubs in the pillow room. In her frayed state of mind she was completely unprepared for the calm that prevailed up at WE. A kind of half-light rested over the deserted office landscape, and the broad iron pillars cast long shadows across the empty workstations; in the mornings, staffing was always at its lowest.

Larry Bloodhound and Field Mouse Pedersen were sitting in the larger of the two conference rooms in the department. Theodore Tapir had come from the station at place St.-Fargeau. Of Tourquai's four police precincts, only the largest station, at place St.-Fargeau, had a well-equipped forensics laboratory. Tapir had come to give the brief run-through that Bloodhound asked for yesterday, and would leave again as soon as he was finished. Derek Hare from the Technical Department was there to listen. He was more sprawled than seated in his chair and looked like he wished he were back in bed. His personnel had barely had time to start their examination of the components of the crime scene. Falcon Ècu stood in front of the whiteboard on the opposite side of the room. He had a pink scarf around his neck and was wearing a powder-blue jacket over a white shirt. Compared with how the others were dressed, Falcon seemed out of place. Anna did not interrupt anything when she barged in; the run-through had not begun.

"Super-sorry," she panted.

Except for a large, severely worn conference table on which coffee cups, cigarette butts, and keys or knives had left ineradicable traces, there was no room for much else. A row of lightbulbs hung above the table, the seats of the chairs smelled of damp wool. In the window boxes were two potted plants that had died from oxygen deficiency. They'd been there for weeks. Why didn't anyone remove them? Bloodhound asked himself. Through the windows you could look down over the parking lot opposite. On the roof of the lower neighboring building on the other side of the street was a strikingly large, complicated ventilation system; it might have been a modern sculpture of gleaming steel.

"Not that I have much to tell," said Falcon Ècu, "but may I start, if you will?"

Bloodhound nodded tiredly. He had eaten only half a grapefruit that morning and was now regretting that he hadn't had anything else.

"Nova Park is solely owned by Oswald Vulture," said Ècu, who had been at work since dawn, engaged in digging deeper into the company, its owners and history.

"Was owned," Bloodhound growled.

"What?"

Falcon cleared his throat nervously.

"Are your ears plugged up? *Was* owned, I said," the superintendent repeated.

"Was owned? Excuse me, but now I don't think I understand—"

"Vulture is missing a head," explained Derek Hare, who had no patience for games. "The unkind Superintendent Bloodhound means that Vulture does not own, but rather did own, his company."

"Yes, yes, of course," said Falcon, relieved. "Clearly. Excuse me, Superintendent. So stupid of me, Vulture *owned* Nova Park. He built the company from the ground up . . . starting with nothing, he made his first million before age twenty-five. Rather impressive is what he succeeded in creating in a little less than ten years—a successful venture-capital firm. Vulture invested money in ideas he believed in, and got the investment back with interest, if things went well. Most often it must have gone well. Unbelievably well. Bourg Villette, where Nova Park had its offices, is—"

"Has!" barked Bloodhound.

"Excuse me, where Nova Park *has* its offices," Falcon corrected, adjusting his pink scarf and trying to sound unperturbed, "is owned by Nova Park. Bourg Villette is owned by Nova Park."

There was whistling in the room.

"Mm," Falcon nodded, "it's at that level."

"And Vulture was someone everyone liked?" Anna asked.

"He was respected," Falcon replied. "That's the image you get. I spoke with almost everyone at the office yesterday, and got hold of a couple of the directors on Vulture's board this morning. They're shocked, of course. Everyone says roughly the same thing. Hard as flint, but not dishonorable—"

"He wasn't hard as flint," Theodore Tapir interjected.

Field Mouse Pedersen laughed curtly, but no one else cracked a smile at the tired joke.

"No one up at Nova Park has anything in particular to tell about what happened yesterday," Falcon continued. "We have to double-check with the receptionist about an electrician who apparently came and went, and of course take another turn with the secretary, Emanuelle Cobra, who doesn't seem to have seen anyone either enter or leave Vulture's office . . ."

During the course of the briefing Derek Hare had been sinking farther and farther down in his chair, and now with effort he brought himself back to a sitting position so as not to fall down under the table.

"Going to be hard to get a judge to believe in ghosts," Derek interjected. "But if neither the receptionist, who sits right across from the elevators, nor the secretary, who sits outside Vulture's office, has seen anyone come or go—"

"Excuse me, Derek, but that's not really the whole story," Falcon resumed, blushing at the same time over having interrupted the experienced Hare. "We have the inventor, Oleg Earwig, who was the last one to see Vulture alive. Earwig and Vulture have worked together for a few years. It started with the vacuum-cleaning wall . . ."

"I have one of those walls," forensic physician Theodore Tapir admitted.

"Well then, shit on you! Does it make you happy?" Bloodhound was seldom sarcastic, but when he was, it hurt.

"All new houses have vacuum-cleaning walls," Falcon clarified. "The wall was a great success. Earwig became the hottest inventor in Mollisan Town, and he formed a company with Nova Park and Vulture. They called it earWall Inc. There were a few more patents, not equally successful, but . . . in recent years his ideas have been meager, and a few months ago Vulture broke off his arrangement with the inventor."

"Just like that?" asked Anna.

"In the most recent reissue—"

"Reissue?" asked Tapir. "Explain so a medical doctor can understand."

"You issue new shares and sell them on the market to bring in capital. Despite the fact that Vulture was the largest shareholder, he didn't take part in the reissue. And then of course no one else dared to buy, either. EarWall Inc. was out of cash, and Nova Park made a bid for the inventor's shares. They said they would consider taking them over without paying anything, or else the company would go bankrupt and Earwig would be stuck with the debts."

"Can you do that?" asked Tapir.

"Vulture would never do anything that was in violation of the stock exchange rules. Or of any other rules, if I've understood who he is."

"But you're saying that ethically the issue is debatable?" said Tapir.

"That must have been what Oleg Earwig said during their meeting that morning," Falcon noted drily.

"Go to hell," Bloodhound barked. "You look like a little pansy, Ècu, but this shows that you shouldn't judge everyone by their clothes."

There was giggling. Falcon nodded. He had never been praised by Bloodhound before, and it made him confused and proud. He sat down.

"Theodore?" barked the superintendent.

"Yes, well," Theodore Tapir began, as he stiffly positioned himself so that everyone could see him, "it seems like everything is pointing in the same direction. Cobra or Earwig. Anything else doesn't seem possible. But when things are too obvious, I become wary. As far as the forensics report is concerned, I will return tomorrow with a more complete description. But so far, I'll start with the cut. The one who separated Oswald Vulture's head from his neck knew what he was doing. A single cut, from side to side, with a sword or a long knife. More conviction than force. If the edge is sharp and the angle correct, the stroke is like a good golf swing. It's not the strength in the arm, it's . . . the zing in the swing. The murderer stood behind Vulture, either accustomed to the movement or with plenty of time."

"Excuse me, but do you mean that someone sneaked up on him? Or that it was someone he knew well and turned his back on?" asked Falcon.

"My friend with the pink scarf, I don't know who you are," said Tapir, "but that was a stupid question. How would I know that?"

Falcon stared intensely down at the conference table and decided not to say anything else.

"On the other hand what I would ask myself," said Tapir, "was how the murderer concealed his weapon from the victim when he or she entered the room. It must have been a rather bulky object."

"And there was an attack alarm in the desk," Derek Hare pointed out. "If Vulture had sensed trouble he could have easily called for help."

"A brand-new invention?" Anna proposed. "C'mon, Earwig could have possibly pretended he was carrying around some contraption that was a new patent."

Tapir shrugged his shoulders to show that he was not convinced.

"The curtains," said Anna, changing tracks, "are another idea. The crazed animal could have hidden himself behind the curtains already the day before."

"Shut up now," Bloodhound asked. "The question is when did the murder occur?"

"Ah, but that's more difficult," said Tapir. "I prefer to wait for the autopsy before I give any definitive statements."

"If Cobra is telling the truth," said Anna Lynx, "there's not much to talk about. Earwig left, we came, in between someone trimmed the head."

"That doesn't need to be wrong," nodded Tapir. "That was actually what I wanted to say. That doesn't need to be wrong at all."

Tapir never took any risks, and Bloodhound knew that the doctor wouldn't say even this much without being fairly certain.

"Thanks," said the superintendent. "You can go now if you want to, Tapir."

"I do," said Tapir.

The elderly doctor left the room.

"For any of you who think that as usual it's the widow who's guilty, you can get that thought out of your head," the superintendent stated. "Apart from the fact that she was genuinely surprised, suitably dense, and generally incapable of action, she thinks the vulture has swindled her out of all the cash. Rambled on that he was going to donate the fortune to some foundation. Still remains to be seen whether that's true, I assume, but the point is this: she assumes she has less money now than when he was alive."

"But that isn't—" Anna began, but was brusquely interrupted by the superintendent.

"For a hag like Flamingo, I can promise you, money is everything."

Hare squirmed impatiently in his chair.

"Was there anything else?"

"In a hurry, Derek?" asked Bloodhound. "Have you promised some little female she could play with all your fine toys down there?"

"Just tired of you, Larry," Hare replied.

"Children," said Anna, "you'd be happy in day care. In the pillow room. Tell us about Vulture's office, Derek. I know you haven't started your full analysis, but your impressions? Feelings?"

"The office was completely void of personality," said Hare. "I've never seen anything like it. Nothing. The only thing that fell outside the frame was the small laptop computer on the desk. His business correspondence was in the desktop computer. But there were no personal folders or documents. We haven't got into the small machine yet. No, the vulture seems to have had gloves and a face mask on at work. What I think is strange is that the murderer seems to have been equally meticulous. Maybe we'll find something today, but up to now we haven't seen a single trace of the head. I mean, even if the murderer is a ghost, someone must have seen the vulture's head being carried out of there."

Falcon nodded. Now that Tapir had left the room, Inspector Ècu regained some of his courage.

"You've already thought about this, I'm sure, but it struck me that even if we do find the head, it's not a certainty that Vulture can tell us who did it," he pointed out. "Tapir said the stroke did come from behind."

The stuffed animals in the room pondered this truth in silence.

"Surveillance cameras?" asked Anna. "Shouldn't there be some?"

"In the reception area," Hare replied. "I've asked for all recorded material since before the weekend. Perhaps the murderer's been caught on tape. We'll soon see."

Bloodhound got up.

"Well, we can't sit here fiddling with our belly buttons any longer," Superintendent Bloodhound said. "This is actually a classic case. A murder has been committed in a room with only one entrance. And the murderer does not seem to have either gone out or come in. Two suspects. We'll question them right away. I'm going back to Nova Park to have another chat with Cobra. Anna, you take the newcomer with you and have a visit with that inventor . . ."

Derek Hare stood up leisurely.

"Does this mean I can go now?"

"Get out of here," Bloodhound barked.

2.3

This will only take a sec," said Anna Lynx less than an hour later.

"Not when—"

"No, come on now, I just didn't have time," she nagged.

"But we're on our way to—"

"C'mon—please?"

Falcon Ècu sighed theatrically and parked. Anna hurried. She threw open the car door and ran the few steps across the sidewalk into Springergaast. When she returned a few minutes later, she smelled like fresh-brewed coffee and blueberry muffins. She handed a croissant dripping with butter to Falcon in a conciliatory gesture.

"My morning was a circus," she said. "But you'll see. One fine day you'll have cubs."

"Right now I'm prioritizing my work," Falcon mumbled.

"That's ridiculous," Anna laughed. "Don't become one of those bitter old guys at the station who think they made a choice at some point. They never chose."

Falcon had rolled down the window on his side, and the

scent of the city filled the inside of the car once they were on the road again. The mild breeze had just blown in through the city. They took the route along orange-colored rue Leblanc, one of the quickest shortcuts through Tourquai if you wanted to avoid the main streets and avenues. The neighborhood was empty and silent; at this time of day the stuffed animals had already gone to work.

"We're just at different stages in our lives," Falcon attempted.

"What's that my ears are hearing? That I'm ancient?"

"No, no, but . . . I mean, I don't even have a . . . friend."

"They're not going to throw themselves into your arms automatically, if that's what you think. You have to try a little, Falcon," Anna replied.

She knew that her advice could get a bit personal, but she was looking after him.

Anna's mother was a light green Shetland pony and one of the most intelligent animals that ever lived in Mollisan Town. And not just according to Anna. She was the youngest ever to graduate from Lancheim's medical school, and she had registered two patents for the treatment of Triklin's disease before she was twenty-four. For the past twelve years, however, she had remained secluded in her two-room apartment in south Tourquai, sedated but bitter. She never went out, she had lost all interest in the world around her, and she barely recognized her daughter on her rare visits. Instead of running with her talent and opportunities, she had fallen in love with a macho firefly who demanded she stay at home. He was going to take care of her, he was the master of the house; she would be his spoiled princess. And the hardworking scholar, the highly promising research scientist, accepted the idea. Because that is, sometimes, what love does to us.

The subtle terror already began when Anna was delivered. And year by year, Anna's brilliant mother turned into a pill-eating wreck, deprived of a will of her own. Without even trying—or trying because of that—the firefly closed the door on the Shetland pony's life, inch by inch. He spoiled her, and she grew accustomed to it. When he finally left her, she was already an addict. Years before that Anna had stopped calling him "father." She swore that what happened to her mom would never happen to her. Perhaps the idea of joining the police force was rooted there, in her mother's tragedy.

Falcon had found out that Earwig was a denizen of honey yellow Carrer de Carrera in north Yok. Rue Leblanc led down to Western Avenue; after that it was only a matter of driving through the Star and into the southeast part of the city.

"I did a little research this morning," he said as he stopped at a red light. "Nothing to speak of, but I thought it would be good to be prepared. Oleg Earwig is thirty-eight years old. He has no criminal history, has never been arrested, and, apart from a few parking tickets many years ago, the authorities have never been interested in him. According to his tax returns, the last few years have been meager. Even a police officer earns more. Earwig owns shares in the company he has with Nova Park, but they're almost worthless."

"Hard to be an inventor," Anna commented, taking a drink from her still-hot coffee as Falcon put the car in first and accelerated.

At the next red light Anna took the opportunity to drink up before she spilled. In the car alongside sat a peacock, looking straight ahead and putting on his seat belt without letting on that he was doing so. The sight of a police car instilled guilt in most. The peacock hesitated when the light turned green.

"I was forced to search eight years back before I found traces of the vacuum-cleaning wall in his tax returns," Falcon continued.

"Do you mean you've searched through eight years of tax returns already this morning?"

Falcon sat quietly. During his career this was the third murder investigation he had ever taken part in. This was major. Coming in early this morning and sitting hunched over a computer a few extra hours was the least he could do.

"I took the opportunity to look in the Patent Office's registry a little, too," Falcon admitted.

"Lunatic. Did you ever go home last night?"

"I got home before midnight," he lied.

"I don't want a partner who spends the nights on research and then isn't sharp when we need it."

"I know," said Falcon.

Anna shared Larry Bloodhound's sense of priorities. Police work was something you did out on the streets; cowardly bureaucrats sat behind desks.

Falcon turned out onto the bloodred avenue and increased speed.

"And the Patent Office?" asked Anna after a moment of silence.

"Oleg Earwig has four new patents being processed right now. He has registered a hundred inventions since 'the wall.' But apart from the self-cleaning oven, none of them seems to have been a success. At least I've never heard of any of the others."

"So, an earwig hungry for cash and recognition," Anna summarized.

"Hmm. Might be right," Ècu agreed.

A few minutes later they drove through the golden Star, Mollisan Town's geographic center and the roundabout from which the four avenues ran. You might get the impression that these broad streets had been the starting point for the city planners when the city was divided into districts, but nothing was farther from the truth. On the contrary, the fact was that before the four independent towns of Amberville, Tourquai, Lanceheim, and Yok grew together, political boundaries were the scene of battles for centuries. Today these boundaries were reduced to multilane expressways; only scattered monuments were a reminder of history.

Western Avenue separated Amberville in the south from Tourquai in the north; Eastern Avenue separated Lanceheim in the north from Yok in the south. When Falcon turned into the poorest part of the district's labyrinthine swarm of cramped, discolored streets and squares, as usual he could not avoid wondering what it would be like to work down here. Larry Bloodhound was the toughest police officer the falcon had ever met, but Bloodhound was also sitting safely in north Tourquai, where things were actually pretty good. The superintendents who worked at the police stations in Yok were made of different stuff. In these neighborhoods you never asked first.

When they arrived, the address on Carrer de Carrera proved to consist of a large, freestanding warehouse, built of corrugated sheet metal, without windows, and bombarded with graffiti. Falcon chose to park a short distance away so as not to attract attention.

"How much of the car do you think will be left when we leave here?" he asked worriedly as he locked the doors.

"Falcon, now you're not thinking right," Anna replied with a broad smile. "You know, the secondhand market for police-car wheel rims is rather limited."

Obviously. The Volgas that the police drove were specially made. The spare parts only fit other police cars. Falcon swore to himself. Every time he tried to drop a comment that he thought sounded police-like, he only revealed his lack of experience. Who did he think he was fooling? Nervously he adjusted his pink scarf again.

There was a doorbell, but after trying it they pounded on the door instead. Nothing happened.

"Do we have the right address?"

Falcon nodded. He was certain.

They decided to see if there was an entrance at the back and went around. The building covered the entire block. On the other side there were tall windows and the sheet-metal walls were exchanged for wooden planks. From inside, the sound of continuous pounding was heard.

"Check it out," said Falcon, nodding.

Through the windows they saw an earwig in a white coat running back and forth in front of a machine that resembled a printing press, but with more indicator lights and gauges.

"C'mon, look, the door's open," Anna noticed, pointing.

They went in. What they had not been able to see from outside was the impressive ceiling height of the space. Mechanical apparatus and technical gadgets were everywhere.

"If I were five years old and imagining an inventor," Anna whispered to Falcon, "it would be exactly like this."

The earwig stood with his back toward the door in front of a massive machine that rattled, hissed, and puffed. What the machine was doing was a mystery. The inventor held an oilcan in his hand, and he could not possibly have heard them arrive.

Anna took a few steps forward, holding up her police badge.

"Oleg Earwig?" she asked.

Without taking his gaze from the oilcan and the machine and without turning around, Oleg shouted back.

"That's me, that's me. Come back later. Come back tomorrow. Or next week. Next week. Right now I'm busy."

"Mr. Earwig," Anna shouted to be heard above the noise, "we're from the police department."

This had a certain effect. Earwig lowered the oilcan and twirled around. He was disgusting to look at, with long, hard feelers that stuck out from his head and razor-sharp fangs that hardly fit in his mouth. Arms and legs were poking out in all directions, it seemed. He was completely black, and the blackness was in sharp contrast to the white coat he was wearing.

"This won't take long, Mr. Earwig," said Falcon. "We only want to ask a few questions."

"Don't you see that I'm busy? Busy!"

"We are, too," Anna replied. "Do you have a place where we can sit down?"

"Sit down? Sit DOWN? This is a cardan filibrator that's about to explode. Explode! I can't sit down!"

"Turn off the machine for now," Falcon ordered. "Otherwise you can come along up to the station. We can talk there instead, if you want."

"The station?" said Earwig, taking a few steps backward, astounded at this lack of respect.

"C'mon, knock it off!" Anna insisted.

Earwig looked from the lynx to the falcon and back again. He realized they were serious. Under protest, he turned off the hissing machine, muttering about irreversible processes and days of work that were now wasted. Then he led the police officers through the mechanical garbage dump that was his place of work. Among piles of potting soil, cans of fertilizer, and clay flowerpots was a round table where he sat down. With a preoccupied gesture from one of his many legs, he invited the police officers to be seated. He explained that the dirt on the floor was the remains of the unbelievably successful work he'd done on the organic toothbrush—on which new bristles grew by themselves.

"Oswald Vulture," said Anna, without revealing that she had never heard of such a toothbrush. "Does that name mean anything to you?"

"Vulture?" Earwig repeated. "Oswald Vulture? Does that mean anything? To me? A bigger fraud than Oswald Vulture has never walked the streets of Mollisan Town. A more cold-blooded liar has never been fabricated! He is a disgrace to his breed, a disgrace to all breeds, to our society. Oswald Vulture should—"

"Someone cut Oswald Vulture's head off yesterday morning," Falcon interrupted.

"Good!" Earwig exclaimed with feeling. "Amazing! Not

a day too soon. Not a single day. It should have been done a long time ago. I should have done it myself! A long time ago."

"That leads us to the next question," said Anna without changing expression. "Where were you yesterday morning?"

"Me?" Earwig was offended. "Me? Where was I? That's none of your damn business!"

"I must remind you that a murder has been committed," said Falcon. "You seem to be taking this lightly."

"He's missing a head, you say?" Earwig continued. "He's truly missing a head? Well, I'll be damned. Not a day too soon. Not a day. I have an alibi, don't worry about that, sweet little cat."

"I am not a—"

"Headless, headless, headless," the inventor sang. "Yes, what the hell . . ."

"Hasn't Nova Park invested considerable money in your company?" asked Falcon.

Oleg Earwig was not listening.

"How did they cut his head off?"

"For investigative reasons we can't comment on that," Anna interjected before Falcon said too much.

"No," Earwig replied, nodding. "No, that doesn't matter. Yes, the company. Yes, can it be any more rotten than that? He betrayed me, that SWINE! He betrayed me. I was in the middle of great, revolutionary work on my Dry-o-plex, and—"

"Dry-o-plex?" asked Falcon.

"The drying cabinet," Earwig explained. "I was in the process of transforming our dreary drying cabinets into four-dimensional cinemas! Instead of standing there, drying for hours, you have flat screens around you, above your head and under your claws. You're standing on the movie! The experience is . . . it can't be described. Not a single wet stuffed animal in this city is going to want to be without a Dry-o-plex."

Earwig fell silent and considered this. Then he nodded in agreement with himself.

"It sounds . . ." Falcon began, uncertain of how it sounded.

"But that SWINE pulled out. That SWINE! He betrayed me. Betrayed me. Pulled the rug out. I was there yesterday morning and talked with him. I'm sure you know that. He let me fall. I fell. I'm falling. But now . . . now I'm falling with a smile!"

"And your . . . alibi?" asked Anna. "You may have been the last person to see him alive. As you know, it's hard to determine exact times during the latter half of the Morning Weather. Can you account for your whereabouts yesterday morning?"

Oleg Earwig stood up.

"Of course I can. Foolishness. Now I have to get back to my cardan filibrator," he explained. "I don't have time for this. Arrest me, if you want!"

He held out a pair of his arms theatrically. Anna shook her head.

"No, exactly," said Earwig triumphantly. "I didn't think so. I refuse to disclose what I was doing yesterday after the meeting with the cursed Vulture. I have personal reasons. Personal! But Balder Toad will vouch for me. I spent the rest of the morning together with Toad. For personal reasons I'm not saying more. But that should be enough. Toad is my guarantor."

Falcon recorded the toad's name in his notebook.

"You've put me in a very good mood, little cat!" Earwig said to Anna. "This may turn out to be a good day!"

And he disappeared behind the scrap iron. Soon the racket of the big machine was heard again, and Ècu and Lynx left the inventor's peculiar world on Carrer de Carrera.

2.4

Superintendent Larry Bloodhound went straight back to his office after the morning meeting with Tapir, Hare, Ècu, and Lynx. He shut the door to the office area; the shades on the window were already lowered; it was mid-morning but it could have been any time of day. He sat down behind his desk, belched audibly, and looked around. The office was claustrophobic. The thought of how many hours of his life he had spent in there overwhelmed him. All those papers. Carelessly spread out, piled in collapsing heaps, wadded up in little balls, or stuck into coffee-stained plastic folders. On the cheap bookshelves behind him were white, gray, and black binders he had inherited from whoever had been in the office before him. The bloodhound's own contributions to the bookshelf were of a different type. Half-consumed mugs of coffee. Concealed, half-eaten lunches so moldy they no longer smelled, and too disgusting for the cleaning people to dispose of. A novel or two testified to cultural ambitions; heaps of crossword-puzzle magazines suggested melancholy. On the only empty wall in the office hung a large, framed piece of art: a blurry charcoal drawing possibly depicting a barn, which he'd won when he was a member of the station's art club. The musty odor in the room—Larry's aftershave mixed with bacon and stale beer—had forever settled into the black-and-white-striped carpet.

He took out paper and pen and decided to calculate how many carbohydrates he had put away yesterday—to figure out what he could allow himself today. But before he could even begin, he remembered the piece of chocolate he'd eaten en route to the widow Flamingo. He put the pen aside. His thoughts went to yesterday evening and the cocaine that kept him from drinking up the cream in the fridge. If it hadn't been for the struggle against weight, he would never have started using the drug. Besides, the first few months had been successful. He'd lost a lot of weight, and the urge for sugar disappeared. But then, after about a year, the desire for food slowly returned. Despite coke in the evenings—and sometimes at lunch—he again started fantasizing about warm syrup, caramel sauces, and meringues. It was inexplicable, but true nonetheless.

Perhaps a different strategy. Phasing out. Instead of counting carbohydrates, would it perhaps be enough to simply eat less today than yesterday? Start a slower but perhaps more realistic journey toward the perfect body? In the lower right-hand desk drawer he expected to find the remnants of a honey-glazed pineapple, but the drawer was empty. Larry sighed and got up. Might as well head out to Nova Park and have a serious talk with the cobra. Maybe he could stop on the way and pick up a little something?

In Bourg Villette's entry hall the frog recognized the superintendent. After an astoundingly rapid elevator ride sixty-one floors up through the building's incomprehensible metal body, Bloodhound got out at Nova Park's office. He went up to the young goat in reception, smiling broadly.

"You remember me, right?"

"Quite frankly . . . ," the goat replied, looking embarrassed, "I believe so . . . Don't say a word. I'll think of it—"

The superintendent took out his identification. "Magnus gives to some and takes from others," he growled. "What's your name?"

"Goat Croix-Valmer," the goat replied.

"Croix-Valmer," Bloodhound repeated as he wrote down the goat's name in his book. "Good. Listen up, Croix-Valmer. I'd like to speak with Emanuelle Cobra first. Is she here?"

Goat nodded toward the corridor.

Bloodhound found Emanuelle Cobra at the desk where she had been sitting yesterday. Today she was wearing a turquoise top not quite as revealing as the blouse she'd had on the day before.

"Bloodhound," the superintendent barked as he entered the office. "We've already met, of course. I have a few questions."

Cobra inspected him up and down. He wore a large-checked shirt under a jacket so stained and tattered that its filth couldn't be described. His jeans were worn smooth even on the thighs, and the heavy boots might possibly have been suited to a nighttime walk in the forest. Bloodhound suddenly felt uncomfortable.

"I've already answered questions, my friend," said Cobra.

"And you're going to answer more questions, 'friend,'" Bloodhound barked angrily.

Cobra sighed, but didn't contradict him.

So as not to be at a disadvantage, the superintendent avoided the vacant chair across from the secretary, sitting instead on the edge of the desk. But in doing so he knocked over a pen-holder, which fell to the floor with a crash.

"Do you want to watch me pick it up?" asked Cobra, smiling derisively. "I can do it really slow."

Bloodhound was ashamed. Partly about how clumsy he'd

been, partly because she'd embarrassed him. He decided to go on the offensive.

"You realize of course that you're in a bad situation," he began. "Someone cut the head off your boss while you're sitting outside, and you maintain that no one has gone in or out. Then, my little dear, there's only one suspect."

"Nonsense," Cobra answered.

"Nonsense?"

"Nonsense," she repeated firmly. "Besides, I told the falcon everything. Both Earthworm and Earwig were in to see Oswald yesterday morning."

"Those were just regular meetings?"

"I have no idea what sort of meetings they were," Cobra replied. "Oswald never has the door open. You can ask Earthworm, he's here today. As far as that inventor is concerned, I've always thought that he was disgusting."

"Did Oleg Earwig visit often?"

"Before. But yesterday was the first time in a long while. Maybe six months?"

"Did you speak with Vulture after Earwig had left?"

"No."

"Did you see Vulture when Earwig left?"

"Yes," said Cobra less certainly. "Yes, I think so. We didn't talk to each other, but I think I saw him through the doorway."

"You think? You have to know whether you saw him or not."

"I saw him," Cobra repeated.

But it was apparent that she had lost interest in the conversation. After the initial provocations, she now seemed almost bored.

"And how long was it between the time Earwig left and we arrived?" Bloodhound continued.

"I don't really know," Cobra answered. "Half an hour maybe? An hour? It's always hard to say before lunch."

What she was saying was true; the weather and therefore

time were impossible to interpret in detail before the Lunch Breeze because nothing changed.

"And you still maintain that you were sitting at your desk the whole morning?" the superintendent asked.

Cobra sat silently awhile, considering how she should answer. Then she decided, met the superintendent's gaze, and nodded.

"Yes," she said. "Yes, I was."

"This is just idiotic," Bloodhound growled. "Idiotic! I don't believe you. I'm asking you again. Did you ever leave your desk?"

Emanuelle Cobra looked at him with her large walnut eyes. She had already answered the question. Finally he turned his gaze away and got up.

"Idiotic!" he growled again, leaving her in the beautiful office.

The superintendent was so upset by the interview with Emanuelle Cobra that he stormed out of Nova Park, sat in the car, and ate up the spun-sugar chocolate sticks he had intended to save for the afternoon, even before he started the engine. Quickly and aggressively he then drove the short way home, ran up the stairs, and, once inside the apartment, went straight to the refrigerator, where he ate up all there was to eat. Cordelia gave him a friendly chirp from her golden cage, and after a few minutes the superintendent relaxed.

"Ah," he growled, "I'm sorry, little one, but I was so upset. I'll have to have a good day tomorrow instead."

Cordelia looked out through the window. Or so it appeared to Larry. It was tricky to know with a budgie.

"Have I told you my theory?" he asked, sitting down on the couch with a package of alphabet cookies on his lap.

There was never a risk of being interrupted by a caged bird.

"We have to hope that this involves a perpetrator who did

not find his destiny right there, in Vulture's office," Blood-hound said pensively. "Because I always say that chance, Cordelia, chance is like an automatic weapon. Chance is a ma-chine gun that loads the chamber with bullets of fate. Chance doesn't care about us stuffed animals, at least about us as indi-viduals, because for chance the whole is more important than the component parts. Chance is just and blind. It doesn't care who's standing in the way when it shoots."

Bloodhound took a "g" and an "h" and put them in his mouth. The cookies were sweet but dry.

"Chance fires its weapon when it has the desire, Cordelia, and we stuffed animals have no protection against these bul-lets of fate. There's nothing we can do to avoid them. That's the way it goes. If chance was waiting like a sniper up at Nova Park yesterday and hit the murderer with one of his bullets, then this could be . . . a little hell . . ."

He ate up an "r" and a "k," and then got up to get a beer.

"Do you understand what I'm saying?" Bloodhound growled softly. "It's not so difficult. We're delivered. It's our fate. To be delivered. To a certain address, a certain family, and there's nothing we can do about it. Reincarnation is non-sense. We can talk about the soul another time."

He took a swig from the bottle as he was returning to the couch.

"We're delivered, Cordelia, and fate puts our lives in motion. Whether we want it or not. There's nothing we can do about it. The limits are set from the first moment. Do you call that freedom? Or justice? Bullshit. Fate has staked out your life even before life has managed to begin. It's about how we look. Who we are. Dog or bumblebee. If we're smart or dumb. What neighborhood we grow up in, and whether we're rich or poor. What age we live in, and the values of the age. Can our particular kind of talent be used in Mollisan Town at this point in time? It's about what school we go to, who else is in the same grade, who our parents' friends are, and what values they have. You get stuck in a social network before you even grasp what that means. Do you understand, Cordelia? There's not much you can do about it. You become what you become."

Superintendent Larry Bloodhound had repeated this monologue—with minor variations—to all the police officers at rue de Cadix over the years.

He poured the rest of the cookies straight from the carton into his mouth, washing them down with beer.

"Fate puts you in motion, Cordelia, like a stone rolling down a slope. Cause and effect. It's about cause and effect. You do something good and get rewarded. You get to know someone who knows someone else who knows a third person who tells a story that you then always carry with you. That marks you. One of your father's friends that you admired was a policeman, and you become a policeman yourself. A teacher in school pats you on the head because you stayed within the lines the first time you used crayons and you always want to be praised because you did something someone else decided was good. Or else you're punished. Because you talked too loud, or dressed too carelessly. Logic rules your life. Fate puts it in motion, but then you roll down that slope in a rut that is the most reasonable. It can be predicted. It can be calculated. And that's what police work is about. We can trace anyone whosoever back in time, back to the time when they were delivered, by seeing how cause and effect have led the criminal, step by step, up to the criminal deed. We think we're free in this life, Cordelia, but who the hell is free? We live with the conditions that the Deliverymen gave us when they placed us in a certain home at a certain time. No bastard is free. And through careful detective work, we can put away anyone."

A long belch gave him an opportunity to catch his breath before he continued.

"We can put away anyone whosoever, if chance hasn't loaded its machine gun and put a bullet in the murderer yesterday morning. Because sometimes it happens that stuffed animals are struck by something outside themselves, something they have no control over, something that causes their lives to depart from the course fate set out. And if that happens, everything that led up to that point when the deed is committed becomes irrelevant. Then no police work in the world will help. Then this case with Vulture is going to be a fine mess . . ."

2.5

They were in a red, black, and yellow police car. Anna was driving in tense silence. The Afternoon Rain had ended a few minutes earlier and Field Mouse Pedersen refused to give up his attempts to carry on a lighthearted conversation.

"I know why you didn't ask Falcon," Field Mouse chuckled to himself. "In nine cases out of ten you ask your partner. But in the tenth case—you ask me."

"Very nice of you to volunteer," Anna replied, but her tone was neutral and she didn't look at him.

"I'm guessing, of course," Field Mouse corrected himself. "But I think I know. Why you didn't ask Falcon."

Field Mouse Pedersen did not know where they were going or what was expected of him, and his nature was such that he was not one to ask straight out. He was loyal, and he was proud of that. His colleagues should know that they could always count on him.

"You're easier to convince," said Anna.

They were driving along bright yellow North Avenue. A full-grown lane of willows divided the northbound and southbound traffic, but there weren't many cars at the moment. The memory of the recently fallen rain had left the avenue in a pleasant fog, and Anna was driving with the lights on.

"Easier to convince, huh? That sounds ominous."

The spiked wall around Les Trois Maggots showed up in front of them to the left, and Anna put on her turn signal.

"Are we going shopping?" Pedersen commented.

They turned left and drove up onto the massive asphalt meadow that was the shopping center's parking lot. Even though it was a late Tuesday afternoon in early June, she couldn't find a parking place. Finally she parked the police car on the sidewalk outside one of the smaller entrances, turned off the engine, and turned with a serious and worried expression toward Pedersen.

"Inside here there is someone," she explained, "that I want you to arrest. Take him out to the car, drive over to the station. There you can let him go."

Pedersen looked like a living question mark.

"Arrest and then release? But . . . has he done anything or not?"

"He's done something," Anna maintained.

"So why do I let him go?"

"He hasn't done anything we can arrest him for."

Pedersen stared at her.

"Now I understand why you didn't ask Falcon," he said at last. "Falcon wouldn't do it, would he?"

"And you?" she asked, looking him in the eyes. "Can you do it? For my sake? I promise he doesn't deserve better."

Field Mouse Pedersen nodded curtly and opened the car door. Anna did the same. With determined steps they walked beside each other across the sidewalk toward the entrance.

The theme for Les Trois Maggots was fertility. The dimensions of the shopping center were enormous, as expected, and along the hundreds of escalators, across the entire glass ceiling, and up along the monumental pillars grapevines and clematis were growing. In built-in planters on the main floor stood rows of oaks, whose magnificent crowns reached all the way up to the fifth-floor level. And everywhere on the floors, rose petals were strewn; Anna had read somewhere that five thousand roses a day went on to the floors in Les Trois Maggots. She didn't know if that was true.

"Where is he?" Field Mouse asked.

"Don't know."

"You're joking? If we're going to search at random this is going to take hours."

"I know what stores she likes," said Anna.

"She?"

"We're doing this for her sake. And I promise, she's worth it. We'll start with Missonno."

Missonno's flagship boutique was on the second-floor level, across from a restaurant that boasted Yokian specialties in the window. The police giggled at this—nothing good had ever come from Yok. The Missonno boutique was furnished in mauve from floor to ceiling, and behind the registers a waterfall rumbled and foamed. The whole thing was very theatrical.

Anna saw Cow Hellwig at a distance. She was trying on a knee-length skirt that caused her hips to look unusually wide. Across from Cow sat her husband on a stool, acting as her adviser.

"That's him," said Anna, pointing. "Can you manage it?"

"Won't you be along?"

"Fool," she said. "I know him."

Field Mouse Pedersen pondered this, then shrugged his shoulders. Without further ado he went over to the couple Anna had pointed out, as Anna fled the boutique, positioning herself to watch from inside the Yokian restaurant. It took a few minutes, and then Pedersen came out with Cow's worse half. He had even succeeded in getting Cow to remain behind in the boutique.

———

"You!"

"Wait, let me say—" said Anna Lynx.

"Of course it was you," Cow Hellwig shouted. "But this is crazy!"

They were standing inside Missonno, shouting at each other, partly to be heard over the waterfall.

"Cow," said Anna, "you must come to your senses. I've seen what he's done to you. I've heard what he says. That . . . no female can accept."

"Anna, I accept it," said Cow.

"But think of all the others. Think of all those who, through the years, have been oppressed, set aside, and treated like, well, cattle. If not for your own sake, then do it for the sake of others. For the sake of all females."

"Do what?"

"Leave him. Now. Come along with me. There's a secure apartment where you can—"

"Secure apartment?"

"He's never going to find you there. You can be safe."

Cow stared at her friend. She was furious. At the same time she felt laughter bubbling up in her throat.

"What have you done with him?" she asked.

"Nothing," Anna answered. "Don't worry about him. The only thing I've done is give you a chance. Now."

"You're out of your mind," said Cow, as the laughter reached up to her eyes. "You're out of your mind. But there's something sweet about the whole thing anyway."

Anna didn't know how to interpret this laughter.

"Cow, I—"

"Anna, listen now. Don't ever do this again. Or I'll report you."

"Me? Me? C'mon, I'm not the one who—"

But Cow Hellwig was on her way out of the shop, and she did not intend to let Lynx stop her.

IGOR PANDA 2

Jake Golden Retriever put out the cigarette and summoned the waiter. He was always impatient after he'd finished his coffee; he hated sitting, waiting for the check. There was something degrading about asking to pay so you could leave the restaurant.

The outdoor café at Trois Étoiles in Bois de Dalida was in pleasant shade, and the mild breeze nudged the heat away under the artfully suspended sails that served as a roof, which shone in all the colors of the rainbow. Somehow this eccentric appendix fit in with the café's old-fashioned elegance.

As usual, the restaurant was packed. Since Chef Pig Laînotre returned to Trois Étoiles last year, it was almost impossible to get a table. No reservations were taken for the outdoor café, however, and Jake had been lucky.

He waved a bill in the air as the waitress went past, but she didn't see him. He was used to that. He was a dog who was easy to ignore. He was not one to make a fuss, and his appearance had a tendency to slip past an observer's awareness. His fur was almost white with streaks of beige, his eyes were brown and imploring. His manner was accommodating and pleasant, and he had learned many years ago to dress discreetly.

Jake lit a cigarette and made a new attempt to get the waitress to see him.

Bois de Dalida, the park that came to form the northwest boundary of Tourquai and Mollisan Town toward the great forests, came into existence during the first decade of the twentieth century. In the beginning, the park was no more than a few pen strokes on a map, a simple act of clearing an existing forest; a small gravel path was constructed that enclosed an area of a few square miles. Then a competition was announced. Entries were submitted by the foremost architects of the day. They surpassed one another with lavish oak avenues and dramatic waterfalls, elaborate boxwood labyrinths and romantic water-lily ponds. After a drawn-out, heated jury process, a winner was announced and the work begun.

When the great depression struck Mollisan Town, the park was almost halfway completed, and the Yokian pavilion was on its way to completion. The winning entry had included four buildings representing the four districts of the city, but the Yokian pavilion was the only one actually erected. With the depression, all activity in the city came to a standstill overnight. The workers refused to return to work because they would not get paid, and the employers were secretly relieved at the interruption of work because they couldn't pay.

It would be five years before the Yokian pavilion, with its arched glass veranda, its three towers, and its integrated greenhouse, would be completed. It would take another ten years before the garden in front of the pavilion was put in order, with its delta of small rivers between the ponds and twenty or so artificial islands with equally high but short bridges between them.

With that, however, the Bois de Dalida was finished; just a little more than half of the original project had been realized. Even today, the northern part of the park consists of wild forest that differentiates itself from the surrounding forests only by the fact that it is located inside the gravel path.

The Trois Étoiles restaurant opened in the Yokian pavilion during the late fifties. From the very first moment it became a particularly popular destination for the well-to-do in the city, but the cuisine had varied in quality over the years. Pig Laînotre created his reputation as a master chef at Trois Étoiles, and after several years at restaurants in town he finally returned. And with him a large following.

Jake Retriever put out his cigarette.

He figured out himself how much he owed and left the money—with a tip—on the saucer under the coffee cup. Then he got up and left the restaurant.

Golden Retriever chose to take the route across the islands. He was not in a hurry, and he liked the high, small bridges. Out on the walking path he continued northward at a pleasant pace. Even though it was the middle of the week, and the middle of the day, there were many out walking.

A little more than halfway between the Yokian pavilion and the northernmost point of the gravel path, Jake Golden Retriever unexpectedly climbed over the low hedge and continued into the forest. He did this with a self-assurance that would have convinced any observer that the dog knew exactly what he was doing and thereby even had the right to do so.

Deviating from the gravel path and wandering in among the trees was not forbidden. Berries and mushrooms grew in the forest; there was a stillness that a stressed modern animal might well need, and an isolation that couples in love sometimes appreciated.

But Jake Golden Retriever was no philosopher or berry picker, and he had always lived alone.

He continued deeper and deeper in among the trees, and after a few minutes the growth thinned out and Jake approached the hill that many in Tourquai called a mountain. Through the hill ran a ravine, which in certain places was only wide enough for one animal at a time to pass, and when Jake had gone halfway he could see Igor Panda standing and waiting at the northernmost end.

"Finally!" Panda groaned, obviously irritated.

Jake did not reply.

"Well, say it, then!" said Panda.

Panda was aggressive, and he seemed nervous besides. He stamped his foot and had a hard time standing still.

"Say it!" he repeated.

"What do you want me to say?" Jake asked, when he was close enough to use a normal conversational tone.

"Say that you want the money," said Panda. "Say that you want your share."

Jake Golden Retriever's expression did not reveal what he thought about the contentious Panda.

"I would gladly take my share of the money," he said obediently.

"Never," Panda replied and laughed. He took a few steps backward, changed his mind, and went up to Golden Retriever again.

"Never," he repeated. "You're only a bungler. An artistic bungler. I know your type. It's a joke that you should have half."

"Without me you have nothing to sell," Jake Golden Retriever pointed out quietly.

This caused Igor Panda to explode.

"Sell?" he screamed. "I'm a prerequisite for you to have anything to sell! Without me your Esperanza-Santiagos would be worthless! However damned cleverly you may make them!

Without me you're not even a forger, you're only an epigone. Everyone knows that she lets only *me* sell her things! Everyone knows that, everyone who might conceivably have the means to buy. Without me . . . if you tried to go to any other dealer . . . whoever . . . even the cursed Janzon . . . you wouldn't have a chance!"

Panda had taken two steps forward and thus was standing so close to Golden Retriever that the dog felt the panda's breath.

"You," Panda whispered, "are not worth fifty percent."

Panda had complained about the division before, but never so explicitly. Golden Retriever stood silently, staring into the stuffed animal's eyes without averting his gaze.

"And I don't intend to give you fifty percent. I intend to give you . . . a hundred thousand."

Jake did not react now, either; Panda took a few steps back.

"A hundred thousand," he repeated.

He turned around, leaving Jake alone in the ravine. When he returned after a few minutes, he had the attaché case with him. Jake was still standing on the exact same spot.

Igor Panda found the silent, patient dog unbelievably irritating. There was something triumphant about the golden retriever's attitude, and he felt a desire to shake him up, produce a crack in the tight-buttoned façade.

"What if I had a gun in the case?" said Panda. "What would you do then?"

Golden Retriever raised one white eyebrow.

"I could kill you," Panda continued. "Here, in this ravine. Then you wouldn't get a penny."

Golden Retriever lowered the eyebrow. He looked neither happy nor sad, neither angry nor afraid.

"Whatever!" Panda hissed. "A hundred thousand. That's what I'm offering. What do you say about that?"

"Seven hundred fifty thousand. If you want to keep on doing business," Jake replied.

There was nothing threatening in his tone of voice, it was a simple statement.

"But you're not going to succeed without me!" Panda screamed. "Don't you get it? 'Keep on doing business'—without me there is no business!"

"Seven hundred fifty thousand," Jake repeated calmly.

In frustration, Panda took two tight turns in the thicket where he was standing. He sat down on his haunches and opened the briefcase. Hesitated. Closed it again, got up, and started to leave. Changed his mind, came back to Golden Retriever and placed himself quite close, as if to say something. But he did not get out a word. Finally, he threw the case on the ground.

In silence Igor Panda counted out the seven hundred fifty thousand and gave it to the dog, who took the money just as quietly.

Swearing, Panda left.

DAY THREE

3.1

The police station at place St.-Fargeau was a paragon of power, a freestanding brick palace in the middle of densely built-up Tourquai. The building was crowned by three towers rising above the roofs of the surrounding buildings; the entryway consisted of heavy oak doors in the middle of a massive portal, ornamented with stone sculptures that were reminders of the eternal victory of justice over wickedness.

"Imagine working here, looking at this every morning," Falcon Ècu whispered longingly.

"Really," Anna Lynx whispered back, "that would be tough . . ."

Not wanting to seem like a careerist, Falcon refrained from answering.

As they entered the building, the difference between this police station and their little station down on rue de Cadix became embarrassing. In the stairwells, behind the counters, and this way and that on the large stone floor, police officers of all types and departments walked and ran in regulation dress, en route to defending the city. Falcon sighed in admiration. Anna misunderstood him again.

"I know," she said. "But we'll just listen to the run-through, then we'll leave, quicker than quick."

Two levels belowground was the Forensics Department where Theodore Tapir had ruled since time immemorial; there was a faint odor of formalin and disinfectant as soon as the elevator doors opened. Falcon and Anna hurried through corridors edged by closed doors. Soon they came to a reception desk, where they were shown the way to Tapir's office, large enough to hold half a department from rue de Cadix. Bloodhound and Pedersen were already there, waiting.

"Morning traffic," Anna mumbled, late as usual dropping off Todd at day care.

They sat down with their colleagues at a white, polished conference table with room for at least fifteen more stuffed, animals. Tapir smiled broadly at them all.

"Good," he said. "I hope you're awake, despite the early morning hour. This may get a bit complicated."

Anna noticed what everyone had already seen: Tapir was giddy. He was wearing his customary white coat—which showed that he was a researcher and a medical doctor, not a simple police officer—but he was glowing. He had something to tell.

"We'll take the formalities first," he said. "You can do that, can't you, Bramstoke?"

The turnover of Tapir's browbeaten assistants was endless. Tapir wore them out during the course of a few months, and then they were never seen again. This month's version, Bramstoke, who as far as could be judged was a tuna fish, started recounting the well-known circumstances around Oswald Vulture's departure. The clinical nature of the office, Vulture's general condition—which was average, apart from a slightly enlarged liver and a hearing deficiency in the left ear since he was young—and finally the cut itself. But here Tapir took over.

"Do you recall what I said the other day?" he began. "About the fact that the perpetrator carried out the deed from behind?"

"Excuse me, but as I recall it—" Falcon began, who remembered exactly what his words had been.

Tapir was not pleased at being interrupted.

"Yes, yes," he drowned out the falcon, "now I can state that it was exactly as I believed. After an analysis of the murder weapon there is no doubt. I would like to show you a few pictures."

Tapir nodded to Bramstoke to turn off the lights. On the white screen that mechanically glided down from the ceiling, something that resembled a field plowed by a slightly intoxicated farmer was projected. Anna had been through this before and did not expect to understand what she was looking at.

"This is Vulture's neck," Tapir explained. "Note the structure of the fabric . . . Fascinating, isn't it?"

With a long pointer Tapir indicated a new, linear pattern that mostly resembled an unsuccessful batch of spaghetti.

"This type of pliability, let me call it elegance, is very seldom seen," Tapir maintained, putting his long experience as a forensic physician behind the words. "A single stroke, without a doubt from behind, an unbroken movement from above. Whoever executed the stroke was standing; Vulture was sitting down. I am quite certain that he was not moved to the chair afterward. The rigidity of the limbs, especially in the knees, is unambiguous. I repeat, exactly as I have already said, that technique may very well have replaced force. But . . . there must be two arms, at least."

"Excuse me, but what do you mean?" asked Falcon. "Are you saying that you're . . . ruling out snakes?"

"In my job," Tapir snorted, "we do not talk in terms of stuffed animals. This is about science. If you are asking whether a snake could stand up on the floor and at the same time, coiled around the handle of the sword, swing the blade with such precision, I would judge it to be highly improbable. There may possibly be a boa who somehow could have managed it, but . . . a snake of normal size . . . no, it's not likely."

Bloodhound growled quietly. Everyone around the table was thinking about Emanuelle Cobra, and trying to imagine how it might have been done. But, as Tapir had just said, it was difficult, not to say impossible, to picture it.

Theodore Tapir continued to instruct the gathering for ten minutes about cutting surfaces and textile singularities, the roughness of fibers and the possibility of establishing individual differences. Oblivious to the other stuffed animals' boredom with these scientific subtleties, he finally got to the point.

"And now to the question of time."

Bloodhound sat up. Falcon stopped taking notes. Tapir made a theatrical pause so that everyone would notice the silence spreading, and then asked Bramstoke to operate the projector. As Tapir talked, his assistant clicked new enlargements onto the white screen.

"I don't need to go over the background, you all know how it is. From midnight until the Afternoon Weather the temperature increases by one degree per hour. Then the temperature falls again in a corresponding manner. We divide a single degree into sixty units. By studying the humidity structure in Vulture's open wounds, as you see here, we can determine the time of the decapitation with great precision. What causes problems is the air-conditioning in the Nova Park offices. Next picture, Bramstoke. Here. You see what's happening with the humidity? Yesterday we put a fabric corresponding to Vulture's on his office chair, and then we followed the change in the textile. Here you see the development. Then it was a matter of extrapolating this process from the natural circadian temperature, without resorting to simple subtraction. The pictures that Bramstoke is showing now are simulations of how we think it might have appeared. This entire process thus depicts the gaping wound that is Vulture's neck opening from the cut that exposed the fibers, until we arrived at the office and could interrupt the process by closing the body hermetically according to our customary procedure. Fascinating, isn't it?"

"And?" growled Bloodhound.

"And I can with more than ninety percent certainty say that the temperature was higher than sixty-eight degrees outside when Vulture lost his head. Not much, that I admit, at the most a tenth of a sixtieth. But that makes the margin limited, I would say."

Theodore Tapir looked as though he expected some type of prize after this run-through, and Bloodhound growled with approval, even if still not impressed.

When they left the police station at place St.-Fargeau, Pedersen noted in a low voice that Tapir's observation had not changed anything. Oleg Earwig and Oswald Vulture had started their meeting when the breeze died out and the Morning Weather began. Cobra had a clear recollection that the meeting lasted half an hour rather than an hour, and this time frame had been confirmed by the goat in reception. Cobra had also consistently stated that Vulture was alive when Earwig left.

"Tapir said nothing new," Pedersen repeated.

"He never does," Anna said. "It's only on TV that medical examiners decide murder cases."

3.2

I have to go downstairs and do some shooting," said Falcon. "I'm sorry. I know the superintendent told us to leave right away to talk to the toad, but we'll still make it, won't we?"

Anna concealed her smile.

"Again? You have to shoot again?"

"Yes, I really have to."

Falcon was not pleased. He unlocked the topmost drawer and took out the pistol and holster. He was one of the few police officers at WE who stored his weapon in accordance with regulations.

"I thought you passed the first time. Larry's going to be out of his mind if he sees we haven't left. C'mon, I'll talk with him."

"It won't take more than half an hour," said Falcon, running toward the stairs.

There was a shooting range in the basement below the police station at rue de Cadix, and in order to carry a service weapon, the police officers had to pass an annual shooting test. Falcon had unique qualities as a police officer; for him, this test was a major challenge.

Anna stayed behind in her seat, watching her nervous colleague as her telephone rang. She picked up the receiver.

"This is Lynx."

"Anna? It's Charlie."

It took a few moments before she made the connection. Charlie, down at tech, whom yesterday she'd asked to help her with information on the tipster.

"Charlie? Have you—?"

"Yep," he said. "It wasn't even difficult. But I don't know if this will make you any happier. The call you asked about came from a phone booth. Rue de Montyon, almost at the corner of rue le Brun."

"All three? Two to Bloodhound and one to Falcon?"

"Exactly. They were made later during the Afternoon Weather. The second one came shortly after the first. The third, the one to Falcon, was a little later, less than ten minutes. I would say about ten minutes before the Lunch Breeze."

"Charlie, thanks a lot," said Anna and hung up.

Rue de Montyon. That was a blue street, and she knew exactly where the phone booth at the corner of rue le Brun was. So the mysterious tipster had not phoned from Nova Park. Anna Lynx thought about this. It was no more than ten minutes from Bourg Villette to rue de Montyon. If you ran, perhaps you could make it in an even shorter time. But was that likely? That someone happened to see the body on the sixty-second floor and then took the elevator down to Boulevard de la Villette and ran like a lunatic to a phone booth?

Considering the tight time frame, one alternative would be to suspect Cobra of being the tipster. She must be involved in some way. But why would Cobra want the police there? And in that case, why run off to a phone booth? Anna had brooded a great deal about Cobra, but what she could not put together was that the secretary so obviously put herself in a bad situation by being at the office when the police arrived.

Trying to secure clues in the phone booth itself was fruitless. If the tipster left any behind, it would be impossible to determine which were his in particular. She could of course take a swing past rue de Montyon a little later—there were police animals with improbable luck, but up to now she had not been one of them. Falcon Ècu kept her waiting, which indicated that the shooting exercise was not going according to plan. Anna Lynx returned to the reports she had started yesterday, but the going was sluggish. Animals came and went around her, they shouted and laughed, talked loudly in telephones and across tables; it was hard to concentrate. Over and over again her thoughts kept returning to her friend Cow Hellwig. Why wouldn't she listen to reason?

After an unfocused quarter of an hour, Anna Lynx turned on her computer and logged in to the Ministry of Finance database. If the report writing was not going well, the time was better used checking the blocks around the tipster's phone booth via the building registry. There was an ongoing debate about the authorities' coordination of data registries, but during the last year the protests had been confined to occasional articles.

Police work, she thought. Randomly skimming through lists of names of tenants and condominium owners without knowing what you were looking for. Falcon Ècu would consider what she was doing wasted time; he didn't believe in intuition.

Anna Lynx scrolled through stuffed animals who lived in the blocks around rue de Montyon and rue le Brun. Slowly she let one name after another scroll up and off the screen, life stories she knew nothing about, and after a few minutes she inevitably started to get tired. It was just when she raised her paw to rub her eyes that it suddenly showed up: Claude Siamese.

She jerked back from the keyboard as if she'd burned herself. Leaned back in the chair and stared at the screen.

Claude Siamese. At 42 rue de Montyon, fifth floor.

If Anna Lynx had been given the task of compiling a list

of the hundred stuffed animals with the heaviest criminal involvement in Mollisan Town, Claude Siamese would have been on that list. If she were to rank the twenty most dangerous animals in Tourquai, Claude Siamese would be at the top. He'd been involved in everything: prostitution, drugs, assault, blackmail. He had served a few short sentences at King's Cross but never been convicted of any major offenses. Everyone in the legal system knew that the city would be a better place if Claude Siamese were arrested and thrown into prison. Yet they couldn't arrest him. There was no evidence. There were no witnesses. There was, Bloodhound asserted, no justice.

"Excuse me, but what are you doing?"

Falcon's question startled Anna and she lost her balance. A reflex caused her to take hold of the desk. Falcon smiled.

"You scared me!"

"I'm sorry. That wasn't the idea. What are you doing?"

"How'd it go?"

"They probably won't be calling me when they need sharpshooters," Falcon sighed. "But I passed."

"Good." Anna pointed at the computer. "I'm checking the thing with the tipster a little more."

"Who?"

"The stuffed animal who called you and said that Vulture was dead. The tipster."

"Cobra," said Falcon.

"You think?"

"Depends on what you mean by think. I realize that Cobra didn't do it, not after what Tapir said this morning. But that doesn't mean she didn't have anything to do with it."

"Then I'm going to make it a little harder." Anna smiled. "The call came from a phone booth on rue de Montyon. Do you think that little piece of latex slithered there, called, and slithered back again?"

"A phone booth?" said Falcon. "Hmm. Yes, compared to

you, Anna, I don't have much to offer where investigations are concerned, but I still think it might be her. I don't know. She doesn't act rationally. She goes in to her boss, he's sitting at the desk without a head. She runs out, confused and contrite, and she can't handle the situation. She has to call someone, she calls the police, but she doesn't want to end up in a lengthy interrogation where she has to give her name and have her life turned upside down. So she calls anonymously."

"Sounds completely unbelievable," said Anna.

Falcon nodded. He agreed.

"Besides, look at this," said Anna, moving the computer screen in Falcon's direction. "Claude Siamese lives in the building by the phone booth."

Falcon sat down at the desk.

"Excuse me, but I don't understand. What does this mean?" he asked after a pensive silence.

"No idea," Anna replied.

"No idea?"

"Do you have a theory?"

Falcon thought about that.

"Yes, if you ask straight out like that . . . I don't know, of course, but . . . one of the animals that hated Vulture hired a hit man from Siamese? When the hit man carried out the deed, he calls Siamese, who in turn tips off the police," Falcon proposed.

"Okay," laughed Anna. "And why would Claude Siamese tip off the police?"

"I don't know, of course, but it may have something to do with the alibi," Falcon continued freely out of his imagination. "Siamese wants the police to find the body as quickly as possible, because the hit man has an alibi for just that point in time . . ."

Anna remained sitting, serious and silent. She was staring at Falcon. There was a glimmer of respect in her eyes. He saw that.

"Excuse me, but you don't believe it's like that, do you?" he asked in surprise.

"No," she said, "that was just bullshit. I have no idea where Siamese comes into the picture. But that other thing . . . that actually doesn't sound too bad. That the reason someone calls several times, that someone is so urgent, is because they have an alibi for just that time of the morning."

They did not leave until the Morning Breeze. They had located the Balder Toad that Oleg Earwig provided as his alibi at a junkyard up in north Tourquai, and they were on their way there. It was Falcon again who drove, and he parked outside the gates of the junkyard a few minutes before the breeze intensified.

"Have you been here before?" he asked.

"Never," Anna replied.

They got out of the car and went up to the wrought-iron gates, which were open.

"I guess we can just go in," said Falcon.

The wrecks of scrapped cars towered over them on both sides. It was not a big junkyard, but the pathways between the piles of metal skeletons were many and narrow. On the other side they could see the forest; large trees protectively held out their leafy branches over the dead cars. The police officers could see no building or any animals, so they continued farther into the area. The breeze after the rain caused towers of precariously balanced cowcatchers and hubcaps to screech from friction.

"Hello!" Falcon called.

His outburst gave Anna a start. She was about to say something about his carelessness when they heard someone answer. The police officers rounded a pair of burned-out truck cabs and saw a small, dilapidated wooden shed standing next to a thick tree trunk.

"Stop!" a voice was heard at a distance.

Falcon and Anna stopped.

"Who are you?" called the voice.

"We're from the police," Falcon answered in a loud voice. "The inventor Oleg Earwig suggested that we should meet you."

There was silence from the shed. The police officers stood quietly, waiting for something to happen. When no invitation came, Anna took a step forward.

The explosion was unexpected. An old-style shotgun was fired, and a sheaf of buckshot struck the sheet metal a few yards to the right of Falcon.

The police officers threw themselves to the ground—just as the next salvo was fired.

3.3

The weather was just after lunch when Field Mouse Pedersen arrived at the police station with Goat Croix-Valmer in tow. The choice had been between questioning the receptionist at Nova Park or going down and ordering a pizza with pineapple and honey. The interview took priority.

Bloodhound had never thought that Emanuelle Cobra did it. Instinct, experience, gut feeling, call it what you will: whether she was involved or not he left unsaid—she might be—but she was not the one who cut off the vulture's head. Which Tapir had established this morning.

Earwig remained, and because Bloodhound had not met the inventor in question the superintendent had no perception other than that he hoped it was Earwig who was guilty. Because if it wasn't Earwig . . . this investigation would drag on. While waiting for Anna and Falcon, whom he had sent off to check the inventor's alibi, Bloodhound had no desire to start anything new. So he sent Pedersen out after Croix-Valmer. The investigation called for an additional interview with the little goat, and if Bloodhound did it over lunch he would avoid stuffing himself with more unhealthy things.

"This is my lunchtime!" Goat Croix-Valmer protested as Pedersen pushed him down onto the empty chair beside Bloodhound's desk.

He was dressed in a pair of bright yellow slacks that took attention away from his shoes and shirt.

"Shut up," Bloodhound growled. "And think of all the calories I'm saving you."

"Calories?" Goat repeated. "That's not my problem. If you feel fat you shou'dn't think that—"

"Fat!" roared Bloodhound. "Listen up, you cross-stitched little mama's boy, now you shut up and think. I'm a cop. I can lock you up in King's Cross for the rest of your life. I'm the one you want to stay friends with."

Croix-Valmer glared angrily at the superintendent but said nothing. Pedersen cleared his throat.

"Perhaps you'd like me to record the interview, Superintendent?" he asked.

"Thanks, Pedersen, but I think it's better if you leave us. If I have to rough up this poor goat I'd prefer not to have any witnesses."

Goat did not see Field Mouse Pedersen's sly smile before he left Bloodhound's office, and thus the comment had the desired effect. Croix-Valmer decided to cooperate.

"Well, we might as well start at the beginning," said Bloodhound, taking out his writing implements. "And see if this degenerates or whether you can manage a little common courtesy. When did you start at Nova Park?"

"Almost two years ago," Croix-Valmer replied. "It will be two years in July."

"And before that?"

"I was a receptionist at Incubator. And before that I worked at Banque Mollisan. But only a little while, right after school."

Croix-Valmer answered rapidly and honestly. He wanted to get this over with as quickly as possible.

"And how do you get along at Nova Park?" Bloodhound asked, picking his nose with one of his long, black claws. "Compared with your previous experiences?"

"It's the best," the goat replied with emphasis. "Like, ten animals total, good pay, no one gets upset if you arrive a little late or leave a little early . . ."

"And the reason why you quit your previous job . . . at Incubator?"

"They fired me," the goat said in a lower voice. "I don't know any more than that. You'll have to ask them."

Bloodhound made a notation. Pedersen would have to make that call.

"I want to ask you about Monday morning," Bloodhound growled.

"Super-hectic!" Croix-Valmer exclaimed, throwing out his hooves. "They were going to repair the server in Anastasia's office and kept running back and forth several times. And then the police officers who came . . ."

"I was the police officer who came," Bloodhound commented. "Repair the server?"

"An electrician," Croix-Valmer confirmed, nodding. "I made him show his identification every time he went past. Two times. Or three times. I don't know . . ."

"And otherwise?"

"Otherwise I guess it was as usual, more or less. Quiet."

"Any visitors?"

"No visitors. Not many calls. A few deliveries."

"Deliveries? Were there deliveries to reception Monday morning?"

"No. No, there weren't any deliveries on Monday. I meant that normally there are deliveries. Sometimes."

"There weren't any visitors?" Bloodhound asked. "None at all?"

"Well . . ." Croix-Valmer hesitated. "Well, there must have been a few."

"Who?"

"Well, now I'm not sure. Were there any? Not many, anyway."

For someone who worked at a reception desk, the goat was inconceivably vague. Pedersen probably didn't need to make that call; it seemed obvious why Goat had been fired from Incubator.

"Oleg Earwig?" asked Bloodhound.

"That's right!" Goat exclaimed, relieved. "Exactly. I'm sure that unpleasant earwig came and went."

"Was he carrying anything when he left?"

"Like, a suitcase, or something?"

"Did he have a suitcase?"

"No. Nothing. I think. But there were so many arms and legs sticking out, it's hard to say. I don't know. I don't think so."

"When did he leave?"

"Don't know exactly. A few minutes before Emanuelle."

"Emanuelle Cobra?"

"Are there any other Emanuelles?"

"Did Cobra leave the office during the morning?"

"She went out for a smoke. It was right after the earwig left. Smoking is prohibited at Nova Park. The smokers are forced to go all the way down to the street. Emanuelle's trying to quit. Personally . . . I've never started."

"Did Cobra leave the office several times during the morning?" Bloodhound asked, trying to sound neutral.

"No," the goat answered firmly. "Once in the morning and once in the afternoon. No more. No more than that."

"So she left right after Earwig," Bloodhound repeated in order to give the goat a chance to change his mind. "And then she came back?"

"She was out for ten minutes, maybe fifteen. Then the police arrived, but that was a while later . . ."

"And when Cobra was down on the street, smoking," Bloodhound asked, speaking very slowly, "did anyone else go past reception then?"

"Like I said, I don't know," Croix-Valmer replied unhappily. "I don't know. The electrician, I think. Maybe."

"Think about it," Bloodhound growled.

"I don't know. The electrician? I don't know."

"You lousy little woolen mitten," the superintendent clarified, "this is important. I get it that thinking isn't your best subject. But surprise me. Did anyone go past your reception counter while Cobra was down on the street, smoking?"

Goat Croix-Valmer nodded, looking Bloodhound in the eyes, as if he could thereby produce an answer. But not a word passed his lips, and finally the superintendent realized that the only thing to do was give up. For this fool of a receptionist, the pressure was paralyzing.

"Think it over," the superintendent said. "I'm going to repeat the question another time and it would be excellent if you had an answer."

Goat Croix-Valmer nodded again, but Bloodhound doubted that there was capacity for reflection in the goat's confused brain.

3.4

Anna Lynx's pulse was pounding so hard she couldn't hear what she was thinking. She was lying stretched out behind three heaps of worn tires, holding her service pistol in her right paw.

"Excuse me, Anna, but what do we do now?" Falcon Ècu shouted.

He had landed a little farther away, in the driver's seat of a worn-out tractor. Anna could see him fumbling with the buttons on his holster, but before he got his weapon out Balder Toad had fired off the next swarm of buckshot.

The police officers crouched; Falcon dove under the steering wheel of the tractor.

The sound of ricochets cut through the air, after which silence spread over the junkyard.

Anna peered out from behind the tires. She saw the barrel of a shotgun sticking out through the only window in the decrepit shed. She called, "We've only come to—"

She didn't get further than that.

"Go away!" Toad screamed, firing a third salvo.

This time it was in earnest. The windows of the tractor's cab rained down over Falcon in small, sharp pieces. There was no room for negotiations.

Anna Lynx released the safety on her weapon and called, "On three."

She hoped Ècu was experienced enough to understand what she meant, and then she counted down.

"Three," she shouted, "two, one!"

Without waiting for her colleague, she threw herself out to the side of the heap of tires and fired six shots in quick succession into the shed. Out of the corner of her eye she saw Falcon standing with legs wide apart in the approved shooting position a few yards away, firing his gun at the same time. She managed to see that the door to the shed was torn apart by the bullets, then she threw herself back behind the tires.

"Help!" was heard from the shed. "Help! Don't shoot! Stop!"

"Come out with your arms above your head!" Falcon shouted.

A good deal of rattling was heard. Anna peeped up over the edge of her rubber barricade. Toad had come out and positioned himself—on quivering legs—in front of the damaged door, with his arms in the air. He was a thin, green stuffed animal with a white belly and slender, long limbs.

Falcon ran toward him.

"Assaulting an officer," the inspector shouted.

He held his gun aimed at the toad.

"Attacking police officers on duty, this is going to cost you dearly!"

"Police?" Toad answered, looking confused. "Didn't you say Earwig sent you?"

Falcon stopped a few yards away.

"We said that . . ." said Falcon, slowing his speed. "We said that . . . true, we did say that Earwig had—but we identified ourselves. We said we were police officers."

"Police officers," Toad repeated in confusion. "Police officers. Lord Magnus. I didn't know . . . I thought you came from Earwig . . ."

He stood quietly with his arms above his head. Falcon lowered his weapon, Anna was right behind, and together the police officers led the contrite toad into the shed, the door to which they had just shredded with gunfire.

They sat down at a small kitchen table where there were freshly picked wood anemones in an eggcup. The sink was full of filthy plates, but Anna Lynx found a somewhat clean glass. She poured cold water and set the glass in front of the toad. He was so nervous he could hardly swallow.

Balder Toad tried to explain himself. He had seen two strangers and heard them shout Oleg Earwig's name. Toad had never used the gun before. He bought it a few years ago, to keep for self-defense. At that time unpleasant characters were wandering around the junkyard at night. The name Earwig now caused him to bring out the gun and fire it.

He begged pardon once again.

He realized, said Balder Toad, that they were going to arrest him.

"We'll just have to see. It depends on how well you cooperate," Falcon replied. "Tell us about Earwig. Why should he send animals here who . . . who want to harm you, Toad?"

Balder Toad took another gulp of water, stared right into Falcon's hard little eyes, and answered slowly: "I hate him."

Falcon Ècu did not reply.

"A month ago," Toad continued, "I'd never met Earwig. I didn't know he existed. I don't have any . . . vacuum-cleaning walls . . ."

"Tell your story, Toad," Anna coaxed.

It had been a day like any other when Oleg Earwig showed up a month ago at Balder Toad's junkyard. As far as he could recall, Balder had been struggling with a warped car hood when the black stuffed animal arrived on foot. He had introduced himself as one of the "greatest geniuses of our time" and excitedly gestured toward the car cemetery with his many arms and legs.

"This," he had said, "may soon be history. History!"

Toad had, in his hospitable manner—because he was basically a hospitable animal, even if he realized that the police thought differently—invited Earwig in for coffee.

"We sat here," said Balder Toad to Anna, pointing at the table. "Right at this table."

Earwig told about himself. Toad realized that the earwig was boasting, knowing that anyone who considered himself to be the greatest genius of the present day could not possibly be the greatest genius of the present day. But after a while, Earwig nonetheless succeeded in convincing Toad that there was something to what he was saying.

"And I checked him out later. He really did make that wall, didn't he?"

Anna nodded.

Earwig had described a new invention he was working on. It was sensational, it would make everything he'd done up until then pale in comparison.

He had asked for paper and pen and then shown formulas and processes that were behind what he was calling his Matter Processor. He pointed, calculated, and explained. The energy that went into these pedagogical attempts was almost inspiring. Toad put on a good face, even though he didn't understand a thing. Earwig seemed more and more content as time went by.

"I still have all the formulas," said Toad. "I saved them, everything he wrote. I thought they might be valuable someday."

"I have chosen you, Toad!" Earwig said finally. "Of all

the stuffed animals in Mollisan Town, of all the animals that could have helped, I have chosen you. You."

It had to do with the cars at the junkyard.

"I'm a humble animal," Toad explained to Falcon and Anna. "I knew it wasn't on my account that Earwig had come."

According to the inventor, the car was the object best suited to getting the city's stuffed animals to understand in one stroke what the Matter Processor was capable of. A car was not simply a means of transportation and a status object; for the hoi polloi, cars represented the mystery and perfection of technology.

"I need your help, Toad," Oleg Earwig had said that morning a month before. "I need your help. And as thanks, as payment, you'll get a Matter Processor. You'll get it so cheap that I'm almost ashamed. I'm almost ashamed. With a Matter Processor here at the junkyard, your work will be transformed forever. Now and forever. It's going to be so much simpler. So much more efficient. So much cheaper. You're going to be a rich toad, Toad. Thanks to the Matter Processor."

First Earwig described in detail how the Matter Processor looked. Toad was imagining a sort of advanced cannon, some sort of artillery piece. The rays that came out of the weapon were invisible, but had the ability to reduce or enlarge the matter that was "shot at."

In other words, Earwig explained, as if the toad were a little cub, with a Matter Processor at the junkyard, Toad could shrink all newly arrived wrecked cars. He could sort them on shelves or compartments instead of in these enormous heaps of metal. When he needed a particular spare part, it was only a matter of enlarging it.

"But is that possible?" Toad had exclaimed.

Whereupon Earwig picked up the paper and pen and, with even greater energy, fury, and zeal, drew and pointed and calculated in order to convince Balder Toad of the project's feasibility.

"Together," Earwig had said, "we will shake up Mollisan Town completely. Nothing will be the way it was. Nothing! Ever!"

Balder Toad did not reply. Earwig frightened him.

The idea was to summon a press conference, a real demonstration, at the Marktplatz in Lanceheim. During the night Oleg Earwig would assemble the first full-scale Matter Processor in the city's history on a large, newly constructed stage. The apparatus would be concealed under a golden cloth. Toad would contribute a couple of the largest vehicles he had at the junkyard. Tractors or trucks. The assembled press would arrive, along with curious onlookers, and Earwig would let the covering fall.

"The murmur," the inventor imagined at the toad's kitchen table, "will be ear-splitting."

Then Earwig would turn on the Matter Processor and shrink Toad's trucks into little toys.

No more difficult than that.

"It's inconceivable," Toad said to Anna Lynx. "In hindsight like this it's inconceivable, but he managed to convince me. I thought I would be part of something historic. And because I believed in him, I made the mistake not only of inviting my friends, I asked Mom and Dad to get over to Marktplatz. And when Dad refused—he never took time off without a reason—I told him everything. First he thought I was joking. Then he laughed. I was offended, of course. I cajoled and argued and staked my honor on it. Finally he promised to come."

Balder Toad appeared to be on the verge of tears at the memory of the conversation with his father, and Anna Lynx put a consoling paw on his shoulder.

The day arrived.

Toad's friends were there, the press was there, and animals had gathered at Marktplatz by the hundreds. Earwig pulled the cloth off his machine, and a murmur actually passed through the audience. It looked impressive. Toad had contributed a truck that had come into the junkyard a week before; it was almost in the middle of the square, and Toad himself was standing on the large stage alongside Earwig. His gaze was searching for his father in the sea of stuffed animals below.

The demonstration could begin.

Earwig shouted that now it was time to turn on the Matter Processor, and he warned the animals about standing in the way of the radiation. Then, with dignified steps, he went up to the apparatus and flipped the switch.

At about the same time Toad saw his father. He was smiling.

A bluish ray shot through the air, straight toward the truck, and . . . nothing happened.

Fiasco.

Toad's dad's smile got wider.

Oleg Earwig panicked up on the stage. He threw himself toward the machine and started fiddling and pounding on it. But the animals on the square started to laugh. They laughed at Earwig, and they laughed at Toad, and—his dad was laughing the loudest of them all.

"How could he fool me?" Toad asked. "How could I subject myself to such ridicule?"

Falcon and Anna both sat silently.

"Oleg Earwig says you can give him an alibi . . ." Falcon Ècu said when Balder Toad's silence had lasted long enough. "He says that—"

"An alibi?" Toad said. "That I'll give him an alibi? Is he crazy? The only thing I want to give him is a punch in the jaw. That's all he's ever going to get from me."

3.5

Anna Lynx was sitting on the very edge of a hard couch, feeling uncomfortable. A cup of tea was on the table in front of her, and normally the aroma of jasmine would have soothed her nerves. Cow Hellwig was sitting in the armchair across from her, staring. From out in the kitchen Anna could hear fresh tea water boiling. She did not know what she should say.

Cow Hellwig had called right before the Evening Storm and asked whether Anna could come over to her place. It wouldn't take more than an hour. Despite the fact that Anna was tired, dazed after the experience at the junkyard, she answered yes. She called her mom and asked if she could keep Todd company a little while.

Mom was old at this point, and she couldn't manage more than an hour on her own with her intense cubcub. The last five years had been hard on her; she was not made to live alone.

The Chauffeurs had fetched Anna's dad many years too early. In most cases stuffed animals managed to get old and worn before the day the Chauffeurs showed up in their red pickup. No one knew where the old animals were taken, or what awaited them there. The church, of course, supplied its answers, the Proclamations spoke of a magnificent paradise, but Anna's mom was no more than moderately religious. They fetched Dad at the office; the lawyers in the adjacent rooms had carefully closed their doors as the Chauffeurs brutally carried him away. Despite the fact that Anna had not been there personally and seen it happen, this scene recurred often in her nightmares. And afterward it was as though Mom slowly withered away, the energy ran out of her, and now Anna was almost as much a mother to her own mom as she was to Todd.

What a fool she'd been, she thought now. She had run over to Cow in solidarity, in the belief that Cow had finally listened to reason.

Anna felt so strongly about this issue. During her entire adult life she had seen males get their way at the expense of females. She was not dogmatic, not a fanatical zealot of equality. She knew and acknowledged that the care-taking instincts that marked so many of her actions would be called "maternal" if anyone were to put a label on them. She was even trying to bring up Falcon Ècu. But she was proud of that. She wanted to be a good mom, just as she wanted to be an attractive female. What she refused to accept was that these instincts—motherliness and vanity—should reduce her in the eyes of the patriarchy. No one looked down on a careerist or a materialist, if they were male. The personal consequences of the need for affirmation were always taken in dead earnest, as long as it concerned males. And Anna refused to let herself be treated degradingly due to feminine characteristics that the factory had filled her with in some way when she was sewn together. She often spoke about this with her girlfriends, and Cow Hellwig had always been one of her most ardent sympathizers.

Anna had bounded up the stairs to Cow, rung the doorbell, and it had been . . . him . . . who had opened.

"The crazy lynx is here now!" he had called in to the apartment, then disappeared into the living room as Anna was taking off her coat.

Now she was sitting across from the married couple, on the edge of the couch, doing her best to avoid . . . his . . . gaze. She raised the teacup and sipped the tea.

"Anna," said Cow, "I saw no other way than to invite you over. So we can work this out."

"Work what out?"

"Well, whatever there is to be worked out. You just can't let your constables go around arresting Simon simply because . . . you've imagined something."

"C'mon, imagined something . . . ?"

"Yes. There has to be something."

Was she joking? But this was not a jocular presentation, and in the cow's eyes Anna read a sincere lack of understanding that shocked her.

"But . . . but . . ." she stammered. "But everything we said the other evening . . . ?"

"I still don't understand," said Cow. "What does that have to do with Simon? When you said I should move in with you . . . I thought you were joking!"

"But you were the one who said that," said Anna, flabbergasted. "You said it yourself. That you were thinking about taking that job at the Ministry of Finance, but that . . . he . . . said that it was too far to drive the whole way down to Amberville every day."

The silence in the Hellwig family's living room was deafening.

"You had me arrested because I thought it was too far to drive down to Amberville?" Simon asked at last.

Anna did not reply.

"Well, she's just *sick*," he said, turning to his wife.

"It sounds completely crazy, Anna," Cow agreed. "Do you mean that's the reason for all this? You can't mean that. There's something else, isn't there?"

"But . . . I don't get it," said Anna. "This is exactly what we've been talking about all these years. This is what it's about. It's not big things, this is the way oppression looks. Getting you to abstain from a job, from a career, by hinting. Threatening, but only indirectly. In practice *this is what it's about*. I thought that—"

Anna fell silent. She realized that she was still holding the teacup, and she carefully set it down on the table. She was ashamed. She tried to remember what had triggered all this, why she had been so sure that Cow Hellwig must be liberated from her . . . Simon. But she couldn't think of it. The redness rose in her face. She got up from the couch.

"Anna, there must—" Cow began.

"Forgive me," said Anna Lynx.

And like so many times before when her protective instincts had taken over and forced logic and common sense from her brain, she knew she'd gone too far. She took a few steps toward the hall.

"Forgive me," she repeated.

And then she fled. It would be months before she dared call Cow Hellwig again.

IGOR PANDA 3

A wide, black Volga Deluxe came driving at high speed along salt and pepper Bardowicker Strasse. The sun was still high in the clear blue sky, and even though the lunch rush was over, numerous stuffed animals were still moving about on the streets.

The black car did not veer for anyone.

It passed the Radio Building at high speed, and slipped past the red lights on Konviktstrasse even though it could have stopped for yellow. A hundred yards or so farther east the car pulled up along the sidewalk. The tires screeched against the asphalt as the driver put on the brakes. Igor Panda turned the engine off, and it was obvious that he did not intend to park in a more orderly manner than this.

He threw open the door and got out. He was holding the black attaché case in his paw and entered the gallery with rapid steps.

"Igor!" Arthur Rhinoceros called out, getting up from his chair.

Arthur had been working at Gallery Panda for six months.

He got no compensation for taking care of the gallery, but thanks to the job he had somewhere to hang out, and he could truthfully tell his friends he was working in the art business. He was still studying art history during the day, but there were few mandatory lectures, and taking care of the gallery at the same time worked out. Apart from openings, they did not get very many visitors.

"Don't think I was sitting there sleeping!"

But Igor Panda paid no attention to Arthur.

Panda rushed furiously past the simple, low reception counter and on into his office. He slammed the door behind him.

Wide awake, Arthur stood looking after him. The weather was hard to determine and Arthur had no idea if he had only dozed off or if he'd been sleeping for several hours.

With his hoof, he scratched the curved white horn in the middle of his muzzle that kept others from mistaking him for a donkey or a horse.

Right now Gallery Panda was showing a young, talented badger who worked with photography and collage. Across from the reception desk hung one of the larger pieces, an enormous enlargement of a money clip in which a birch leaf was pinned. The leaf was bright green, everything else was in black-and-white, and why Arthur Rhinoceros disliked that particular picture so much he could not explain. Perhaps the motif was so simple, and the result so successful, making Arthur's own artistic attempts stand out as forced and overburdened? He painted at night, but no one was allowed to see what he did. He was not ready for criticism yet. If he ever would be.

He was basically a good-hearted rhino, but like many others in the field, he had an envious side. That side could rejoice in the fact that since the opening—and the sympathetic reviews—there had been no more than a dozen visitors to the badger's exhibition. Of this dozen, five had asked for a price list, and of these five, only a single animal had made a low-ball offer on one of the larger collages, an offer that the artist firmly refused.

In a few words: even if the badger was talented, even if he had his own opening at Gallery Panda, he had sold no more pictures than Arthur.

If life as an artist was hard, life as an art dealer did not seem any easier. Igor Panda was Hummingbird Esperanza-Santiago's dealer, everyone knew that, and it afforded Panda a certain amount of reflected glory. Unfortunately it did not give him any other salable artists to exhibit. On the contrary, Igor seemed to have an unfailing ability to sign technical mediocrities whose work couldn't be hung in ordinary homes. Like the young badger.

Arthur sighed. Hummingbird Esperanza-Santiago was something completely special. She had not exhibited in more than ten years. Her demands on herself were high. Arthur saw her as a role model.

"Forgive me if I'm disturbing you," said the rhinoceros as he opened the door to Igor's office.

He knew that he would get told off. He scratched his horn, bearing in silence the harangues about what a closed door meant. When Panda had let out the worst of it, Arthur cleared his throat.

"The sky's starting to get foggy," he said. "And today was the day you were going to visit Hummingbird . . ."

Panda fell silent. He remembered.

"Then why the hell haven't you said anything?" he shouted.

"I—"

"Were you sitting there sleeping again?" Panda screamed.

"I—"

"How the hell do you find reliable employees!" the black-and-white bear finally spewed out as he scraped together a few things from the desk and tossed them into an attaché case.

Then he ran out to the street and threw himself into the large, black car.

Hummingbird Esperanza-Santiago lived outside the city.

To the north, east, and south, dense forest surrounded Mollisan Town. To the west, on the other hand, was a pleasantly rolling landscape all the way to the coast and Hillevie, the place where the more well-to-do animals spent their vacations. The road there—you could take the train from Central Station in Amberville if you didn't have a car—was bordered by cultivated fields and vast country estates. There were also some settlements not belonging to any of the farms, isolated houses in beautifully blossoming groves and meadows.

Calculated from the city line, where Western Avenue turned into a country road, Hummingbird Esperanza-Santiago lived two hours outside the city. The last few miles you were forced to drive on the narrow paths that the farmers used to get from one field to another. Igor Panda's wide Volga Deluxe was not built for such terrain. The rains had gouged deep holes in the narrow roads, the shock absorbers labored, and Panda was swearing.

It was only after having visited Esperanza-Santiago ten or so times that Panda knew the way. The artist's house was embedded in a kind of transplanted grove of old, heavy oaks. When Igor got a little closer, he could see the narrow, low house with its typical grass roof, dark blue exterior, and white windows and doors. The house looked abandoned. Despite a garden that blossomed and blazed, signs of decay were visible even at a distance. A few window shutters were hanging on their last hinge, others were missing completely. There was a hole in the grass roof so large that Panda saw it from the last side road, and the closer he got, the more holes he discovered. The exterior was deteriorated from the wind, the paint had peeled in some places, and Igor thought the whole thing was depressing. Why did Esperanza-Santiago choose this life when she didn't need to?

Carefully he drove the whole way up to the little yard. As usual he had to force his way through the army of red hollyhocks standing at attention in front of the well, and just as he got to the hyacinth beds the door opened.

Out came a duck.

Under its wing the duck was carrying a folded easel and with its other wing was lugging a massive suitcase spattered with paint.

"Stop!" said Panda.

The duck stopped, looking compliantly at Igor.

"I have to hurry," he said. "I have to get home. Mama is already wondering where I—"

"What are you doing here?" Panda demanded.

"I've just been getting some help . . . that is . . . Miss Esperanza-Santiago has—"

"'Miss'?" Panda cried out without restraining his fury. "Did you call her 'Miss'?"

"Yes . . . I did," the terrified young duck stammered. He realized that he had given the wrong answer, but not in what way.

With a careless motion Igor Panda shoved the duck off the front stoop, going straight into the run-down house. He looked angrily around in the semidarkness. Hummingbird was standing over at the sink, rinsing brushes. She was the smallest stuffed animal he knew; she hardly came up to his waist. She was light blue, with a long, narrow beak and large, sincere eyes.

"Hello?" he called.

Igor was so angry he was about to explode. At the same time all he could do was to carefully—extremely carefully— try to get Esperanza-Santiago to understand that what she had just done was wrong.

"Igor?" asked Hummingbird, looking up from her work.

There was no electricity in the house. The light that came in through the door was blinding the artist, and all she saw was a dark silhouette.

"It's me," Igor Panda answered. "We did agree to meet today, didn't we?"

"I'd completely forgotten! Igor, forgive me. I haven't even put on any coffee."

"That's no problem, I—"

"I'll get it ready . . ."

She hurried over to the stove, where she started putting wood into the oven door to make a fire. With a heavy sigh, Igor sat down at the kitchen table. He was careful, knowing the chairs were ramshackle and treacherous.

"I met a duck on the way in," he began.

Hummingbird was in search of a saucepan in the cupboard and hummed an acknowledgment. Through the window above the kitchen counter the daylight fell in and the transom painted a shadow cross over the little bird body.

"I thought we'd talked about that," Igor continued. "The energy you can devote to painting you should prioritize for your own work."

"Oh, I'm working," the hummingbird informed him.

She had found a chipped saucepan, and she filled it with water that she ladled up from a bucket standing next to the stove. Was it rainwater? Hummingbird sometimes complained that the well had gone dry. Whatever, thought Panda, if she boils the water there shouldn't be any danger.

"I know you don't like me taking in pupils," Hummingbird continued in a gentle tone, "but I have to answer to someone who is even more important than you, Igor."

Hummingbird Esperanza-Santiago was talking about Magnus, our Lord. The artist was deeply religious, and her relationship to the spiritual world in general, and Magnus in particular, was complicated, as well as deeply anxiety-ridden.

"You're not going to be able to do much for your pupils if

you don't have food on the table for yourself," Igor answered quietly. "You have to develop yourself to be able to develop someone else."

"It's nice of you to want to help," said Hummingbird.

The water was starting to boil and she put in the coffee.

"My friend," Igor continued, somewhat more insistently, "it's more than three years since you completed anything. You have to stop . . . it's not the case that your creations are less . . . magnificent now, yet . . . it's about fundamental . . . we're talking about survival."

"Yours or mine?" asked Hummingbird, but immediately regretted it. "Igor, forgive me. I know you wish me well. I have nothing to complain about. I have my pupils. They bring food along and . . . the things I need. You're friendly and pay my bills down at the store. And I'm . . . working. Even if it's . . . hard."

As far as Igor knew, Hummingbird had not been in Mollisan Town for many years. She lived on her little plot, calling down to the store to order food and necessities, which they drove up to the house once a week. And she agonized in front of her easel. Sometimes she would show him the canvases she was working on. There were a number of pieces, all of which were magnificent, amazing, at least as good if not better than anything she had shown before.

Still, she was dissatisfied.

"There are critics who are harder to convince than you, Igor, my friend," she would say.

He knew that once again she was referring to our Lord Magnus. He knew that Hummingbird devoted endless amounts of time at night—and for that matter during the day as well—to discussing her artistic creations with Magnus. On a few occasions Panda had unintentionally been a witness to one of Hummingbird's long, complaining monologues, and thereby gained an unexpected key to the artist's spiritual life. She was so filled with guilt, so filled with shame, that Panda, who could tolerate most things, could hardly bear to keep listening.

Still, he did.

It was clear that the hummingbird did not feel she deserved either success or talent. She painted for His sake, but satisfying Him was nearly impossible. If she exerted herself to the breaking point in the form of technique and expectations, she was putting on airs. If she held back her ambitions and instead tried to find the simplest possible expression, it was unworthy.

Igor Panda, who had dealt with many artists over the years, realized that as long as Hummingbird Esperanza-Santiago continued to "fail," this granted her a certain satisfaction. For a guilt-ridden stuffed animal of Esperanza-Santiago's type, defeat was one of the few bright spots in existence. It also explained why she chose to live the way she did, why she refused herself comforts or a social life, and why she was not interested in the money that was within reach if she would be more productive.

"But it's not time there's a shortage of, Igor," she would say. "It's talent."

And she devoted hours to trying to prove the opposite.

They drank their coffee in darkness at the kitchen table. They talked about the sorts of things that have nothing to do with art. Panda tried to keep the conversation light and flowing. It was impossible to pressure her. No threat was worse than the inner demands that constantly threatened to blow her apart.

Jake Golden Retriever had shown up a few years ago when the situation was about to degenerate. Igor Panda had been six months behind on rent for the gallery and owed money to all the city's banks and loan sharks. The golden retriever seemed to be a stuffed animal without background or context, but his forgeries were brilliant. Suddenly Hummingbird's eccentricities became fruitful.

As long as she persisted in rejecting honor and gallantry—

and society in general—there was no risk that she would ever discover what was happening in Mollisan Town. Suddenly many of the more established collectors could boast about an Esperanza-Santiago in their collections—canvases that had never been subjected to the artist's scrutinizing gaze, had never stood in any relationship to Magnus, and hence equaled easy money for Igor Panda.

"I'll see you in a few weeks, okay?" said Panda as usual when he finally left her.

She nodded and waved to him through the kitchen window.

DAY FOUR

4.1

Derek Hare thought it over.

"It's not impossible," he said at last.

"I'm only a beginner, of course," said Falcon, "so I don't quite understand. Are you saying it's not likely?"

They were sitting on the second floor at the rue de Cadix police station, where the Tech Department was located. If on the fourth floor up at WE you found yourself in a dark, hostile, steel forest, two floors down you were a tourist in a white, sterile futuristic landscape. They were in Derek Hare's office. Outside, the dark clouds had not even moved in for the Morning Rain; dawn was still a memory on the horizon. Hare hated speculation about what was reasonable and unreasonable, and he squirmed uncomfortably in his seat.

"I can't judge whether it's likely," he said at last. "All I can say is that nowhere in Oswald Vulture's office is there a trace indicating that the head might have been destroyed or cut into smaller pieces."

"So the murderer carried the head out of Nova Park in one piece?" asked Falcon.

Not least for his own sake, he wanted to understand where the hare's conclusion was leading.

"The windows can't be opened. A stuffed animal's head is too large to flush down the toilet. And, once again, neither in the bathroom nor in the office are there any traces of the head being deconstructed. But . . . a careful animal with insight into how we work can always remove traces after himself."

The technical investigation of the murder scene had been concluded during the night, and Hare had been summoned to an emergency meeting. It was believed that the murder weapon—a sword—had been found, and tests during the early morning hours had shown this assumption to be correct.

Along with a clearly sleepy Superintendent Larry Bloodhound, who did not cover his mouth when he yawned, Falcon Ècu sat taking careful notes. Falcon was wearing a pink checked shirt under a dark red striped sweater, and the day's socks were blue with a red shaft. Not that anyone would notice them, thought Falcon, feeling both bitter and relieved at this. Hare reported his conclusions in his inimitable, boring manner; this cop was no entertainer.

"And the surveillance cameras in reception?" asked Falcon. "We must at least be able to see if there's anyone carrying anything onto the elevators."

"Haven't you told him?" asked Hare.

"I didn't have time," Bloodhound mumbled, shrugging his shoulders.

"The cameras were broken," Hare reported. "That's what the electrician running around up there was supposed to fix. The hard drive was inside one of the offices. If I understand correctly it's all working now?"

"Broken?" Falcon repeated.

"He's quick, that bird," said Bloodhound.

Falcon had tried to get hold of Lynx and Pedersen, but without success. It was understandable that Anna had Todd to think about, but Field Mouse Pedersen had not answered his phone at this early hour, either. This upset Falcon; according to regulations, an inspector should always be accessible. The superintendent, however, had only growled in a manner that was impossible to interpret. The same indefinable growling had been Bloodhound's reaction when Falcon told him about Toad at the junkyard. Obviously the many-armed inventor had no alibi.

"Back to the sword," said Bloodhound. "I didn't understand a thing. Was only one of the swords real?"

Derek Hare looked down at his papers. He leafed through the pages and got stuck somewhere. Read, then looked up.

"Yes. Only the one, the one on the right. The sword with the suit of armor on the left you couldn't even slice a banana with. Both suits of armor are copies. A little surprising, almost, in a place like Nova Park. You'd think they'd have the money for real antiques. We asked around. Nobody at the office knew the sword was razor sharp, and nobody could say whether it had been that way the whole time."

"So the murderer may have placed the murder weapon there in advance?" Falcon concluded.

"Or else it was just a long shot," Bloodhound growled. "A damn impulse."

"Theoretically both scenarios are possible," Hare confirmed, looking unhappy. "But I won't get involved in that. On the other hand, I am one hundred percent certain that the sword was used to cut the head off of Vulture. Rather smart, actually. Putting it back."

"Smart?" Bloodhound growled. "You discovered that right away."

"But I found no other traces. Neither on the handle of the sword nor on the armor," Hare replied. "Whoever swung that sword was clever about covering his tracks."

"Which brings us back to the vanished head," Falcon commented.

"As I said," Hare repeated, "I don't deal in speculations. There is no trace of the head."

"There are damn few leads in general," Bloodhound grunted.

The Tech Department's search confirmed that Oswald Vulture's office had been almost clinically free of personal effects. In one of the desk drawers they found a business card from a dry cleaners; but otherwise, nothing.

There were two computers on the desk. In the larger desktop computer only work-related documents had been found. In the smaller laptop, there was only a single folder. The folder was locked with a password, and the police had not yet deciphered it, but there was hope that they would find something that would lead them forward.

"A paranoid individual, if you ask me," said Derek Hare. "Without a doubt Vulture had something to conceal. No desk drawers can be that empty, no corporate manager is so lacking in calendars, binders, phone books, and memos. But whatever Vulture was hiding, he did it well. 'Cause I have no idea."

Hare sighed, shuffling together some papers he had placed on the table.

"I figured you'd want to know about the sword as soon as possible. I'll get back to you as soon as we can read the folder in the laptop."

Superintendent Bloodhound growled something that was meant as a "thanks" and got up. With Ècu in his wake, he left Hare's office.

As soon as they came out into the sterile corridor and began walking toward the stairs, the falcon hurried to catch up with the tired dog.

"Excuse me, Superintendent, but I had an idea. Perhaps this is just their corporate culture. I mean, I didn't see any personal things in the other offices, either. And I was actually thinking about how empty the desks were. I said something about that,

I don't recall to whom, and was told that in their industry the competition is so keen, discretion is imperative."

"Hmm," Bloodhound growled. "Could be."

They were in the west part of the police station, so they took the stairs down to the main entrance, only to take the elevator from there up to the fourth floor. As they were passing reception, the police officer on duty called to Ècu from behind the counter, "A message has arrived, Falcon."

The tone was condescending, the voice a whisper, almost as if the police officer hoped that Falcon Ècu would not hear. Bloodhound reacted but said nothing. Falcon ought to comment on this. He ought to indicate that you don't address an inspector that way. But Falcon said nothing. He went over to the reception counter, nodded, and reached for the envelope that was extended. The police officer behind the counter, with a rude smile, pulled back the envelope at the last moment. Falcon remained standing with his wing outstretched.

"What the hell?" growled Bloodhound.

In a second the superintendent was at the reception counter. The police officer with the envelope froze. Bloodhound did not stop in front of the counter but instead went around and placed himself so close to the officer that Larry's smoked-sausage breath went straight up the officer's nose.

"I get it that those ugly little pieces of glass for pig eyes make it hard to see," the superintendent growled, "but are you too nearsighted to take deliveries?"

"Er, I, uh . . ." stammered the desk officer, whose smile suddenly seemed far away.

"Ècu works for me at WE. You know that, don't you?"

"I . . . I . . . sure . . ."

"And if I hear you addressing any of my inspectors that way again, you can't even count on a job at a lousy security company tomorrow."

"I'm sorry, Superintendent, but—"

"Shut up," said Bloodhound, turning his back to him and going over to the elevators.

Falcon snatched up the envelope still lying on the counter and hurried after the superintendent. The inspector did not know what he should say. Embarrassed at having been exposed to ridicule, even more embarrassed at having been helped, he cleared his throat in an attempt to regain his professional status.

"What's in the envelope?" the superintendent asked.

"I've requisitioned a will. Vulture's will," Falcon explained. "I was thinking—"

"Well done," Bloodhound interrupted, seizing the envelope. "And, Falcon, next time someone messes with you, don't be such a soggy little amoeba."

4.2

Anna Lynx threw her coat across the chair and ran over to the ladies' dressing room without even saying hello to Ècu. Once again she hadn't made it to day care on time, or to work before the Morning Rain. Falcon understood her hurried entrance; the coat smelled of damp wool. When Anna returned, after ten minutes in the warm drying cabinet, her tufted ears were again standing up the way they'd been made.

"Whew," she said, sitting down on her chair. "You always forget how late it can get. Nice shirt, Ècu. What did Larry say about Balder Toad?"

Falcon laughed awkwardly and unconsciously adjusted his pink cuff. The office felt lifeless somehow; in the ceiling the drainage pipes were rattling aggressively as they always did in the morning, and the few police officers at their desks hardly seemed awake. Ècu explained that Bloodhound had no reaction at all to the fact that Earwig did not seem to have an alibi.

"Forget it, it's too early in the morning for Larry," Anna giggled. "He heard what you said. We'll talk with him a little later."

Then Ècu briefly reported on the morning meeting with Hare, and about the sword that had served as a murder weapon.

"Then it must have been planned! The fact that someone, just like that, takes a sword from an antique suit of armor and cuts the head off Vulture seems . . . too much."

But before Falcon could comment on this, they both heard a loud bark from inside the superintendent's office.

"In here! Both of you. Bring something to eat!"

"Eat?" Falcon asked, looking unhappy.

Anna shrugged her shoulders to relay that she didn't have anything edible with her.

"Not tomorrow," Bloodhound shouted. "Now!"

They got up and took the few steps into the superintendent's office. Falcon closed the door.

"I'm extremely sorry, Superintendent," said Falcon, "but I didn't know you wanted something to eat. If I'd known, of course I would have—"

"Shut up, Ècu!" the dog ordered, holding up a couple of densely covered pages with one paw. "This, you understand, this is damned interesting."

Anna shook her head inquisitively while Falcon nodded in understanding.

"Vulture's will," said Bloodhound, waving the papers in the air. "Not a foundation as far as the eye can see. The widow can exhale, even if she won't get all of the pie."

"I thought that perhaps it might be—" Falcon began.

"A will?" asked Anna. "Vulture's? Listen . . . isn't that suspicious? That there's a will at all? I mean, Vulture was neither old nor sickly."

"Forgive me for pointing this out," said Falcon, "but Vulture was rich. Rich enough to be convinced by lawyers, who charge by the hour, to be safe rather than sorry."

"Falcon may be as freshly hatched as I am wrinkled," Bloodhound barked, "but he's right. Nothing strange about

a will in Vulture's circles. Not when money is gushing from
the estate."

"Okay," said Anna. "What does it say?"

"The wife and son get most of it," said Bloodhound.

"I am of course shockingly inexperienced," said Falcon,
"but I actually forgot to ask. What did the son say, Superintendent?" Falcon asked.

Bloodhound was embarrassed. He hadn't managed to reach
Oswald Vulture's son, even though he had left several messages on the answering machine. The moment he dismissed
the widow, the rich Flamingo, he had also lowered the priority of her son. He had a recollection of having delegated the
matter to Pedersen, but perhaps he'd forgotten to ask?

"You two will have to look up the son immediately, get
his alibi, and give him the bad news. I don't think he has any
contact with his parents," said Bloodhound. "Do that during
the day. And it's not just bad news . . ." The superintendent
nodded at the papers and said, bitterly, "There's more money
than you think."

"And it all goes to the wife and son?" asked Anna.

"No. No, Vulture was no doubt a cunning devil . . . I don't
know . . . Well, read it yourself."

Bloodhound pushed the will over to the inspectors.

"It's only formalities at the beginning. Start on page three."

Anna leafed through to page three, leaving the papers on
the table so Falcon could read too:

> . . . and to my chauffeur Kai Gnu I leave both my
> black Volga Deluxe and the red Volga Kombi that my
> wife uses. To Fritz Burma, who clipped my hedges for
> so many years and fertilized my flower beds, I leave the
> bathroom furnishings at Mina Road. He may take the
> fixtures he finds valuable (he will have to disassemble
> them himself, and this applies both to the gold faucets in
> the guest bathroom as well as to the diamond-studded

mirror on the top floor). Ellen Spider, my reliable cook, is awarded two million and Chameleon Raukanomaa, who ironed my shirts and underwear, is awarded one million: the money shall be deposited into their respective bank accounts no later than two months after my demise. To Jasmine Squirrel shall go a monthly payment of fifty thousand as long as she lives. The doorman at Nova Park and likewise my personal factotum George Llama shall be guaranteed a workshop of no less but possibly larger than two thousand square feet in Bourg Villette, to be furnished and equipped according to Llama's instructions. To Daniel Lamb, my faithful assistant, a sum of fifty million shall be paid, in installments of ten million on the fifteenth of January for five years. Pugdog Owen, in the event she loses her job as domestic servant at Mina Road, shall be compensated with the equivalent of the monthly salary she had at the time of her termination until she reaches the age of seventy. My masseuse Cow Bonvie is awarded my collection of antique cuff links.

"Several suspects," said Falcon Ècu when he was finished. "In any event, several who have a motive."

"Too many to worry about now," Bloodhound growled. "But there is something else remarkable about this will."

"Excuse me, but now I don't really know what you mean, Superintendent," Falcon asked.

"Think about it," Bloodhound growled.

Falcon thought.

"Injustice, possibly," he said at last. "That . . . the masseuse . . . gets nothing more than a collection of cuff links. Can anyone have known about the will in advance, and felt provoked?"

Anna Lynx was squirming in her seat.

"Cuff links must cost a pretty penny," she said. "We're

talking about someone who has gold bathtub faucets, apparently. No, I see what you're getting at, Larry. It's Squirrel."

"Exactly," Bloodhound confirmed.

"The squirrel?"

Falcon wasn't following. Bloodhound explained.

"Everywhere in the will Vulture is careful to describe the
details. Who's done what, and why. Nothing is left to chance
here. But this . . ."

Bloodhound picked up the papers and read to himself.

" 'Jasmine Squirrel'—who is she?"

"No idea," said Falcon.

"That was a so-called rhetorical question," the superintendent growled.

"Excuse me, Superintendent."

On the other side of the blinds the sky had cleared, and the
wind was as absent as Falcon's sense of humor. Bloodhound
sighed.

"I don't know if any prosecutor is going to request it, but
we'll probably have to check up on every poor pile of shit mentioned in the will. Where they were at the time of the murder,
how their relationship to Vulture appeared . . . you know," he
said.

"C'mon, can't we ask Pedersen?" Anna asked.

"It sounds like Pedersen's type of assignment," Bloodhound
nodded. "I'll let him know. His group can check everyone
who's mentioned in the will."

"Perfect," Anna nodded.

"Except Squirrel," said Bloodhound. "First I want a little
background on Squirrel, Ècu. And you'll also have to take
care of the son, if Pedersen's going to have time for the rest."

"Excuse me, but what's the son's name?" asked Falcon,
ready with his notepad.

Superintendent Bloodhound eyeballed the file again to refresh his memory.

"Igor Panda," he said. "Oswald Vulture and Irina Flamingo

have a son whose name is Igor Panda, and even though he doesn't know it himself yet, he has become exceedingly rich."

Falcon and Anna got up, and as they were on their way out of the superintendent's office, Bloodhound added, "And bring in that inventor, too. We'll let him spend the night down in the jail, then I'll get to him early tomorrow. How stupid can he be? Did he really think you wouldn't check up on Toad?"

4.3

I don't want to put on airs," said Falcon Ècu, adjusting his blue scarf, which matched his socks, and which he had put on when they left rue de Cadix in an unmarked police car, "but wasn't it you who taught me that chance is a method for mystery authors and not for real police officers?"

They were standing at an espresso bar across from Gallery Panda. The place was no more than a hole in the wall, a long, narrow bar that cut through the building like the core through a pineapple. Six small, high tables were attached to the wall across from the bar, and the passage between the tables and bar was cramped. A lizard in a white apron had set down a double espresso for each of them, and the detectives sipped the strong coffee from small white cups. The place was packed with animals; it was crowded and smoky and full of energy: before lunch no one had time for more than a quick cup of coffee.

"C'mon, it's not chance that's important," Anna Lynx hissed, irritated for once. "The call came from a phone booth right across from Claude Siamese's building. That's a fact."

"That is a fact. But with all due respect, Anna, the next thought, whatever it is, is speculation, based on chance. Nothing else."

"There's chance, and then there's chance," Anna maintained. "And this is the latter."

Falcon laughed curtly, shaking his wings slightly. It was Thursday, and he had another match this evening. After the humiliating loss to Pedersen on Monday, he'd been pondering his failures on the court. He realized that a lack of match training was hampering him, that he let himself be driven back and forth along the baseline because he was more concerned about saving the ball than winning it. Volley and half-volley had always been natural strokes for him; this evening he would show them.

"I don't know," he sighed, trying to return to the matter at hand. "There's an explanation, of course. But unfortunately I think we're far from it."

"C'mon, there must be a connection," Anna insisted, "between Siamese and the Oswald Vulture case. The tipster called looking for you and Larry because he knew who you were. Have you had anything to do with Siamese, Falcon?"

"Never," said Falcon.

"But Larry must have had something to do with that criminal cat at some point over the years."

"Anna, forgive me for pointing this out, but you've taught me that discernible connections are everywhere. Two red cars drive past. The same day you meet two cats who both comment on the weather. Thousands of such events occur every day. And interpreting them as intentional is simply absurd. Those are your own words."

Anna's face darkened. There was something dishonorable in refuting her theories with her own objections. She was about to answer, but someone bumped into her and she almost dropped the little espresso cup. She stared angrily at the back of a suit that had already hurried out onto salt and pepper Bardowicker Strasse.

She was standing so that she had a view of the gallery across the street. A rhinoceros in reception had informed them that the dealer himself, Igor Panda, was at a meeting but was expected back in fifteen minutes. That was half an hour ago, but no Panda had arrived yet.

"It would be good if we got out of here before the Breeze," said Falcon, showing an unusual sign of impatience. "I don't want to eat too late. My body feels heavy until the afternoon. My backhand doesn't seem to function like it should if I haven't had time to digest my food."

He leaned over and looked out through the narrow windows toward the street. It looked as if someone was about to enter the gallery, but the animal in question changed its mind at the last moment and continued walking.

"I still think the tipster is decisive," Anna nagged. "But Larry seems to be turning a deaf ear to that. And yet he has such long ears . . ."

"Really?"

"Have you heard him utter a word about it?" asked Anna. "Nope. Nothing. It's, like, 'Tipster, what tipster?' But at the same time I haven't said anything about Siamese. And you aren't allowed to either, Falcon. I know Larry. If I don't have anything concrete to show, he'll just get angry."

"And perhaps the very fact that you don't have anything to show has an explanation?" Falcon hinted. "Namely that perhaps there isn't one?"

"Listen . . ." Anna started, but stopped herself and nodded toward the window. "We'll have to discuss this later. Now it's time to meet Panda."

Falcon could see for himself how a panda was getting out of a big, black Volga Deluxe that had just parked outside the gallery. With rapid steps the panda crossed the sidewalk.

"Judging by the car, he doesn't appear to need an inheritance," Falcon noted.

"Nice. We don't need more animals with motives."

Anna left payment on the counter and, without waiting for the barista, forced her way toward the exit.

"We're looking for Igor Panda," said Anna Lynx.

Arthur Rhinoceros was sitting behind the reception counter inside the gallery, staring at the police officers. They had been there half an hour ago and identified themselves. What was it about police officers that made him react defensively?

"I don't know if that will work," he replied.

"Excuse me?"

Arthur scratched his horn nervously and continued.

"Mr. Panda has just been in a meeting with the directors of the Modern Museum. It's about a very valuable painting of Hummingbird Esperanza-Santiago that will be loaned out for a retrospective exhibition. I—"

"Esperanza-Santiago?" exclaimed Falcon Ècu. "I knew I'd heard that name before!"

"Esperanza-Santiago?" said Anna.

"No, no. Gallery Panda. I knew I'd heard Igor Panda's name before, but I couldn't remember where. Panda, of course, is Esperanza-Santiago's dealer!"

"That's right," said Arthur overbearingly, and more than a little proud.

"Fantastic!" said Falcon. "And you were speaking of a retrospective exhibition at the Modern?"

"Still only in the planning stages."

"That's unbelievable." Falcon turned to Anna. "This has never happened before. Esperanza-Santiago's works have been shown at openings, it must have been at this gallery? But that was many, many years ago. An exhibition—to see her collected works—this is going to be an experience."

This unexpected outburst surprised the sullen Arthur Rhinoceros, who forgot that he was trying to make the officers leave. Anna was surprised, too. She had certainly heard of Hummingbird Esperanza-Santiago, but that Falcon Ècu appeared to be an art lover came as a surprise.

"In any event, we would appreciate having a few words with Panda," she repeated.

Rhinoceros nodded.

"I'll go see . . ."

He left the reception and walked down the corridor toward Panda's office. Anna and Falcon followed. When Rhinoceros knocked, there was no answer. He knocked a second time, but instead of waiting for a reaction Anna forced her way past him and opened the door. The office was empty.

Anna stared at the rhinoceros.

"Are you joking with us?" she asked sternly.

"No, no, I . . ." Arthur began, confused, but then he saw.

All three of them saw it.

The veranda doors facing the courtyard were open. Anna went quickly through the room and out into the back, but Panda had gotten away. She came back into the office.

"He's gone," she stated.

She stood, slightly perplexed, looking at the two males. Falcon reacted first.

"Can you please ask Igor Panda to call us?" he said, giving Rhinoceros his card. "We have tragic news to convey to him."

Rhinoceros nodded.

Disappointed, the inspectors left the gallery.

4.4

Anna drove. They had stopped by the station to get a new car after their visit to Gallery Panda; she refused to drive another mile in the one they'd had in the morning. The unmarked police cars were bewilderingly alike to an untrained eye. All were neutral gray with black leather seats and air-conditioning that didn't work. But there were differences. Certain engines were more robust than others, and in many cars it was impossible to remove the vestiges of panic and anxiety, vomit and blood. Now she had requisitioned one of her favorites. The Volga reacted sensitively to her commands, and the pinecone-scented disinfectant that the cleaners used lingered in the car.

They drove through north Tourquai in neighborhoods more reminiscent of small, self-sustaining villages than parts of a big city. Parks and cafés, bakeries and the kind of old-fashioned textile shops that had almost disappeared with factory production of clothing. Certain parts of north Tourquai reminded Anna of Lanceheim, where she had grown up and where her parents still lived. Stuffed animals sat on benches with their eyes closed in the sunshine or stood on street corners conversing; there was a calm and a coziness that felt timeless in some way.

"I wouldn't have anything against living here," she said.

Then the street scene changed. Traffic got heavier, one lane was added to another, and the sidewalks were as deserted as they were wide. The compact brick apartment buildings grew to massive monuments of glass and steel, and they were again in the heart of the district where they worked.

Anna had an impulse and turned right on emerald green rue Primatice. Falcon did not react. When Anna drove, he relied completely on her taking them to the right place in the shortest possible time. Not even when Anna turned left a few minutes later onto blue rue de Montyon did he realize where she was heading. In his thoughts he was on the tennis court, up at the net, and he was just making a distinct backhand volley that decided both game and set when they unexpectedly pulled up next to the sidewalk.

"There," she said, nodding across the street.

It took a few moments before Falcon understood.

"The tipster's phone booth?" he asked.

Anna nodded.

"And there's Siamese's doorway," she said.

The windows of the car were fogging up again, and she rolled down the window.

"Forgive me for asking, but why are we stopping here?"

"Claude Siamese lives in that building," Anna repeated. "Get it? Siamese. And it's from that phone booth right next to it that someone calls you with a tip about Vulture."

"Anna, for one thing, Siamese is part of Tourquai's drug syndicate. I'm sorry, but you'll have to find the connection in order to get me interested. Was there anything in Vulture's or Nova Park's business deals that may have had a bearing on the drug trade up here?"

"Good," said Anna. "Now you're thinking constructively."

"And we haven't found anything that even suggests that," Falcon continued.

"But no one has looked for the drug connection," Anna objected.

"True."

"Then we have something to do this evening, too."

"This evening it's tennis," Ècu protested. "Tomorrow, you mean. Tomorrow we can have a go at it."

She got out of the car. Falcon followed. Together they made a pass around the phone booth. They didn't know what they were looking for and didn't find anything, either. The lynx could not refrain from glancing toward the doorway to number 42. It was strange that Claude Siamese lived so modestly, she thought. She had never met him, but the stories were many and she imagined a cunning stuffed animal, arrogant and dangerous. Apparently, however, he was wise enough to live a low-key life. She noted that the paint was flaking on the entry to the building.

"No," she said out loud, "we won't get any wiser here. Let's go get Earwig."

Honey yellow Carrer de Carrera was abandoned and quiet, just like on Tuesday. This time Anna parked outside the building; there was no longer any reason to be discreet.

They got out of the car. Falcon quickly confirmed that the cuffs were hanging on his belt. He had misgivings about Earwig.

"This is going to go fine," said Anna to calm him, as if she had read his thoughts.

If anyone else had spoken to him that way, he would never have taken the concern seriously. Now he nodded. But he noted that Anna unconsciously felt to see if her pistol was resting securely in its holster.

They rounded the edge of the building. Due to the Afternoon Weather the air seemed to be holding its breath. The back courtyard was in shadow; through the windows of the building they tried to catch sight of the inventor, but he didn't appear to be inside. The large machine was working at full steam; it was puffing and groaning in the same ear-splitting manner as last time.

The door was unlocked. Anna took one step into the place and called out, but it was doubtful whether she made herself heard over the din.

"Oleg Earwig!" she shouted. "It's the police!"

No one answered. No one was visible. The inspectors walked beside each other, slowly and carefully. Due to the noise it was hard to communicate. With a nod she directed Falcon straight ahead, along the windows, while she turned left, into the premises.

Suddenly he was standing there. Dressed in his white coat and with arms and legs sticking out in all directions. He had appeared from behind the clattering machine, only a few yards away.

"The police!" he exclaimed.

He sounded furious.

"Oleg Earwig," Anna called in her most formal voice, "we hereby arrest you for the murder of Oswald Vulture."

"An arrest?" The earwig did not sound the least bit surprised, only angrier.

"Come along voluntarily and we'll make it easy for you," Falcon shouted threateningly.

But Falcon's authority was unclear, and Oleg stared at the bird.

"Fools!" the inventor screamed. "Fools! Haven't I said that I didn't do it? Haven't I said that? Haven't I said that I can prove that I didn't do it? Haven't I said that?"

"Oleg Earwig," Anna repeated in a loud voice, remaining calm. "I must ask you to—"

But Oleg Earwig did not intend to wait to hear what she

had to say. He turned and fled in among his machines and scrap metal. Falcon ran after, Anna drew her gun.

"Stop!" she shouted.

She could not see either Earwig or Falcon, nor could she hear them. She squeezed the trigger, firing a shot up at the ceiling.

"Stop," she called again.

The shot had the intended effect. Only seconds later the inventor was standing in front of her again.

"Are you going to kill me?" he asked.

He was shaken.

"Stand still!" Falcon called.

He came running, his gun aimed right at Earwig's head.

"You're out of your minds!" the inventor shouted. "You're out of your minds! I haven't done a damn thing!"

But he did not budge from the spot. His respect for Falcon's pistol was greater than his respect for Falcon.

"You are under arrest for the murder of Oswald Vulture," Anna repeated.

She had a hard time keeping her voice steady. The adrenaline caused her pulse to race, and it was not settling down, even though the situation was under control. When she saw all of Earwig's arms and legs, she realized that the handcuffs would not do the job.

"Follow me," she said, adding, to Falcon, "and follow him. Don't let him out of your sight."

The last was mostly so that Earwig would understand that this was serious.

"But you only need to talk with Balder Toad!" Earwig whimpered. "He's going to vouch for me."

"Shut up," Falcon roared. "And follow Detective Lynx."

4.5

Larry Bloodhound stayed behind in his office when Ècu and Lynx set off to arrest Oleg Earwig. He was sitting with the door closed. Someone had pulled up the blinds facing the parking lot while he was out at lunch. Probably the same animal that emptied the wastebasket, he thought with a grimace. With a groan he got up, took the step over to the window, and pulled down the blinds again. This office felt better in darkness.

He looked out over the mess and recalled that yesterday morning he had tossed half a croissant in the upper-right-hand desk drawer. But for now he let that be—he was resolute, thinking about his weight and feeling like a better stuffed animal as he turned to his work.

Larry Bloodhound really did have a lot to do but couldn't decide where to begin. When the phone rang and Larry saw on the display that it was Derek Hare from tech, he tossed aside pen and paper, opened the drawer with the croissant, and stuffed it in his mouth as he picked up the receiver.

"Bloodhound," he growled. "I'm listening."

"It's Derek," said Hare. "I just wanted to tell you that we were able to open the folder in Vulture's laptop."

"And?"

"Well, that's just it. It's bookkeeping for a company, Domaine d'Or Logistics. Debit and credit. You know, expenditures and deposits."

"And?" the superintendent growled.

"Nothing else," said Derek. "Seems completely uninteresting. Thought I should just mention it. Maybe you'll find out where it fits in. If we find any code or key in the big box that explains what this is about, I'll call again."

Bloodhound hung up. He leaned back and closed his eyes. Tried to concentrate. Oswald Vulture's head was not the only one missing in Mollisan Town at the moment. In a warehouse connected to the Lucretzia Hospital in southwest Tourquai there was a large hall no normally functioning stuffed animal went to without good reason. The living dead were there, stuffed animals that in one way or another had lost their heads but had not yet been taken to the next life by the Chauffeurs. A constant temperature was maintained in the warehouse. The cloth bodies lay on rolling stretchers inside closed cabinets; there were long corridors with drawers of stuffed animals in endless rows. There were stuffed animals whose skulls had burned up or been damaged by mistake. And there were others who had been subjected to assault. Bloodhound had heard someone mention that no more then five percent of all bodies were brought back to life, and this possibility appeared in some way even more unpleasant. Like rising from the dead.

In the mess on the superintendent's desk were folders dealing with at least three of the bodies in Lucretzia's warehouse at the moment.

"What the hell," Bloodhound growled to himself.

Secretary Cobra was lying, he had a hunch. The question was why. Oleg Earwig was lying, he thought. The question was whether it was for the same reason. No one else seems conceivable, Bloodhound decided.

But he had a vague feeling that there was something he was missing, and the uneasiness caused him to get up and leave the enclosed office. He walked quickly through the department. Here and there police officers were sitting, working. A few looked up and greeted him as he went past, others didn't bother. He went to the men's restroom over by the elevators.

Why one of the light fixtures was always broken, why the simple locks on the stalls were hanging to one side, and the reason for the scratches in the stainless-steel sinks were things Larry Bloodhound had never been able to figure out. Nor could he explain why the cleaners put lavender-scented soap in the men's restroom.

Larry met his gaze in the mirror. With all the dark brown, wrinkled, hanging cloth in his face, his expression completed an image of great fatigue.

"Now I'm going to forget about this for today. I've earned a beer, since I didn't eat the croissant," he said to his mirror image.

He knew he'd eaten the croissant. But maybe his mirror image didn't know it.

At Chez Jacques it was unusually smoky. This happened sometimes, even though the smoke level shouldn't vary much since it was usually the same stuffed animals who met there every day. Outside, twilight besieged the sky, casting Mollisan Town's streets and squares in warm, gentle colors. The smoke and the thin curtains hanging at the windows created a muted, restful light inside Chez Jacques.

Private detective Philip Mouse was waiting as usual at the table by the window. Larry nodded at the familiar faces on his way there, ordered and got a beer at the bar, and then sat down across from the mouse.

"No light today?" Philip asked, raising his hat an inch or so on his forehead.

Larry shrugged his shoulders.

"I hear you've made some progress in the Vulture case."

Larry nodded.

"No thanks to me," the superintendent growled.

"That's never stopped you from taking credit for it." The mouse smiled.

"I don't know," Larry growled, ignoring the slight. "An inventor, the last one to see Vulture alive, has every reason in the world to kill him. A real crazy, apparently. Lies about his alibi, but I don't know . . ."

At the next table two gnus left a half-eaten bowl of chips, and Bloodhound managed to grab it before the waitress noticed and took it away.

"An inventor? Do you think it has something to do with Vulture's investments?"

"I don't think anything," Larry maintained, putting a pawful of chips into his mouth.

"Always the wisest," Mouse agreed. "But too wise to be true. Deep inside we always have a feeling."

"There are too many with reasons," Bloodhound said. "A whole will full of possibilities. By the way, have you ever heard of a Jasmine Squirrel?"

Mouse shook his head.

"What about her?"

Larry growled something, but it was unclear what he meant. Chez Jacques was rumbling this evening. The sound from all the police officers who had just got off or would soon go on their shifts—laughter and quarreling, shy confessions and blustering boasts—seemed to settle like a thick, dark brown rug over the black wooden tiles. Philip and Larry were sitting in the midst of a sound porridge, bubbling and boiling on rue de Cadix.

"I guess it is what it is," said Mouse. "Isn't that what you always say? That fate rules us all?"

"That's bullshit," Bloodhound growled. "Don't make yourself ridiculous. Believe in fate. I've never said that. What I *have* said is—"

"I know," Mouse interrupted. "Larry, I know what you've said. Because you've said it so many times. But if you were to be right, it would mean that the future is exactly like history. That everything has already happened, both forward and backward in time."

"I have to think about that," Bloodhound said, digging for the last crushed chips in the bowl.

"Should we get more chips?"

"No way," said Bloodhound. "I'm trying to cut back, you know."

"But that was how you described it," Mouse continued, lighting a cigarette. "Didn't you say that fate is like a train track? We have a certain number of cars to move between. There, in the cars, we can do what we want, and succeed and fail and meet and separate and everything. But the train is moving in the direction that fate determines."

"Yes, yes, just like that," Bloodhound growled. "Smart mouse—excuse me, could we please get a bowl of chips here?"

Stuffed animals came and went, the crowding at the bar waxed and waned. Larry and Philip were sitting half-turned toward the window, so that most of it went on behind their backs. An occasional loud volley of laughter rose up from the spoken Muzak.

"This is what I mean," the private detective said, taking a deep puff on his cigarette. "The consequences of what you're saying are just that everything has already happened."

"You're too smart for me," Bloodhound growled.

He felt tired. He had no desire to listen to Mouse's philosophical digressions. When the waitress came with the chips he ordered another beer, but a light one this time. He longed for Cordelia.

"Imagine a journey in time," Philip said, putting out the

cigarette. "If we go back in time we end up in historic events. Carl the Horse's war, and a hundred years later the resistance movement of Shrew-Mouse, or in the twenties what led up to Goldstein's theories . . . But the same thing if we travel forward in time, to our grandchildren. There, the same sort of events are waiting. If fate has set the rails through the future, we're going to end up in what has already happened, despite the fact that our lives have not yet taken us there. Do you understand? I think of it as a long train, and each car is a tableau, whether or not there is an audience; 'theater cars' in a marketplace that line the road into the future."

"Sounds really strange," said Larry, who hadn't been following his reasoning.

"It's your idea, not mine. I don't even believe in it. But it undeniably raises questions about infinity. Reasonably there must be an end to all these theater cars, no? Your train tracks have to end somewhere. Because you believe in a fate that is waiting for us in the future, you must also believe in a mountain of time, or a sea of time, where everything ends, right?"

"Bullshit. It doesn't end," Bloodhound growled. "That's the whole point of eternity. That it feels hopeless to imagine. I've got to piss."

Whereupon the superintendent got up and waded through the noise over to the toilets. When he came back, Philip Mouse had taken off his hat and set it on the table. But the detective was still talkative and attacked the superintendent as soon as he sat down.

"And love?" asked Mouse.

"Love?"

"Is that fate? Or do you believe it's just something you find on board your train?"

Larry Bloodhound did not answer. He couldn't help that it was the little green budgie waiting for him at home that showed up in his thoughts as soon as Mouse mentioned the word "love." He felt pathetic, which made him angry.

"Love," sighed Bloodhound, "is going around constipated and unsatisfied your whole life. Neither more nor less."

The private detective nodded.

"Unsatisfied? Not bad, Superintendent. For every step you take toward her," the mouse said in a lingering tone of voice, "she takes two steps back. For every word you utter, every word you think builds a bridge, she sinks deeper into herself. It's like a kind of artful labyrinth that leads you farther away, even though you've figured out in advance how you should move ahead."

Private detective Philip Mouse was an animal who lived in his irony; distance was not just in his words but part of his personality. Hearing him talk about love came as a surprise.

"I'll be damned," said Bloodhound. "Superb, Mouse. And insightful."

Mouse blushed.

"Everyone has some kind of hub, right? Another animal, a feeling or an idea that is immovable as an anchor at the base of the soul and means that we never manage to tear ourselves loose. Foolishly we paddle around in more or less wide circles, in our own little sea . . ."

Philip's voice died away. Mumbling, he finished the sentence to himself. Larry sat quietly and observed the private detective with renewed interest.

"I'll be damned, Mouse," he repeated.

Like everyone else, Bloodhound felt comfortable with the predictable, but in reality Larry Bloodhound had always known that it was the surprises that brightened up life. And hearing Mouse reveal his personal thoughts was refreshing.

At the same time, all the talk about love made the superintendent impatient. He wanted to go home, and he got up.

"Will you get the check, Detective?"

Mouse nodded.

"You can pay in the next life," he replied.

4.6

Darkness sat like a hat on top of Mollisan Town, with stars sparkling in a clear sky. On rue de Montyon in north Tourquai the streetlights lit up the deserted sidewalks, shadows of light fell soft as cotton across the blue asphalt. The weather had long since passed midnight, and the low apartment buildings that lined the street stood dark and silent.

The exception was the fourth and topmost floor at 42 rue de Montyon.

From there a warm yellow light flowed out through the windows, suggesting that the entire top floor was a single apartment with a single resident. The music, too, penetrated out onto the street, or parts of the rhythm at least: a bass drum that kept an insistent and unsophisticated tempo, and a wailing voice that stumbled around a familiar melody.

Claude Siamese's apartment was somewhat out of the ordinary. It had room upon room upon room in a row in line with the street, and a wood floor laid so that it was impossible to detect the joints: fifty feet of beautiful, wide oak planks, as if the trees were felled by giants. It was sparsely furnished, but here and there was a lounge chair. On the floor piles of pillows were strewn; they could be used as seats, tables, or beds. The lighting shifted in various colors; for an animal going from one side of the apartment to the other, it was like walking through a rainbow.

Out in the kitchen stood a cat, Claude Siamese himself, dressed only in a pair of leopard-spotted leather trousers, alongside him a pretty little rat in a red polka-dot bikini top and jeans, and right behind her a gazelle in a blue jacket. One of the gazelle's horns seemed to have broken off in the middle. Each of the three was holding a knife and cutting open with concentration some small cans of tuna on the counter.

The apartment was crammed with hi-fi speakers; it was not possible to escape the music anywhere, and the rat and gazelle were singing along.

"But concentrate!" Siamese shouted to be heard above the noise.

The pretty rat only laughed and continued cutting and singing. The gazelle didn't seem to hear anything at all; he was hacking at his can as if in a trance.

"Focus!" Claude screamed. "We have to SUCCEED! My life depends on it!"

The rat laughed louder and made a few halfhearted attempts to actually hit the little can with her massive knife. The kitchen counter was cut to pieces. When Claude Siamese awoke early the next morning, he would have to make a few calls and have the counter replaced with a new one.

At about this time of day Siamese always felt an uncontrollable urge for tuna fish. He knew there was a can opener somewhere, but he couldn't think where. Along with the rat and gazelle he had already turned all the drawers in the kitchen inside out. Silverware and cutting boards, saucepans and place mats, tablecloths and napkins were in piles on the floor around them.

But the can opener was nowhere to be found.

Then he thought of it.

"Wait!" he shouted.

The gazelle and rat both stopped in mid-cut, startled by his tone.

"I KNOW! In the sauna!"

He threw his knife in the sink, the rat did the same, and they ran, paw in paw, out to the corridor. The gazelle followed close behind.

The room outside the kitchen was flooded in orange light. Ten or so animals were lying there in piles across an elegant, austere sofa. In the middle was a large coffee table, full of overturned glasses and liquor bottles, newspapers and pieces of clothing. Around the couch there were still more clothes. A pair of pants, a few bras, and a beige jacket that appeared to have gone through a paper shredder. Claude's candy dishes— small turquoise porcelain bowls with white glass borders where there was always cocaine—were empty.

"Who are all these stuffed animals?" asked Claude Siamese, making a gesture toward the crowd.

The animals on the couches moved; they were conscious.

"You ought to know, right?" the rat giggled.

"But I don't know."

"You invited them, didn't you?" she giggled even more hysterically.

"May I kick them out?" he asked.

She was laughing so that she couldn't answer, but she nodded enthusiastically. The gazelle nodded, too, less positively, however.

Claude Siamese adjusted the lining on his leopard-skin trousers, took a deep breath, and went over to the sofa with dignified steps. He remained standing for a few moments, uncertain about how he should go about the task. Then he raised his voice and screamed, "I am Claude Siamese. Vanish. Otherwise you'll vanish forever!"

Four stuffed animals flew up from the sofa and ran as fast

as they could toward the hall and the outside door. Three animals tried to follow, but stumbled and tripped and did not appear to be getting anywhere. A few animals still lay sleeping, unaware of what had happened.

The rat laughed. The gazelle laughed. Siamese smiled, but then he remembered.

"The tuna fish."

And they resumed their search for the can opener, hurrying on through the rooms on the way to the sauna.

The sauna was large and lovely, and adjacent to Claude Siamese's bedroom. The can opener was on the upper platform.

"Bring the cans here," said Claude Siamese.

"I thought you were bringing them," the rat replied, turning to the gazelle.

"Darling," said the gazelle, "you're talking about canned goods all the time, but I still don't know what you mean."

A moment of uncomfortable silence, then Siamese laughed. The rat laughed, too, it was liberating; the gazelle smiled wryly. And they ran back through rooms where stuffed animals were still busy abusing Siamese's hospitality.

At first they didn't hear the doorbell.

Siamese, the rat, and the gazelle were back in the kitchen, opening cans. The apartment door was unlocked, and sooner or later most tried the handle. But the visitor continued ringing, and the signal cut through the music. The only ones who behaved like that were the neighbors.

"Shit," Siamese swore.

He gave the can opener to the gazelle and instructed him to open the cans. Then he ran out to the hall and opened the front door.

Outside stood Superintendent Bloodhound.

"Larry!" Claude Siamese exclaimed in surprise.

"May I come in?"

Claude took a step to one side, and the police officer entered the apartment.

Siamese ate tuna fish right out of the can while he listened to Superintendent Bloodhound.

"Well, well," said the cat. "That's no problem. It's really no problem. But I'm FURIOUS!"

Bloodhound fell silent. They were sitting in Siamese's office in a part of the apartment where the after-party never made it, the dog on the austere, black leather couch and the cat on one of the soft white armchairs.

"FURIOUS!" Siamese repeated.

He stopped talking and ate. Bloodhound had never heard the cat raise his voice. A single lamp shone on the table, but the glow barely reached the cat and dog.

"You promised," Claude Siamese continued after a few quick bites, "and Magnus knows I've paid you to keep promises. And yet I saw a police car turn in and park on the other side of the street."

Larry shook his head with irritation.

"And?" he asked.

"And it's obvious," Siamese complained. "Despite all you've said, you're after me again!" said Claude. "That makes me FURIOUS!"

Larry was about to raise his voice and put the little fop in his place when Siamese added, "And when I am FURIOUS I'm not going to remember the combination to the cabinet, and your powder is in the cabinet."

It was a simple threat that normally would have provoked Bloodhound. Now his self-esteem was faltering.

"A car that stops across . . ." he growled quietly. "You're paranoid. It may have been a couple of lousy traffic cops out after illegal parking, what do I know?"

"NEVER!" Siamese screamed. "They got out of the car,

they were plainclothes detectives, not regular patrol officers, and they were snooping around the phone booth across the way for several minutes."

"Shit your pants. I never promised that I can take responsibility for what GL is up to," Bloodhound answered morosely.

"THAT is not what I want to HEAR!" Siamese shouted crossly.

Bloodhound's legs were shaking. He was thinking about his hiding place at home in the kitchen cabinet. It wouldn't last long. Self-contempt tormented him; why had he put himself in this situation? The question was a form of self-pity from which it was impossible to gather strength.

"If I see anything that—" he began but was interrupted.

"See to it that they DISAPPEAR!" said Siamese.

"I can't do more than—"

"DISAPPEAR!" Siamese repeated.

"I'm a superintendent at WE," Larry Bloodhound reminded him. "I have a certain influence over the other departments, but I can't stop ongoing investigations. I deal with assaults, with murders."

Siamese got up, took the two steps over to the couch, and sat down so close that his unpleasant eyes ended up an inch or so from Bloodhound's face."

"What if I KILL them," whispered Siamese. "What if I found out who they were and KILL them?"

Later that night Bloodhound was unsure what the exact words had been. What *his* exact words had been. He weighed the bag of cocaine in his paw and knew it wasn't worth it.

Yet.

4.7

Anna Lynx lied about Todd's age, and they accepted her, it was really no problem; anyone who wanted could be involved. But she soon realized that all of the other Parents In Town had cubs that were teenagers. Yet she wanted to make a contribution; it was important to keep cubs off the streets, and as a police officer she knew how severely constrained resources were at the department. Besides, Todd, too, would be a teenager one day, so it was important to understand a few things.

She went with a group from the neighborhood a few times a week. Compared to her job, the nighttime walks were mostly pleasant and social. You gossiped a little about and with each other, and if you encountered some overimbibing cubs you made them listen to reason in a friendly way. Most often no more than that was required. Sometimes there would be a passed-out drunk cub on the ground feeling nauseous who seriously horrified everyone, and Anna was often the animal who led the cub home. When Parents In Town encountered someone who was high on harder drugs and behaving aggressively in the way that Anna came in contact with daily on the job, the night patrol hurried away to call for reinforcements. It was simply not the idea that Parents In Town would do anything other than strengthen neighborhood unity, and at the same time get a little fresh night air.

This evening Anna was walking together with a chameleon who worked as an accountant and lived in the same building as she did, although on the seventh floor, and a semifamous cricket player named Godot who always lagged a few steps behind. She was having a nice time with the accountant, who proved to be a passionate expert on Styrofoam balls, and who had a private collection that included hundreds of colors and forms.

The half-moon was on its way to becoming full, and the air was cool but not yet chilly. Before she left home, she'd had a few glasses of wine with her mom, who always slept with Todd the night that Anna patrolled. Anna also called Falcon to hear how his match had gone, but that was less successful. He sounded defeated in a way that caused her heart to ache, and she hadn't been able to provide any consolation. For that reason, at least, it was nice to walk along the deserted, dark sidewalks and listen to the chameleon expound on the acquisition of Styrofoam balls. She did not give a thought to the fact that they were suddenly walking south on blue rue de Montyon.

The silence was restful. Not dense or frightening. They conversed quietly, not needing to drown out the constant drone from the cars on North Avenue. But when a doorway opened ten or so yards away, the sound cut straight into the stillness, and all three of them stopped, Godot a few steps behind Anna and the chameleon.

From out of the doorway came a sizable stuffed animal in a thick jacket. Anna knew immediately that she recognized him, but it took a few seconds before she could place the figure. He walked out quickly, then paused a few moments on the sidewalk outside the doorway. He looked around, discovered the three night patrollers as they stood in the shadow of a lantern post, and then walked in the opposite direction.

As he turned toward them, Anna Lynx had seen who it was. And a few seconds later, as she herself passed the doorway out of which he had come, there was no longer any doubt.

Larry Bloodhound had come out of the doorway of Claude Siamese's building. The superintendent had been standing a few yards from the phone booth where the tip about Oswald Vulture had been called in. Called in to this same Superintendent Bloodhound.

Anna excused herself and quickly left Godot and the accountant alone in the night. Thoughts were swirling in her head, but so far they were incomprehensible.

IGOR PANDA 4

In his paw he weighed his chips—only black counters—with an inward smile that no one could see.

A fortune is no heavier than this, he thought.

My life is no heavier than this, he thought.

Yesterday evening he had decided how he would bet, and since then, he had waited for this moment. He got up, excused himself to Raven, who was sitting next to him, and squeezed his way to the short staircase. Down on the cold cement floor in front of the screen he put his counters in the green tube. A murmur was heard from the animals in the grandstand. Everyone was there for the same reason, everyone was used to high stakes, but even so this was something out of the ordinary. Igor Panda himself felt a drop of sweat run down his temple as he returned to his place.

There was perhaps five minutes left until it was time.

During those five minutes, Panda lived more intensely than in several weeks at the gallery. This was his drug, the adrenaline was pumping out into his system, and he experienced the familiar feeling of becoming light as a feather. It was a kind of delirium, but a pleasant one.

"I'll be damned," said the raven as Igor sat down again.

But Igor didn't hear a thing.

There was a stuffy odor of dampness and cold. They were seven stories below street level in one of the many parking garages that had been blasted out under Tourquai's city center. The grandstands were set up across from each other and could be assembled in less than ten minutes; six rows held a hundred animals each. The operation was illegal, moving from garage to garage, and where it would turn up next week only the initiated knew. New players were seldom accepted and, when that did happen, it was only after extensive background checks.

"Green, is it?" said the raven in a fresh attempt at conversation.

They all handled the nervousness differently. The raven was obviously the talkative type, the kind who thought the grandstand seats were hard and who feared the moment when the wheel would stop.

It was the opposite with Igor Panda. He enjoyed it. He concentrated on the tension, letting nothing disturb him.

That's why he remained silent.

The raven continued to babble, not caring that the panda didn't answer, and he fell silent only when the Master of Ceremonies appeared.

As usual he arrived without anyone seeing him; suddenly he was simply standing there. Quickly the grandstands became silent. The Master of Ceremonies was wearing a long red mantle and large dark sunglasses. He walked slowly up to the wheel, which was placed on a small stage across from the grandstands, and raised his arms dramatically.

The wheel resembled a shrunken tombola wheel. It lay flat on a table and twirled at great speed. On a large screen hanging on the garage wall, images flickered past. They were replaced at the same rate as the wheel was twirling; it went so fast it was impossible to comprehend what they depicted. But tonight there were no novices in the grandstand; everyone knew what this was about.

Below the screen, six hollow Plexiglas tubes stood on the floor: one black, one red, one blue, one green, one yellow, and one gray. They were all filled with counters. Prior to Panda's bet, red had been the night's most popular color.

"One minute," the Master of Ceremonies announced.

The most indecisive now shuffled down from the grandstand to place their bets in the respective tube. It was always the same animals who waited until last, the tacticians who wanted to be sure they knew what they were betting on. It seldom happened that a single animal could affect the odds, but tonight Igor Panda's enormous bet had exactly this effect. It created a different type of behavior at the tubes; it was necessary to react to the fortune that had been bet on green.

"Half a minute," the Master of Ceremonies called out.

The seconds ticked slowly by, then it was over. The tubes were sealed by the emcee's assistant, and then all the bettors returned to their places in the grandstand.

Finally the Master of Ceremonies lowered his arms, and at the same moment a sharp signal was heard. The wheel slowed down. All attention was directed at the screen on the wall.

Live footage from streets around Mollisan Town were being shown. The rate was still so high that they looked like still photographs.

The wheel's way of reducing speed was clever. It would take a few minutes before it stopped: an endless time, it seemed. The images on the screen lingered longer and longer, and at a given moment you suddenly saw that there was movement, a pedestrian, a car driving past.

It was called VolgaBet.

Who organized and ran the game remained unclear. No one dared investigate it. Before every game night a number of

videocameras—some said there were ten while others maintained there were at least fifty—were placed in different parts
of the city. They were positioned on building exteriors, on
balconies and roofs, keeping their watchful lens eyes on the
deserted streets below. Just as often as the gaming location
was moved between garages in Tourquai, the cameras were
relocated to different streets in Mollisan Town.

The slower the wheel twirled in front of the Master of Ceremonies, the longer the animals in the grandstand were able
to observe the same street.

When the wheel finally stopped, the street for the night was
chosen.

Once again a murmur passed through the audience.

Now it was only a matter of waiting. In the sealed plastic
tubes were the bets. Igor Panda had bet his money that the
first car that showed up on the screen tonight would be green.
This was more than an impulse. It was the result of a careful
strategy in combination with a calculation of the odds based
on a statistically significant investigation Panda himself had
made of the streets of the city. Green was an absolutely sure
card on a night like this.

But it was also an intuitive feeling that it was time at last to
win really big.

It took a while.

Sitting and intently staring at the screen where nothing happened was the part of the game that strained the nerves most.
Sometimes it could take hours before a car drove by, depend-
ing of course on where in the city chance had chosen a camera.

Tonight Panda seemed to recognize the street. But he wasn't
sure, and he disliked players who always claimed to know
where the camera was located. The sort who thought they
could predict the locations and manipulate fate. Panda didn't
care to guess. That's not what this was about.

Then.

At a distance they saw the car approaching. A muted murmur was heard in the grandstand.

It was still so far away that the color could not be discerned, but soon someone called "Red!" right out into the air, whereupon someone else called "Black!" at the next moment, and then the speculations were under way as the car quickly approached the camera.

They saw it at almost the same time.

More than half of the players fell silent, while a few continued to scream hysterically.

The car was red.

Igor Panda made his way down from the grandstand as the Master of Ceremonies started the wheel going again. Panda heard the noise from the stuffed animals preparing to bet again, but he didn't care about that. With heavy steps he walked on the cold, damp cement floor, away from the grandstands and into the shadows in the deserted garage.

The car was parked at a safe distance as usual. A reminder, but a reminder that was not overly insistent. The dark window in the backseat glided down even before Panda had approached.

"Stop right there," came the order from inside the car.

Panda stopped a few yards away.

"I need credit," he said.

"We need payment," someone answered from the backseat.

Panda had never seen the face of the one sitting in the car, but he thought it was the same animal week after week; he thought he recognized the voice.

"You got almost all of it back this evening," Panda replied. "Now I need another small loan."

"You lost exactly everything you just borrowed."

"That's why I need another loan," said Panda, irritated.

"Not tonight, Igor," the voice replied. "You made a repayment, but it was too little. We want five hundred thousand. Six hundred thousand in three days. Seven hundred thousand in six days."

Igor nodded. He'd been through this process so many times he didn't even have the energy to argue about the unreasonable interest rate.

He turned around and went toward the ramp that, like a slithering snake, led up to the street. On the third level he could get reception. He called Jake Golden Retriever. After the fifth ring Jake answered. It was obvious that he'd been sleeping.

"I need another painting," said Igor Panda. "Now. I'm coming by right now to get it."

"I don't have any paintings," the barely awake dog slurred.

"Don't play the fool, dog-devil," Panda bellowed. "I know where you live. I'm coming now."

It was a lie. Panda had no idea where Golden Retriever lived, but it couldn't be very hard to find out.

"I don't have any paintings," Jake said again.

"Then you'll have to scribble one together. Now."

"I don't paint myself, you stupid panda. I'm only the one who makes sure you have paintings to sell."

Igor stopped. Perplexed. Was Golden Retriever only a go-between? A pimp?

"I don't care which," he screamed after a moment's pause. "I want a new painting. NOW!"

DAY FIVE

5.1

Screams and shouts were heard from far off, and Bloodhound quickened his pace along light brown rue de Cadix. The fog had just given way to the faint breeze, and the sky darkened gradually before the coming Morning Rain. Outside his own doorway the superintendent had stepped in something sticky and foul-smelling that he wasn't able to scrape off his shoe, and the stench irritated him. He was not sure how many hours—or minutes—he had slept that night, and the anxiety over having left Cordelia alone far too long gnawed in his chest.

"One day," he mumbled to himself, "I have to resolve all this with that monstrosity of a Siamese cat."

But not today. And the one positive thing about the night's cocaine rush was that the superintendent was certain that he had burned more calories than he had taken in.

Barely a block away from his office he heard a commotion.

At the top of the stone stairs just outside the entry to the police station there was some kind of disturbance going on. There were four or five uniformed police and two plainclothes officers. Arms were gesticulating, threats were hurled—Bloodhound could only make out fragments. But when he saw that one of the stuffed animals in the middle of the small group was Oleg Earwig, the superintendent jogged the final yards up to the stairs.

"What the hell is this all about?" he barked with his harsh, commanding voice.

The police fell silent, settled down, and waited. Even Earwig and his cohort turned their attention to Bloodhound.

"I'm only ensuring that my client gets out of here," the cohort yelled, a well-dressed antelope Larry thought he recognized.

"This is a farce!" Earwig shouted. "A farce! This is going to cost you dearly. Dearly!"

The police officers waited. Bloodhound was up on the stairs, placing his broad, heavy body in front of the earwig.

"And what's going to cost me dearly, you multilimbed laughingstock?"

"We have witnesses," the antelope explained, turning toward the superintendent with a superior smile. "We have hundreds of witnesses. At the same time as your murder was committed, Oleg Earwig was standing on a stage at Marktplatz in Lanceheim, demonstrating an . . . an invention."

"The Matter Processor," Earwig clarified. "Balder Toad and I. In front of hundreds of admiring animals, who sensed that their lives would be changed forever!"

The police officers involuntarily took a step back. They realized where the conversation was heading.

"That invalidates the grounds for the arrest," the antelope said. "The assertion that there is no alibi does not hold up. You have held my client overnight for no reason. And you know that! Don't be surprised if this has legal consequences! Come, Oleg."

Bloodhound didn't move from the spot, and the antelope was forced to go around the considerable superintendent.

Earwig followed his lawyer, and just as he was passing Larry he whispered in the dog's ear, "This is going to cost you dearly . . ."

Larry closed his eyes. Self-control. He took a few deep breaths. None of the police officers around dared say a thing. When Bloodhound opened his eyes again, Earwig was gone. His unpleasant attorney likewise.

"Swine from hell," the superintendent growled.

With these words he left the police out on the stairs and went into the station. He was boiling with rage. Lynx and Ècu had not done their homework. He didn't know what had happened, but that much he understood. No one would have dared release Earwig if there wasn't good reason for it. And it was him, the head of WE, who looked the fool, while the unpleasant insect was triumphant.

Bloodhound stationed himself by the elevators but didn't have the patience to wait. Instead he jogged up the stairs to the fourth floor, but overestimated his physical condition and was forced to drag himself up the last stretch with the help of the railing. Before he entered WE, he caught his breath a few minutes, then felt extremely disappointed when he saw that Lynx's and Ècu's desks were empty. It was too early in the morning, and they hadn't come in yet.

Panting and angry, he marched through the almost deserted morning office.

"When they get here," he growled to Pedersen, who was at his place a few desks over, "send them in to see me. Right away!"

Pedersen nodded. He recognized the tone of voice.

Larry Bloodhound continued into his office, slamming the door shut behind him.

"Damnation!" he swore out loud.

He wriggled out of his jacket and threw it in a corner on the floor.

———

It would be another hour or two before the falcon and lynx came in, but by then Field Mouse Pedersen had already been down to the jail and gathered enough information that he could tell Bloodhound what had happened.

Balder Toad had told the police the truth. On the other hand, he had omitted a significant detail. The demonstration at Marktplatz had happened last Monday. In the morning. The short visit that Oleg Earwig made to Oswald Vulture had been a final attempt to get Vulture interested in investing in the Matter Processor.

Earwig's attorney had known the exact point in time when Vulture lost his head, and thus he had been able to prove Earwig's innocence. No one could answer the question of how the attorney had access to the sensitive information from the technical investigation. Someone had leaked. It could be someone at rue de Cadix, but Bloodhound considered that unlikely. It was more likely one of the civilians in the laboratory at place St.-Fargeau.

While Field Mouse Pedersen expounded on the context of how he interpreted the situation that morning down in the jail, Bloodhound realized at last the lay of the land. Yes, it could probably be proved that Earwig was standing on a stage in front of hundreds of stuffed animals at the moment when Vulture lost his head. True, along with several dozen others, the inventor did have a motive to cut off the head of the capitalist, but that wasn't enough to keep him in jail.

"I guess we have to realize that it wasn't Earwig who did it," Pedersen sighed dejectedly. "Was there anything else, Superintendent?"

"No, no, that's fine," Bloodhound growled.

"Then I'll get back to the will," Pedersen replied, leaving the room.

"Damnation," Bloodhound sighed. "Damnation, damnation, damnation."

Less than an hour later Anna Lynx cracked open the superintendent's door and stuck her head in. Outside, the Morning Rain had ceased, and on the fourth floor at rue de Cadix the large iron pillars cast their sharp shadows across the stuffed animal police working the day shift.

"You were looking for us, I heard," she said.

Bloodhound looked up. At first he didn't seem to recognize her, then he waved her in. Anna took a hesitant step across the threshold. Falcon Ècu, standing behind her, followed right after. They both thought they knew what was waiting; their colleagues had gossiped about the superintendent's mood.

"I'd just like to beg your pardon," Lynx begins.

"We're so sorry," Ècu says. "We're so sorry. Superintendent, from the bottom of my heart I want to say that—"

"Bah, shut up now," Bloodhound growls, waving his paw as if he were waving away cigarette smoke. "Let's just turn the page."

Anna and Falcon were shocked into silence.

"This investigation is shit," the superintendent notes sourly. "We're back to Cobra. And Squirrel. Did you get hold of the son, Panda, yesterday?"

"No, we . . . but we intend to make a new attempt this morning," Anna says.

She realizes that she finds it hard to look Larry in the eye. It's as if she is ashamed about having seen him come out of Siamese's building last night. She tries to shake off the unpleasantness.

"This morning," Bloodhound rumbles from his desk, "there's a lot of shit I have to do. Organizational administration. Or vice versa. It's pointless. Captain Buck has read some management literature and decided we should have 'team building.' I can't ignore it again. When I come back—it will take a few hours at most—I want a folder on Squirrel. Do you understand? I want her background. Complete and exhaustive. I'm going to talk to her myself. After you're finished with Squirrel's background, I want you to find Cobra. And this time you don't have to be nice to her."

Falcon and Lynx nod in agreement and return in silence to their workstations. Anna has decided not to say anything to Falcon about Bloodhound's nighttime visit to Siamese. She may sympathize with the pedantic, vain bird who can't play tennis, but she knows where her loyalties lie. She has worked with Bloodhound so long that the only thing she can do is ask him flat out. What was he doing with Siamese? But it's important to choose the right moment. And she knows for sure that now is not the time. She understood the frustration in her boss's voice. He asked for a report, and it must be delivered. Sometimes the situation is critical, and this is one of those occasions. The leads are getting cold; Anna realizes that the urgency can't be questioned.

The office up at WE is, as usual, only half-staffed; the day shift is already out on the streets again. Where police officers belong. A kind of expectant fatigue has settled over the department, as if everything is in the balance but has not yet decided in which direction it will tip. Over by the elevators Pedersen sits, talking on the phone. Anna doesn't hear what he's saying. She looks out the windows and lets out a deep sigh. She brought her own car to work today, to make it on time to her talk at the Crisis Center seminar in the afternoon. Females from all over Tourquai will be there to hear her. Anna has been working on the lecture for months, and she feels content. "If Gender Meant As Little As Biology" she calls it. A biting satire of how Mollisan Town would appear if the physical differences between a snake and a brown bear were to create the same chasm between species as the normative attitude creates between females and males.

When Falcon asks how it's going, Anna tells him. She feels pressured by the upcoming lecture. Falcon immediately offers to look up Emanuelle Cobra on his own. Anna knows this is not a good idea, but intends to let him do it anyway. Certain obligations simply must be fulfilled, and she can't say no to the Crisis Center.

During the hours that pass, the inspectors sit in front of their computer screens, working diligently. When one of them produces substantial information they briefly pass this on, and slowly a picture of Jasmine Squirrel develops between the desks.

The parents, Hubert and Nicola, get their cub late in life. Hubert is a deacon in one of Amberville's smaller parishes, Nicola works at the large library in Yok. The new mother quits her job in connection with the delivery of Jasmine and never returns to professional life. To all appearances, Squirrel has a secure upbringing in Tourquai, to which the family moves when Jasmine is five years old.

In one of the Ministry of Finance's many digital archives Falcon Ècu finds a lengthy medical record prepared in connection with Jasmine's whooping cough. The doctor reflects on growing up in a clerical home—"never uncomplicated, an enormous need for liberation is built up which in the worst case explodes in puberty"—and about Nicola's maternal concerns: "Seldom does one see the devotion that is found in Mrs. Hubert, and which with all certainty will give the young Jasmine the self-esteem in which to stand strong."

"What kind of doctor is that?" Anna asks with surprise.

Falcon Ècu shrugs his wings and summarizes his impressions of the medical record.

"It seems as if the young Jasmine Squirrel has had all the usual childhood illnesses by the age of eleven, her schooling flows along without problems, and she dreams of becoming a surgeon."

In the registry from the Ministry of Culture's education division, Anna Lynx finds Jasmine Squirrel's transcripts, which support the thesis of a goal-oriented stuffed animal on her way into the world of the natural sciences. Anna also finds confirmation, in another registry from the same agency, of

Jasmine Squirrel's admission to the Teachers College, indicating that Jasmine, if nothing else, has shown evidence of academic talent.

Then it gets harder.

The inspectors sit quietly in front of their computers and attack the keyboards, only to see one computer image after another flutter past without Jasmine Squirrel's name showing up. There are no transcripts from the Teachers College, or from any other college, either; there is no income information included in the annual tax declarations. Neither Banque Mollisan nor the Savings Banks' Bank has any entries on a Jasmine Squirrel. According to the tax forms, she is still living at her parents' home.

They find Squirrel again in the data registries' vast world of ones and zeros about ten years later, after a doctor's visit at a health clinic in Lanceheim. A similar visit to an emergency room in Tourquai is registered thirteen months after that, only two years ago. In neither case is it possible to produce the reasons why Squirrel sought help; the records are confidential. Not even a warrant will help.

However, Falcon notes out loud, the costs of the medical treatments in both cases are paid by a health insurance policy taken out by a company, Domaine d'Or Logistics.

"I have to go now," says Anna Lynx.

She's forgotten the time and is suddenly in a hurry. She logs off her terminal.

"According to Squirrel's tax return from the same year, she gets no salary from Domaine d'Or Logistics," says Falcon without even seeing Lynx get herself ready.

Anna is not listening; she is on her way out the door.

5.2

L arry Bloodhound parked the car on vanilla white Place de la Liberation and stepped out onto the sidewalk. Immediately he noticed the sweet scent of fruit in oil and coconut. The kiosk, located at the intersection of Boulevard St. Rain since the forties, was Mollisan Town's best if you liked pineapple flambé, and the superintendent could seldom resist the temptation.

He crossed the street and devoted a few minutes to looking at the front pages in the newspaper stand next to the little park. He was living in a crazy time, he decided, so self-absorbed that no one even noticed it anymore.

He bought half a pineapple with extra sprinkles, dialing his cell phone as he ate. He got hold of Falcon Ècu, who sounded nervous and stressed.

"Superintendent," Falcon said into the receiver. "I beg your pardon, but the address for Jasmine Squirrel was wrong . . . we've talked with Squirrel's uncle, I think, he lives where Squirrel's parents were listed. He claimed that these days

Squirrel is on orange yellow rue d'Oran, number 18. It says 'Bordeauz' on the door."

"D'Oran? Isn't that—"

"It's right behind Place de la Liberation," Ècu pointed out obligingly. "If you want, Superintendent, we could drive over and—"

"That's not necessary," Larry Bloodhound decided, shoving the last piece of pineapple into his mouth. "I'm in the vicinity. I'll go and talk to her myself."

Brusquely he concluded the call with his inspector and dried his paws on the lining of his jacket.

Number 18 on rue d'Oran proved to be a lovely, burgundy red building from the late nineties. It was six stories high, with barred windows and a deep, dark entryway guarded by two small stone lions sitting on either side of the door. Bloodhound looked for the name Bordeauz on the directory of tenants next to the entry telephone. While he was looking, a rodent came out of the doorway and Bloodhound slipped in. The directory in the stairwell stated that Bordeauz lived on the third floor. To compensate for the pineapple flambé the superintendent avoided the golden elevator cage, which must have been as old as the building, and took the stairs.

He rang the bell without expectations. At this time of day almost everyone was at work, and the likelihood that Jasmine Squirrel was . . .

"Yes?"

Bloodhound did a double take. The door was opened slightly. The squirrel who stood there was light beige. The superintendent had expected someone darker, browner, and he lost his train of thought. She was pretty without being conspicuous. Quickly he let his gaze drop from her face down to her shoes and back up again. She was dressed in a simple skirt and a yellow blouse. No jewelry, no makeup.

He took out his police badge and held it in the door opening so she could see it.

"Superintendent Larry Bloodhound," he introduced himself. "Um . . . may I come in? This will be quick, only a few words."

She studied his identification carefully and seemed extremely hesitant.

"This will be quick," he repeated. "But I can come back another time."

He attempted a smile but it turned out more like a grimace. Her bushy tail waved guardedly back and forth behind her back; then she made up her mind, opened the door, and took a few steps into the apartment.

"Five minutes," she said.

She had a surprisingly husky voice. He thought that perhaps she was a jazz singer. Then he was embarrassed by his clichéd assumption.

"This doesn't need to take very long," he growled softly.

She turned and went before him into the apartment. Quickly and carefully she closed a door that stood open to the right in the corridor and showed the superintendent into the living room. He could not help glancing toward the closed door as he went past, and he thought he heard someone coughing from within.

"Did I disturb you?" he asked as she placed herself behind the armchair where she meant for him to sit.

"Five minutes," she replied. "And, yes, I have a visitor."

There was something in the way she expressed herself that aroused his curiosity. He wondered who was visiting. But that had nothing to do with him. So he didn't ask.

Squirrel sat on the couch. Posture erect, and clearly impatient.

"Well?"

There was a scent of perfume in the living room. There were bouquets of red roses in both windows, and the white furniture seemed quite new. The apartment was simply furnished, yet it exuded luxury.

"This is about Oswald Vulture," Bloodhound began, taking his notepad out of the pocket of his jacket.

Like other police officers, he always had his notepad with him; he even made notes in it sometimes, but he seldom bothered to read what he'd written later. The superintendent leafed through to an empty page, and Jasmine Squirrel answered, "Vulture? I've never heard of him."

Bloodhound froze. Many years of experience rescued him from giving away his reaction. He raised his eyes and scrutinized the squirrel carefully as he slowly said, "Oswald Vulture is dead."

But Jasmine Squirrel, too, was an experienced animal. Larry could see that she reacted, even if she did her utmost not to let it show. If the information came as a surprise or whether she had known about it in advance was impossible to determine.

"I see," she was content to say.

"Are you certain that you don't know who Oswald Vulture is?" Bloodhound asked.

"I meet so many," she retreated somewhat from her position.

"You are Jasmine Squirrel?" he asked.

"Yes."

"And you are registered at this address?"

"Yes."

He made notes about this.

"Employer?"

"I'm between jobs at the moment," she answered.

"Most recent employer?" he asked.

She thought about it.

"NyLon To Go," she said at last.

"The fast-food chain?"

"That's right."

"What did you do there?"

"Worked at the office. Administration. Papers and numbers."

Superintendent Bloodhound made yet another note in his pad.

"And how long ago was that?" he asked.

"What do you mean?" she replied.

"Well, I was thinking . . . this is a beautiful apartment at a nice address. And . . . all this . . . must cost a pretty penny."

"I manage," she said. "And there isn't much time left of your five minutes, Superintendent . . ."

"Excuse me," Bloodhound said. "I'll tell you exactly why I'm here. You are named in Oswald Vulture's will. I'm not an attorney, I don't know exactly how it will work out, but according to the will you are going to be . . . provided for . . . in a generous way."

He observed her. This was without a doubt something she hadn't known about. Her eyes widened, the pupils contracted. She struggled not to reveal herself.

"Really?" she answered at last.

"But you're still certain that you don't know who Vulture was?" said Bloodhound.

"I . . . maybe I remember him," she said without appearing embarrassed at having maintained the opposite only a minute ago. "Vulture? Oswald Vulture? Yes, I think I know. He's dead? And I'm in his will? How unexpected."

"Why," the superintendent continued, seemingly unmoved by her lies, "do you think he's so generous to you?"

"It must be because he liked me," said Squirrel, with a sneering smile on her lips. "Or what do you think?"

"Well," Bloodhound replied, smiling back. "Well, that's often how it goes . . ."

Jasmine Squirrel got up from the couch and looked urgently at Bloodhound.

"Was there anything else, Superintendent?" she asked.

He sat in the armchair with the tip of the pen against the paper of the notebook and thought about it. He had a strong feeling that this would not be the last time he talked with Jasmine Squirrel.

"No. No, I guess not."

"I'll see you to the door, Superintendent," said Jasmine.

She waited while he put the notebook away and got up. Then she followed close behind him to the outside door. He wondered what she would have done if he suddenly stopped and opened the door she had closed in the hall.

"Well," he said as he stood halfway out in the stairwell. "One more thing. Don't you wonder how much you'll be inheriting?"

She held a paw on the door so as to be able to shut it as quickly as possible.

"How much will I inherit?" asked Jasmine Squirrel.

The tail was again waving slowly back and forth behind her.

"Unfortunately, that I can't say," answered Superintendent Bloodhound.

She deserved that, he thought.

There was a reason she was lying, he thought. There was always a reason. And they would have to find out what it was.

5.3

After more than three hours in front of the computer, Falcon Ècu's eyes felt tired and his back ached. In this era of economy measures he had not been allowed to order a new office chair; instead he was forced to use a model that the occupational therapists had rejected long ago.

The superintendent had ordered them to conduct a new interview with Cobra, but it wasn't possible to get hold of her. Falcon had called Nova Park three times during the day and didn't want to call a fourth time. Cobra was not at work. No one missed her there, and no one cared where she was. Falcon got her home phone, but no one answered at that number.

In the registry of the Ministry of Finance he had found her address, and in addition the addresses for her parents and for a brother—Daniel Python—who was several years younger. Her brother was not home, either, but right after the Afternoon Rain, Falcon got hold of the parents. The mother stated that she had neither seen nor heard from Emanuelle in over a month.

Inspector Ècu returned to his registries and discovered that the brother, Python, worked at Monomart's central ware-house. He phoned the main line, and sure enough Daniel Python had just gone on his evening shift. Perhaps he knew where his sister was? But Python could not come to the phone.

"Do ya t'ink dis is a hotel, or what?" asked the animal on the line.

If the police wanted something from Python, Ècu would have to drag himself there.

It was a long shot, but the falcon needed a change of scene; he had been sitting in this chair long enough now. So without additional time for reflection he set off into the field.

Because Falcon Ècu lived alone, he seldom shopped at Monomart. This was a paradise for families, the low-price temple of volume purchases; there was a playroom for the cubs and charge cards that gave discounts to faithful customers. There were a few Monomart stores in every part of town; to Falcon they all looked equally boring. His view was that you saved more money by losing your appetite than on cheap products.

The food chain's central warehouse was in north Lance-heim, in one of the newly built industrial areas. The ware-house was described as a miracle of logistics, but Ècu still had to wait in reception more than fifteen minutes. The logistics didn't seem to extend to keeping track of their employees.

Daniel came slithering from a long corridor. He wore the dark blue uniform that everyone seemed to have on. The snake had frost on his seams and what looked like flakes of ice on his head. He apparently worked in the refrigerated rooms.

"Daniel Python?" asked Falcon, holding up his police badge.

"Yes?"

You could always tell from their tone of voice whether the

stuffed animal in question was accustomed to visits from the police. Python had apparently not been involved with this before. He stopped at a safe distance, looking at the inspector suspiciously.

"We're looking for your sister," Falcon explained, hurrying to add: "She hasn't done anything. We're looking for her as a witness."

"Does this have to do with Vulture?" asked Python.

The stuffed animals in reception perked up their ears. This would be the talk of the evening shift. But Python was not embarrassed.

"So you have spoken with Emanuelle recently," said Falcon.

"I don't know where she is."

"Somewhere she usually goes? A girlfriend's place?"

Python gave him a few names, shaking his head at the same time.

"If I know my sister right, she's out on the town. That seems to be her best therapy."

"This must have been a shock," said Falcon, taking a step closer to the snake.

Daniel nodded.

"Because she'd worked for Vulture for more than five years, if I understand correctly?"

"Might be right," Python agreed.

"And she felt happy there from the start?"

"Felt happy?" Python repeated with surprise. "She loathed it. She's been looking for a new job for years, she's even been here and asked. Oswald Vulture was . . . well . . . when I heard what she earned . . . and the clothes . . . It's not exactly easy to find something equivalent."

"Then why wasn't she happy?" asked Falcon.

This was a mistake. Daniel Python stiffened noticeably, and his eyes narrowed.

"Say what?"

"Any information you can provide makes our work easier."

"I don't know anything. Ask Emanuelle," said Python. "Was there anything else?"

Falcon had nothing more to ask, and the snake slithered back to the refrigeration rooms.

Falcon Ècu had not even made it over the city line when the switchboard called, looking for him. He answered his cell phone, less surprised than he ought to have been. It was Emanuelle Cobra calling. Falcon kept his eyes on the road. The sky was still blue and it would be another hour or so before twilight besieged the city. The afternoon traffic picked up, and Falcon considered avoiding bright yellow North Avenue.

"I'm at Monokowski," said Cobra. "In Amberville. Come here. I'm in the Twilight Salon."

Falcon could not even answer before the secretary had hung up. The sound of her voice made him remember the rest of her, and he swallowed and blinked. She was tasty. The thought made him blush.

He had never been to Casino Monokowski, but he knew that it was one of Nicholas Dove's places. In Falcon's world it was inconceivable that police officers didn't manage to arrest animals like Dove. Convict them, lock them up, and throw the key in the Hole. And it was even more inconceivable that he couldn't express this opinion because it would be considered extremely naïve. Where was Mollisan Town heading?

Instead of taking a few police officers with him in the car, making a raid, and closing Monokowski, Falcon nicely showed his police badge at the door—a container that concealed the casino's entrance on the inside—and was let in by ironically smiling doormen.

In symbiosis with the Mafia, he thought as he stepped into

the sea of blinking slot machines where thousands of greedy stuffed animals drank themselves to intoxication on diluted liquor and were systematically ruined. In symbiosis with evil, that's what the police have degenerated to. Frustration and indignation rose up through his body, and with bold steps he entered the decadent casino.

Falcon took hold of a waiter who was running past with a tray of champagne glasses.

"Excuse me, but the Twilight Salon . . . ?" he asked without taking the waiter's furious look seriously.

"By the gold draperies," the waiter hissed. "And if I'd dropped the champagne, you would have had to pay for it."

"You didn't drop it," Falcon noted meekly.

The Twilight Salon was an inner room where players who weren't interested in small change divided minor fortunes among themselves. Despite the fact that the room was larger than he could immediately survey, he saw her right away. She was sitting at the bar, and her well-filled latex body glistened just as black and invitingly now as it did at Nova Park last Monday.

He made a roundabout movement, and noticed that all the males in the vicinity were aware of her presence. She was smoking a cigarette in a long, black holder and seemed absorbed by a thought that Falcon would be happy to uncover.

"Miss Cobra?" he said.

She turned around and looked at him with an amused smile.

" 'Miss Cobra'? Yes, that's something new. Mr. Ècu. Police working overtime? Because I don't suppose it's for the sake of my eyes that you've come, Mr. Ècu?"

Falcon blushed. The pink color on his neck spread quickly up to his cheeks, and he looked away self-consciously.

"You're blushing," Cobra commented with surprise. "Lord Magnus, I didn't think that was possible anymore . . ."

"I've come to ask a few questions about Oswald Vulture," Falcon said formally, paying no attention to the bar in which they were standing. "It's nothing to worry about, only a routine measure. The better we understand the situation and those involved, the easier time we'll have in solving the mystery."

"You're blushing because I'm teasing you, and at the same time you say you want to understand Oswald Vulture?" Cobra sneered. "Good luck."

"What do you mean?"

Falcon tried to sound professional, but he could hear that he sounded offended.

"Vulture was an animal who . . ." She hesitated before she continued. "My dear police officer, let me give you an example. On Fridays he would lock us in his office. He kept olive oil on the bookshelf, in a crystal carafe. He poured the oil over me, and then I had to slither up and down his long neck. By the end he was moaning so loud it could be heard out in reception."

She took a deep puff on her cigarette and continued.

"Don't look so shocked, little cop. That goat paid for it. There were others he didn't pay. That he degraded. He was capable of frightful things. Me . . . he had to see me again, after all."

Falcon took notes, but mostly to have somewhere to direct his gaze.

"Are you buying me a drink?" she asked.

Falcon waved the bartender over, and Cobra ordered.

"Oswald was a swine," she said, lighting a new cigarette.

"The others," said Falcon, "do you have names of any of the others that Vulture—"

"No names," she said firmly. "He was no amateur. He was a happily married and successful business animal. A family animal."

"But he—"

"You can't even imagine it," said Cobra.

And when her drink arrived she told a story about what

Vulture had requested of her only a few weeks before he lost his head.

Immediately afterward Falcon left Casino Monokowski without even having talked with Cobra about her alibi. He had become accustomed to violence, but that evening he realized that he knew precious little about evil.

His task was still to bring Vulture's murderer to justice. But it would no longer happen with the same satisfaction.

5.4

As she got into the car Anna Lynx could still hear the applause inside her head. Her body was shaking slightly and she rested her paws on the steering wheel; it was the first time since high school she had given a talk before so many stuffed animals. Back then she was captain of the school debate team, but after that public appearances had become infrequent. She'd felt unpracticed and nervous. Now she felt intoxicated, happy, and dazed; they had responded to her thoughts about gender and species in the right way. She would not be surprised if the *Daily News* wrote a line or two about it tomorrow; she thought she'd seen a few journalists in the audience.

She drove north on South Avenue. The Evening Storm pushed clouds of grit across the street; the streetlamps were shaking on their wires and the light swept turbulently back and forth. She managed to hold on to her feeling of ecstasy all the way down to the Star, but there—with the massive Sagrada Bastante and the thirteen towers of the cathedral illuminated from below as a reminder of everyone's insignificance in the larger context—it was no longer possible. The conclusions she'd drawn earlier in the day returned, and in her mind she was again a police officer. The pieces of the puzzle did not fit together.

The first piece: the tipster must be someone from Nova Park. Likely it was the murderer's accomplice, or the murderer himself. In other words, the tipster was either Emanuelle Cobra or the stuffed animal that Cobra had let out of Vulture's office. Anna stopped at a red light on mottled gray rue Houdon. With her black latex body and her big eyes, the secretary might fool Larry and Falcon, but Anna wasn't going along with it. There was no other possibility. Cobra must know more than she's letting on.

The second puzzle piece: on his own, Claude Siamese controlled major portions of the organized crime in north Tourquai. Prostitution, drugs, gambling—all were within reach of his sharp claws. It could of course be a coincidence that the tipster used the phone booth outside Siamese's entry, but that was hard to believe.

And the final piece that Anna had in her head: Superintendent Larry Bloodhound. It was Bloodhound who took the call from the phone booth, and who was unquestionably the one the tipster intended to contact so that he would lead the investigation. Larry Bloodhound, her boss and friend, had some type of relationship with Siamese.

Behind her a mauve Volga Sport was honking, and Anna let out the clutch. The light must have been green for a long time.

Larry, she thought unhappily. What are you up to?

Larry Bloodhound was mixing an egg toddy. He whisked four egg yolks in a small glass and then poured in sugar corresponding to the quantity of egg yolk. Some of the sugar ended up on the floor below the stove, settling like a sparse garnish over the remnants of leeks already lying there. Where did the leeks come from? Larry didn't recall. While he stirred the egg toddy, he thought about how life had to be balanced, at whatever price. If he left the drugs alone for an evening, he simply had to compensate with sugar and carbohydrates. Probably chemical, he thought, sipping his egg drink.

With the glass in hand, Larry went over to Cordelia's cage. He had propped open the little door, which he sometimes did, but Cordelia still chose to remain on her perch. Larry took this as a clear sign that she was happy.

"Do you want a taste, little friend?" he asked, holding the glass with the cream-colored foam up meaningfully.

But Cordelia preferred water and seeds.

Larry made room for himself on the couch by shoving aside a year's worth of level-seven crossword magazines, which had taken him only an evening to solve.

He had found Cordelia almost three years ago, and there was something about the circumstances of their meeting that caused him to return often to the event in his memory. Perhaps, he thought, it was because for once something had happened to him that was beyond the anticipated. Something outside the framework, and thus he, too, reacted in a way that was different for him. It was a quirk of fate that his and Cordelia's paths crossed.

Harbor Seal Flustrup had been semireclined in the backseat of the police car and Pedersen had been sitting alongside, holding him down. The weather was long past midnight, the moon was shining cold and hateful from the black sky, and inside the car it reeked of terror. But it would get worse.

Bloodhound and Pedersen had a place where they would take the hooligans; you drove up North Avenue until it ended and turned onto the little gravel path by the side of the bus stop. The gravel path soon turned into a couple of wheel tracks, but because they always drove up there around midnight, Bloodhound still didn't know how it looked on the sides of the road.

The superintendent stopped the car suddenly. Flustrup

flew against the front seat. The engine was on, the headlight beams shining like two white pipes through the night. Pedersen opened up the back door and shoved the harbor seal out.

"I have no idea!" the seal screamed. "I'm telling you, I have no idea!"

But that's what they all said, and Bloodhound had scared the truth out of one or two animals before. Pedersen kicked Flustrup so that he ended up in the beam of the headlight, while Bloodhound leisurely got out on the other side of the car. He took care of the customary preparations, and when he was ready he let Harbor Seal Flustrup in on his doings.

"This," said the superintendent, "is a tin can with a little fire burning in it. Do you see?"

He held out the tin can under the face of the terrified stuffed animal on the ground. A blue flame was burning inside the can, and the harbor seal could feel its heat.

"And this," said the superintendent, "is a can of water." He showed that, too.

"This is a little game. I intend to set you on fire, a little at a time, Flustrup. And when you tell us what we want to hear, I'll put it out. Do you think that might be fun?"

The harbor seal had listened in silence, but there was no mistaking the terror in his eyes.

"But . . . Holy Magnus . . . I've told you I don't know anything!" he screamed. "I know nothing! I know nothing!"

The superintendent sighed. There was no point in dragging this out. When Pedersen picked up Flustrup from jail, Larry had gone down to the garage and done a line in the restroom. Good thing, too, he thought now. Otherwise he wouldn't have been able to cope tonight.

"Oh well, time to get started . . ."

That was when it happened.

Just as Superintendent Larry Bloodhound was bringing the can with the blue flame toward one of the harbor seal's whiskers, a chirping was heard up in the air, and the next moment

Cordelia flew down from the sky and sat on Bloodhound's shoulder. It was a shock. He had heard about flying creatures, but he thought they only existed by the sea and that they were much bigger. It wasn't until later, at the library, that he figured out that Cordelia was a budgie. Startled, he could only stand and stare. She chirped, the harbor seal was lying on the ground, crying, and Field Mouse Pedersen was sitting in the car, because he despised watching when the superintendent burned the thugs.

What is love? Is it what Superintendent Larry Bloodhound experienced at that moment? For it was more than the feeling of being chosen by fate. It was finding a place of one's own in an infinite universe. An end to loneliness.

Ever since that night, Cordelia had been Larry's life companion, the one to whom he showed his weaknesses and from whom he gathered strength.

Bloodhound took another sip of the egg toddy.

"It's going to be an early one this evening, Cordelia," he said.

There was something on TV he wanted to watch, but he couldn't remember what, and when he reached for the remote control the doorbell rang. This happened very seldom, and, startled, the superintendent went out in the hall and opened the door. Outside stood Anna Lynx.

"Larry, may I come in?" she asked.

Never before had Inspector Lynx come to see him at home, and, as curious as he was surprised, he took a step to one side so that she could come in.

"I don't know how I should say this, Larry," Anna began. "But I know I have to say it."

The Crisis Center and the lecture felt infinitely distant, as if she had given it in another dimension rather than in another part of the city. But she knew she had to do this, however painful it might feel.

"I saw you coming out of Claude Siamese's last night, Larry," she said.

They sat next to one another on the couch and Larry said nothing. He stared at her for a long time, and then growled quietly.

"How do you know that?"

"I saw you. I was out with my Night Patrol and saw you by chance."

"You must never tell that to anyone, Anna," said Larry, looking her deep in the eyes. "Siamese is my best informer."

"Siamese?"

Anna was taken completely by surprise. Whatever she had thought and feared, the possibility that Siamese was a police informer had not even occurred to her.

"No one knows," Bloodhound continued. "And no one can ever know it, either. You have to promise that."

"I . . . promise," said Anna.

"I'm a fool not to be more careful," Larry continued. "If you saw me, that means that anyone at all might have seen me."

"Well, I—"

"Maybe it was luck," Larry Bloodhound continued, casually lying to his friend. "After this I'll just have to be more careful."

And while Larry Bloodhound followed Anna Lynx out to the stairwell, he thought that it was true, anyway. He had to be more careful. But not just that. He would quit. Sooner or later it would have to happen, and today was just as good a day as tomorrow. Stop the lies, and stop the cocaine.

As he closed the door he felt strong and self-confident.

IGOR PANDA 5

Igor Panda was running for his life. That's how he experienced it. He tried to keep in the shadows, but some of the streetlights along Avinguda de Pedrables were functioning, and the unrelenting light sought out the fleeing panda. He heard the car at a distance, and he realized they could see him.

The street was empty; the streets were always empty in Yok. Panda was running as fast as he could, feeling the lactic acid on its way up through his legs. He was no athlete; he never had been. But the fear of what was about to happen gave him energy and strength beyond the usual.

Without slowing down, he twisted his head to see how far away the car was. Much too close. He ran, looking backward, and the impact was as unexpected as it was hard.

A mouse had come out from a small alley.

The two stuffed animals collided, falling in either direction on the sidewalk. Panda got to his feet and realized that the alley from which the mouse had come was too narrow for cars. He fled down it, hearing the sound of tires braking hard, hearing doors being opened and slammed again, and then a kind of whining sound, and he knew what that meant: the adders had roller skates on the tips of their tails.

The narrow Burbage Close ended in a large cul-de-sac. It was as paradoxical as it was typical for Yok: cars couldn't drive in the alley, and yet there was a place to turn around. The darkness was dense, and it took a few seconds before Igor Panda realized he had chosen the wrong way.

There was nowhere to flee.

Right in front of him stood a wall that might be the back of a garage. To the left a windowless exterior that vanished up into the night, and to the right a fifteen-foot-high metal fence, crowned by coiled barbed wire.

Nonetheless Panda continued running. When he saw the boards piled next to the fence he realized that they were his only chance. He threw himself headlong behind the lumber, and a few seconds later came the adders.

Igor Panda held his breath. It was almost impossible for him not to pant. Yet he forced himself not to.

The adders were six in number. They rode slowly into the cul-de-sac on their roller skates, letting the flashlight beams dance across the building façades, high above Igor. These were adders with black hoods and the customary overalls. Three of them were Holders, the other three Shooters. They always worked in pairs, one holding the weapon and the other firing it, one holding the victim tight and the other biting.

When they realized they were in a cul-de-sac, the snakes skated around and around in circles as they shone their flashlights and investigated every nook and cranny. Panda pulled back farther and farther into the darkness behind the planks. The hiding place was better than he'd thought at first; there was considerably more trash around the cul-de-sac than he'd seen initially, and more hiding places to investigate.

The snakes worked systematically. Panda pressed against the metal fence and closed his eyes. The sound of the hissing snakes and their whining skates became more and more hesitant, he thought, and without wanting to admit it this aroused hope in his chest.

Could he have fooled them?

The next moment through his closed eyes he felt a flashlight aimed right toward his face, and even though he was lying completely still it was too late. One of them pulled him out, and they got him up on his feet.

One of the snakes wound itself around his wrists, binding them behind his back. Another crawled around his right ankle to keep him from running away. A third coiled around his neck, and a fourth closed its mouth around Igor's right paw so that he could feel the razor-sharp fangs against his thin cloth. The fifth and sixth snakes positioned themselves in front of him, smiling venomously.

"Igor," said one of them, shaking his head. "Igor."

He looked up. They were still aiming the flashlight right at his eyes. He was forced to squint.

"You ought to know better," the snake that spoke for them continued, hissing and whispering. "We do know one another, Igor. You know we'll always find you. Don't you?"

Igor did not reply. The light was blinding him, and he closed his eyes.

"But you almost get the feeling you were trying to fool us, Igor," the snake continued. "It hasn't been easy to find you. Not at home, not at work. But you must work, my friend. Otherwise how are you going to pay us?"

Igor still did not reply.

"How?" repeated the snake.

And the snake that was around the panda's neck tensed the muscles in its narrow, long body, curling itself up. This happened slowly, so that Igor felt how the initial unpleasantness of something pressing against his throat slowly changed to panic as it became harder and harder to breathe.

"How?" repeated the snake.

"I don't know," Igor forced out.

"That was not a good answer," the adder hissed.

The snake around his neck let up on the pressure and Igor coughed. He relaxed somewhat and was completely unprepared when the snake around his foot tugged on it. He fell like a pine tree. When he opened his eyes again the snake who was talking was only an inch from his face.

"The money has to be paid back tomorrow, Saturday," he hissed.

"But—"

"No explanations. If you can't settle it by tomorrow, you're never going to settle it. Better to write you off completely than wait and hope. We have our orders. You're history, Panda."

"But—"

"Tomorrow," said the adder. "You have until evening. Not a day longer. And go ahead and try to hide. We're going to find you. We always find you."

The snake spit in Igor's face.

Then they were gone.

Tomorrow?

It was impossible.

DAY SIX

6.1

They gathered in the small conference room where the rotting geraniums still remained. Falcon Ècu brought everyone coffee and Anna Lynx picked up Danish pastry on her way from the day care.

Superintendent Larry Bloodhound grunted with irritation at the Danish pastry, but quickly decided to have one right away instead of agonizing for twenty minutes and then giving in. Crumbs fell in flakes over the white laminated table where there were already brown, half-moon-shaped rings from yesterday's coffee cups and the remnants of blueberry muffins from the day before that.

"Well," he growled, "let's hear it."

Pedersen cleared his throat. But just as he was about to begin his report, the door opened and Captain Jan Buck came in.

"Good morning, colleagues," Buck said quickly. "If you don't mind, Superintendent Bloodhound, I thought I'd sit in on your morning meeting."

Without waiting for a reply, Buck sat down on one of the

uncomfortable, rickety chairs around the conference table. He smiled encouragingly at all those present.

"But the way it looks in here . . ." he commented. "Larry, don't you ever have it cleaned?"

Bloodhound growled.

Falcon Ècu did not know where he should look. He was suddenly sitting alongside the police station's highest commander, and this made him nervous. Buck's commentary made him feel ashamed, besides. It *was* truly filthy in here. The air was bad, crumbs and grit crunched when you walked on the floor—and why hadn't anyone put curtains up on the windows?

Why was Buck here? Falcon didn't know.

"You're always welcome, Jan," the superintendent forced out.

Anna Lynx discreetly hid a smile. Before the case of the upside-down shoe, Larry Bloodhound had persisted with a collegially patronizing attitude toward his young captain; since then, Bloodhound did not mince words. Of all the ingratiating politicians that had crossed his path, Buck was the worst by a long shot. Thus Bloodhound's perceptibly pained expression.

"But," Buck nodded, "don't let me interrupt. Just continue as you were. Pretend like I'm not here. Or . . . just consider me part of the group."

He smiled ingratiatingly.

" 'Part of the group'?" the superintendent repeated, wisely holding back his comment. "Pedersen, have at it now."

Pedersen was used to the young captain's desire to take part in police work; Pedersen had been around so long it no longer concerned him.

"My group and I have gone through the individuals who are named in Oswald Vulture's will," Pedersen explained to Buck. "We actually finished yesterday, even though I didn't think that was possible. Shall I take them one by one, or shall I do a summary?"

"The summary," the superintendent growled.

"Personally, I would love to hear how you've gone about this in more detail," said Buck.

Pedersen looked questioningly around the room, and Bloodhound shrugged his shoulders.

"Well," Pedersen began, leafing through his notes, "first there was the chauffeur and the cook. They, uh, live together. They still work for Flamingo, Vulture's widow, on Mina Road, and we got hold of them there. They were shopping at the indoor market in Amberville on Monday morning when the murder was committed. We checked with . . . I think it was the butcher, the one who's just to the right of the entrance from Gruba Street?"

"Podovski," Buck called out. "I buy cutlets from him."

"The landscaper," Pedersen continued. "The one who's getting the bathroom furnishings—"

"What are you saying?" Buck interrupted. "Bathroom furnishings? Is someone inheriting bathroom furnishings?"

"The landscaper is out of town and won't be home before Sunday. He knew nothing about what had happened, he's in Hillevie with his wife, he's been there for ten days and . . . I judge him to be credible."

Falcon Ècu intensely made notes as if his career depended on it. It was the least he could do to prove he was on the ball in front of Captain Buck.

"Then we have the cook and Raukanomaa," Pedersen continued, "who is some kind of domestic servant. We got hold of Raukanomaa late in the evening, she goes to, uh, dance meditation class, it goes on half the night. Both she and the cook have Mrs. Flamingo, the widow, as an alibi. All three were at the house on Monday. Either they've concocted a story together or else they're telling the truth. Their accounts agree. Moving on, uh, that pug that Vulture in the will realized would be fired. She was fired last Tuesday. Her alibi is doubtful . . . I think it's wobbly . . . she changed her story when we pressured her. Sleeping in late suddenly became a shopping trip. But she's one of the small stuffed animals, really small. To cut the head off of Oswald Vulture she would have needed a ladder. Moving on. The masseuse was working in his office all of Monday, so he's clean. There's only the lamb and the llama, who . . . perhaps require more work."

"The lamb and the llama?" asked Anna.

"The llama was the security guard at Nova Park. The lamb was Vulture's personal secretary."

"I thought Cobra was his secretary," Ècu said.

"He had two, apparently," Pedersen observed. "One at work—Cobra—and another at home. Daniel Lamb. Lamb alleges that he never went to work until just before the Breeze in the morning, and last Monday he had to do some personal errands first. He came to Mina Road at lunchtime. We only had time to check one of his 'personal errands,' and it corresponded. He was at the pharmacy to pick up some thread. But there remains a good deal to check to cover the time of the murder."

"And Lamb?" asked Ècu.

"That was Lamb," Pedersen replied.

"I mean Llama," said Ècu, his cheeks turning bright pink.

"Llama is the same. He says he was in his car the greater part of the morning, on his way out to the workshop in Lanceheim to repair a lawn mower. Then he drove back again, and the errand took until lunch. But we didn't manage to get that confirmed by the workshop. I'll try to reach them again this morning."

Pedersen sat down.

"Thanks," said Bloodhound.

"Perhaps we should do a summary of the overall situation, for the captain's sake?" Falcon suggested.

"That's a good idea," Anna hurried to agree, simply to rescue her colleague from enduring Bloodhound's wrath afterward alone.

The superintendent glared bitterly at his inspectors.

"I don't know if Jan feels any need for a sum—" he began.

"That would be excellent," Jan Buck anticipated. "Go ahead, Larry."

"I see."

Superintendent Larry Bloodhound stuffed the rest of the Danish into his mouth. It had been lying there on the table, waiting for him, and now he suddenly felt a need for sugar. Perhaps he could skip lunch instead? He chewed slowly, with all gazes directed toward him.

"Last Monday," he said, although he hadn't swallowed yet, "Oswald Vulture was murdered."

"Good," said Buck enthusiastically. "Take it from the beginning."

"In other words," Bloodhound growled, "it looked like a classic twister. A room with one door. The deed happens without anyone seeing the murderer go in or out. Then it appears that the secretary, Cobra, who sits outside the door, was actually gone for fifteen minutes. And the time agrees with what the stuck-up Tapir states as the time of the decapitation. The murder weapon is found at the scene of the crime. The head, on the other hand, is still gone, no leads. There are tons of stuffed animals who had reason to cut the head off of Vulture, who apparently was an unsympathetic devil. And rich. The widow will inherit a fortune."

"Do we believe the widow did it?" asked Buck.

"We don't *believe* anything about the widow," Bloodhound replied. "I only state facts. She had the most to gain from his death, and at the same time she thought she was married to a real pile of shit. We ought to question her again, that's what I believe."

"Good," said Falcon, taking notes.

Bloodhound looked at his inspector as if he had a contagious disease.

"Rather quickly suspicion fell upon an inventor, Oleg Earwig, who was the last one to see Vulture alive. He had the motive and the opportunity. He was there. We thought. Then we wasted half a damn week on that repulsive insect, despite the fact that we could simply have dismissed him by double-checking his alibi . . ."

The color on Falcon's cheeks intensified, but Anna could not keep from smiling. This was Bloodhound's immediate revenge for Ècu having suggested this idiotic summary.

"And the secretary?" asked Buck.

"Cobra. That she had something to do with the matter is . . . probable. But she's not our murderer. The oracle at place St.-Fargeau has told us that. And Tapir is intolerable in many ways, but he's always right. The murderer had arms."

Anna noticed that Bloodhound chose not to say anything about the tipster and the phone booth. Captain Jan Buck had, anyway, received more information than he could handle.

"And now?"

"We still don't know how the murderer made his way into the office. There is a rather advanced alarm system. We think that possibly he may have disguised himself as an electrician in order to get in and out. There were repairs going on that morning. We're still checking the stuffed animals in Vulture's will. As you heard, Jan, we've gone through the majority of the ones who are named, and . . . well . . . I saved a favorite until last. Jasmine Squirrel. Anna did a background check yesterday."

"Together with Falcon," said Anna. "Perhaps you'd like to do the honors?"

Falcon Ècu not only wanted to, he was looking forward to it. After the conversation with Cobra he had returned to rue de Cadix and worked until long after midnight. He hadn't even had time to tell Anna what he had found. He leafed through his papers.

"Perhaps you can relay the background first?" he said loyally.

Anna recounted briefly what they knew about Jasmine Squirrel's cubdom and youth. This gave Falcon a foundation on which to construct his presentation, and he took over.

"Thus," he said authoritatively, "there were two matters we could continue working on yesterday evening. One was that Squirrel was not found in any registry, apart from two recorded hospital visits. And, second, that Domaine d'Or Logistics paid her health insurance, despite the fact that she never listed them as an employer in her personal tax returns."

"Domaine d'Or Logistics?" Bloodhound repeated with surprise.

"Are you familiar with that company, Superintendent?"

"No," Bloodhound replied, "but in Vulture's laptop there was a locked folder. It contained accounting for Domaine d'Or Logistics."

"Did Jasmine Squirrel work for Vulture?" asked Anna.

"She said to me that she worked at that loathsome fast-food chain . . . whatever it's called," Bloodhound growled.

"A complete lie," Ècu dismissed firmly.

"Yet another," Bloodhound growled.

"And?" Anna reminded.

"This is exciting," said Falcon, smiling slyly. "I started looking for Domaine d'Or Logistics yesterday. I thought they ought to have information about Squirrel that might lead us further."

"Otherwise there's tax cheating going on," Buck pointed out.

"Captain, it's better than that. Domaine d'Or Logistics, the company that has paid health insurance for Jasmine Squirrel for eighteen years, does not exist."

"Doesn't exist?" Anna exclaimed.

"No. Well, that depends on what you mean. There is no company where tangible goods or services are actually produced, where there are employees and, well, you understand? All that exists are minutes from a corporate meeting held

every year that approves a balance sheet that is submitted to
the Ministry of Finance. The representative for all sharehold-
ers, likewise the CEO of the company and the keeper of the
minutes at the annual meeting, is one Alfredo Wasp."

Falcon Ècu made a stage pause. No one in the room had
ever heard of Alfredo Wasp and therefore the pause made no
great impression.

"Wasp has a lot of experience with company meetings,"
Falcon continued. "He keeps the minutes for Nova Park's
board meetings and shareholder meetings."

Pedersen whistled.

"So it's Vulture behind Domaine d'Or, then," Anna
concluded.

"It gets better," said Falcon.

Bloodhound still looked angry, but he could not conceal the
fact that he was interested.

"I took a closer look at that health insurance coverage,"
said Ècu. "It seems that Squirrel isn't the only one who has
medical care paid for by Domaine d'Or. There are between
four and eight names per year. A total of fifteen individuals.
Certain names only appear a couple of years, others recur
almost as often as Squirrel. One of the names is . . . Emanuelle
Cobra."

"What?" Buck exclaimed. "The secretary? The one you just
said was a suspect but who didn't do it?"

"The same," Ècu nodded. "And of the other names—you're
not going to believe this—of the other fifteen names on the
list, six of them have been convicted of sex offenses. I checked
with GL, and they knew about another three."

"What are you saying?" asked Anna.

"They're hookers," Bloodhound clarified brutally.

Field Mouse Pedersen struck the table with his paw.

"But . . . now I get it," he said. "*Logistics* . . . get it? Pro-
curement? Someone's trying to be funny. Domaine d'Or is an
escort service."

"Jasmine Squirrel and Emanuelle Cobra are escort animals," said Falcon. "And if it's as the superintendent says, that Oswald Vulture had information about Domaine d'Or's business transactions in his computer—"

"Vulture is running some kind of brothel operation!" Anna exclaimed. "And his colleagues at Nova Park who testified that Vulture would never do anything criminal?"

Ècu had to smile.

"Okay," said Bloodhound, standing up. "Damn good, Falcon, I have to say. Damn good."

Ècu straightened up.

"Pedersen," Bloodhound continued. "Get the final story on Llama and Lamb. And Falcon and Anna, see about finding the auditor, Wasp. If you don't find him, bring in Cobra. Get her to tell everything she knows about Squirrel. Hell. This may loosen things up a little. Was there anything else, Jan?"

Buck shook his head. He was just as impressed as the others at Falcon's nighttime detective work.

6.2

Alfredo Wasp was in the phone book, and he had nothing against them coming by and asking their questions. He was waiting at his office on emerald green rue Primatice, one of Tourquai's many dark, gloomy backstreets that were neglected in order to keep up all the grandiose avenues. Wasp worked alone, the office more or less resembled a living room, and apart from a failed attempt to create a sort of ficus jungle in the little alcove toward the street, the result was pleasant.

Anna Lynx and Falcon Ècu were shown to a worn couch, where they sat down. Wasp, dressed in a stained but well-ironed suit and a hard-knotted bow tie around his neck, offered them coffee, which they both refused.

"We would like to ask a few questions," Ècu began, "about a company that you've audited. Domaine d'Or Logistics."

"That rings a bell," Wasp replied, smiling.

"It's a company that . . . doesn't have any business operations," Falcon said in order to help refresh his memory.

"I have lots of those," Wasp chuckled contentedly. "You might say it's somewhat of a specialty for me."

"Companies without operations?"

"That's right," Wasp nodded. "You have no idea how many large companies and organizations there are that, instead of liquidating some small subsidiary, let it lie fallow. Someday perhaps it will be activated again, and until then I take care of the formalities."

"How many such . . . fallow companies do you take care of?" asked Anna.

"A couple thousand," Wasp replied. "It varies."

"A couple thousand?" Anna repeated.

"It sounds like a lot, and it is quite a lot, I guess, but if you're careful, and I am, it's not hard."

"But Nova Park . . . ?" asked Falcon.

"A typical example," Wasp answered. "Venture capitalists start and close down operations at a furious pace. They let their companies go in rotation."

"And Domaine d'Or . . . ?" asked Falcon.

Wasp nodded, asking the police officers to remain seated while he disappeared into something that resembled a broom closet by the outside door. After only a few minutes he came back with a binder under his wing.

"Here," he said. "Domaine d'Or."

He folded back a half-dried palm leaf, sat down in the armchair, and leafed through the binder, stopped here and there and scrutinized something a little more carefully, but then quickly went forward. This went on for several minutes.

"No," he said. "I'm sorry. Nothing. The most remarkable thing is that the company has existed for so many years."

"And these payments of payroll taxes and health insurance premiums?"

"There have been employees in the company. Nothing strange about that."

"But no income?" Falcon pointed out.

"No. Only personnel expenses. That may seem strange, but it's not unusual. There may be legal reasons for choosing to allocate expenses and income. Later, when you look at the operation organizationally, you bring the various entries together."

"Did Vulture go in for a lot of this type of shadow games?"

"Vulture? You mean Oswald Vulture, who was killed last Monday?"

"Yes."

"Well, Vulture wasn't born yesterday exactly. But he kept to the rules most of the time."

"And the operation that was run in Domaine d'Or?" asked Anna.

"But Inspector," Wasp replied in an impatient tone, "that's just the point. No operation was being run. Here, you can see for yourselves."

Wasp pushed the binder over to the police officers, who leafed through the formal questionnaires filled out with a typewriter.

"We'll borrow these," said Falcon, shutting the binder. "As evidence."

"That's fine," Wasp nodded, getting up. "Although I really wonder what it's supposed to prove."

The police officers were on their way out to the street again when Anna couldn't refrain from slowing down her steps and asking the question that still lingered.

"Excuse me," she called back. "But why were you surprised when we asked about Vulture? Wasn't it at his request that you managed Domaine d'Or Logistics?"

"No. No, not at all," Wasp replied. "True, Nova Park paid my fees, but it wasn't Vulture who was my contact with respect to Domaine d'Or."

"It wasn't?"

"No, not at all," said Wasp. "It's all in the binder. The owner of all the shares in the company is a Jasmine Squirrel."

"Squirrel?" said Falcon. "Is it Squirrel who is behind Domaine d'Or? But what about Vulture?"

"As far as I know he has absolutely nothing to do with this," Wasp replied.

6.3

There were two interview rooms connected directly to the jail on the bottom floor at rue de Cadix. They were generally called the "north" room and the "south" room, and they were furnished identically. A short table with two chairs on either side, a mirror along the wall—which could be seen through from the other side—and a single lightbulb hanging down from the ceiling, the room's only illumination. On the table was a small tape recorder to which a microphone, fastened to a small tabletop tripod, was connected. The equipment looked old-fashioned.

They were sitting in the north room. Without knowing why, Anna Lynx preferred the north room. She glanced at Falcon, who was sitting next to her. He was making a few quick notations.

They had picked up Emanuelle Cobra on the way back from questioning Alfredo Wasp. When they came into her office, she had sighed heavily.

"What do you want?"

The feeling that first time they stepped into the massive

office had been slightly absurd, the sexy, glistening black secretary misplaced in a modernistic office chair behind a small desk in front of the overwhelming view of Tourquai's futuristic skyline. Today the magic had disappeared. The situation was different, they knew more than they had known then, and besides, Cobra was apparently exactly what she appeared to be.

"Only a few short questions," said Falcon.

"But not here, down at the station," said Lynx.

Now they were sitting in the north room. Falcon was noticeably nervous, aware of the fact that both Buck and Bloodhound were watching from outside. He started, stumbled through the formalities, stated, to the tape recorder, the date and time, who was present, and what it concerned. But when he was about to begin the interview itself, Anna took over.

"We know you've answered a number of questions before," she said. "Forget about that. Now we want you to tell us about Domaine d'Or Logistics."

"Tell about what?"

"The company paid your health insurance and workmen's comp. Is that correct?"

"And salary," said Cobra nonchalantly. "I got a salary, too."

"Excuse me, but weren't you paid by Nova Park?" asked Falcon.

"Listen, on that pitiful secretary salary you don't get far," Cobra smiled scornfully.

"And to get a salary from Domaine d'Or required that you performed what services?"

"The way it usually works."

"Would you like to tell us about these services?"

"I've already done that. For your blushing colleague here," Cobra answered, nodding toward Falcon, who blushed again as if he were programmed.

"I would really appreciate it if you'd tell us again," said Anna.

"I went with males, most often older males, up to their anonymous but rather luxurious hotel rooms and did what they asked me to," Cobra replied.

"You were paid by Domaine d'Or to prostitute yourself?" asked Anna.

"Little lady," Cobra replied, giving Lynx an inexpressibly tired look, "I've been at it a little too long to think that sort of thing is hard work. You can call me what you want—"

"And with whom did you negotiate your pay?" said Anna.

Cobra showed interest in the question, but she did not answer immediately.

"What do you mean?"

"The compensation from Domaine d'Or," said Anna. "How was it decided? Who decided how much you would get paid?"

"Is this still about Oswald?" Cobra asked, turning directly toward Falcon. "Or is it about something else?"

"Answer the question," said Falcon, looking down at the table.

"Jasmine Squirrel," said Cobra, meeting Anna Lynx's gaze. "Jasmine paid me."

"Jasmine Squirrel?" Anna Lynx repeated, articulating every syllable, so that the substandard tape recorder on the table would not mistake it.

"Yes."

"Domaine d'Or is an escort service," Anna stated. "Why does Nova Park pay administrative fees to run an escort service? Why does Nova Park pay Squirrel's bills?"

"You must be joking," said Cobra, and she turned toward Falcon again. "If she hasn't figured it out yet, she probably shouldn't be a cop. But she's pretty. Maybe I can arrange a job for you, lady?"

"We'd like to hear you tell us," said Falcon politely.

He felt that he was forced to take over the interview from Anna. The bosses were watching, and until now he had made a pale impression, he realized that. Now he leaned across the table, the very image of attentiveness.

"Oswald Vulture was Jasmine's john to start with. That went on for ages, until Jasmine got tired of it. Then she placed me outside his office, so he got what he wanted without wait time, so to speak. 'Administrative fees' was probably the least he paid—"

"It was Jasmine Squirrel who got you the job at Nova Park?"

"Dictation isn't my strong suit," Cobra smiled.

"Do you realize that sex trafficking is a serious crime, and that Jasmine Squirrel is going to pay dearly for what you've revealed?" asked Falcon Ècu.

He was troubled by the ease with which Cobra told her story. Considering both of the bigwigs were on the other side of the mirrored glass, this interview was hardly something to brag about, at least not from a technical angle.

Emanuelle Cobra raised one eyebrow.

"Have I been disobedient, Falcon?" she asked.

Involuntarily he blushed again.

"Why would I want to back her up?" she continued. "Haven't I brought in enough money?"

Falcon's blush intensified, and he stammered the next question.

"How . . . would you . . . describe Jasmine Squirrel and Oswald Vulture's relationship . . . recently?"

"Their relationship?" Cobra repeated, shaking her head. "I don't know. She extorts money from him. He lets himself be extorted. And I'm sitting in the middle of it all, which makes the situation tolerable for both of them."

"When did they last meet?" asked Falcon.

"No idea."

"How are the payments from Vulture to Domaine d'Or made?"

"Is it my salary you're talking about now?"

Falcon disregarded the reply, which reduced the brilliance of his question.

"When you say that Vulture let himself be extorted for money," he continued, with forced aggressiveness, "what exactly do you mean?"

"That she extorted him for money." Cobra sneered.

"Were there threats?"

"Little friend, how else do you imagine it would be done?"

"Written threats?"

"No idea. Darling falcon, do you feel like you're starting to be done with this now?"

Cobra concealed a yawn behind the tip of her tail.

On the other side of the mirrored glass Buck and Bloodhound followed the conversation. Buck made continuous commentary on the interview with small outcries: "Oy!" "Fantastic!" and "We didn't know that, or did we?" Bloodhound did not reply.

From the captain's comments it seemed that he was impressed; everything Cobra said he perceived as sensational. In reality there was little new that came out, Bloodhound thought. They were in the middle of a murder investigation; prostitution was not WE's concern. The purpose of interviewing Cobra was to create a basis for the next interview, with Jasmine Squirrel. It was Squirrel who was interesting, and as soon as they were finished, the inspectors would bring her into the station.

"Oy," Buck commented. "She has apparently extorted him for money. We didn't know that, did we?"

The superintendent couldn't bear it.

"I've got to go," he said, although he could just as well have stayed another half hour. "If anyone says anything spectacular, I guess you can call."

"Spectacular?" Captain Buck repeated. "But this is spectacular, the whole thing."

Bloodhound left.

In the north interview room Falcon Ècu was forced to continue the attack. He changed tactics, and instead of asking questions he tossed out theories.

"Vulture must have felt pressured," said Falcon, "since someone knew so much that was unfavorable. He must have wanted to change the situation. He must have been prepared to do whatever it took—"

"You think so?" asked Cobra. "I think he thought I was worth it all, and a little more. Wouldn't you think so?"

Falcon could not produce a sound, and nervously leafed through his papers to find a new thread to tug on.

Anna Lynx was about to explode.

She had been sitting silently, observing her colleague being annihilated by the meddlesome latex tart. Centuries of gender roles were being volleyed back and forth across the wobbly table, and Anna realized that this behavior, this ancient game between male and female, was what marked the investigation from the first moment. Bloodhound and Ècu's way of excusing and dismissing Cobra's lies; that never would have happened if she had been a he. The same way with Squirrel. Without a doubt the superintendent would have pushed harder, if the squirrel had been less attractive.

This double standard was exactly what Anna had talked about at the seminar at the Crisis Center. Gender that overshadows species. Gender that drew a veil in front of Falcon's eyes, meaning that he did not see the hard-boiled criminal before him but was instead confused by Cobra's attributes. It was loathsome.

Anna got up from her chair.

Surprised, Falcon fell silent in the middle of a line of reasoning. Cobra leaned toward the lynx.

"Your lies," said the police officer, "are not impressive. C'mon, don't you get it that you're in a really bad situation? Weren't you the one who extorted Vulture for money?"

"No."

"I'm asking you again," Lynx repeated, leaning even farther across the table so that her large claws moved right next to the snake's shiny black head. "Weren't you the one who extorted Vulture for money? Weren't you the one who conveyed the offer to Squirrel?"

"No."

"Were you the one who exhausted Vulture so that finally he no longer accepted what you were up to? Were you the one who pushed him to make an ultimatum and change from your little fatted calf to a major problem?"

Cobra was about to answer, but Lynx pressed her large paw against the snake's mouth and silenced her. The gesture was so aggressive that the chair on which Cobra was sitting tipped backward.

"C'mon, think it over now, little tart," Lynx advised.

The supercilious gleam that had been in Cobra's eyes was less distinct when she answered.

"It wasn't me. I don't know how or what Jasmine said to him."

"When did you last speak with Jasmine Squirrel?" asked Lynx.

Cobra closed her eyes. She sat like that awhile, absorbed in thought, and then she looked up. It was impossible to interpret her facial expression.

"I was just wondering if you were going to ask that . . ." she said lingeringly.

"C'mon, listen careful now," Lynx hissed, "because now we're asking."

" . . . I was wondering about that on the way here. What I would answer. If you asked that question."

Lynx cast a quick glance at Falcon. He didn't know what Cobra was talking about either.

"But I decided to answer truthfully," said Cobra, with a malevolent smile. "Because I think it can be verified. The last time I spoke with Jasmine was on Monday morning. She called at work. It was after Oleg Earwig left Oswald's office. She called and said that she thought it was time for me to go down in the elevator and have a cigarette out on the street."

Falcon and Anna Lynx stared at the snake.

"Just what I thought," Cobra smiled. "I knew you'd be interested."

6.4

They drove straight from the interview with Emanuelle Cobra to Jasmine Squirrel, from Vulture's latest lover to the former. Falcon drove; Anna Lynx sat alongside and concentrated on her . . . what was it she felt? Mostly she wanted to lock both Cobra and Squirrel up in King's Cross. She didn't understand why she reacted to these two females so strongly. She had worked as a police officer long enough not to be morally shocked or indignant anymore. She must have brought in a hundred prostitutes, and unfortunately only a fraction as many pimps and brothel owners. Cobra's and Squirrel's history was not unique. What set them apart from the crowd?

Falcon was stuck in lunch-hour traffic on North Avenue. It didn't seem possible to stem the increase in the number of cars in Mollisan Town; the only limitation was the capacity of the Volga factories. Falcon honked. Anna laughed.

"C'mon, what are you thinking?" she asked.

"He pulled right in front of me."

Falcon pointed at the cars standing, waiting for the traffic to ease up on one of the off-ramps.

"You're in a police car," Anna pointed out with a smile. "Either you turn on the sirens and force your way ahead, or else you set a good example and be patient. Sitting in a police car and honking—"

"Can I turn on the siren?" he asked hopefully.

She shook her head.

"No. It's better that you practice being a good example. We won't move any faster with the sirens on."

He mumbled something, she didn't hear what, and she laughed out loud.

And then it hit her.

The reason for her feelings had nothing to do with Cobra. It was Falcon. It was his servile manner, politeness, and obvious enchantment with the little tart.

Lord Magnus, thought Anna Lynx, I'm jealous. She tittered tipsily.

Field Mouse Pedersen was sitting in the library where Irina Flamingo had put Superintendent Bloodhound on Tuesday. The Morning Weather's clear blue sky had just passed lunchtime and the warm breeze was blowing again. Pedersen was in agony. He had a hard time sitting still on the couch. No one had offered him anything to drink, and no one was going to.

The widow was dressed up, had put on several layers of makeup, and was wearing a multiple-strand pearl necklace coiled layer upon layer around her long, slender neck. She had unwillingly asked the police officer to come in, but explained that she was on her way out and didn't want to be late. After that she answered his questions negatively and a few times outright unpleasantly.

"What do you want to know about Lamb?" Irina Flamingo was now wondering.

"Yes, can you tell us anything about him? Your husband,

Mr. Vulture, was a . . . demanding employer. Do you think Lamb experienced it that way?"

"You'll just have to ask him," Flamingo hissed.

Flamingo's heavy, sweet perfume made Pedersen's nose itch. The aroma was so insistent that the police officer involuntarily started breathing through his mouth.

"We intend to do that, Mrs. Flamingo," he said patiently. "But now we're asking you."

"I have no idea. What Oswald said or did with his employees was not my concern."

During the morning, Pedersen had managed to get Llama's alibi confirmed by the garage; now only Lamb remained. At first Pedersen had been properly careful with the widow, but now he was starting to get tired.

"Your husband has been murdered, Mrs. Flamingo," the field mouse said with a certain emphasis. "It's in our mutual interest to find out who did it, and why. It can't be overlooked that you yourself will inherit a fortune. The foundation you indicated that your husband threatened you with . . . it doesn't exist. You, Mrs. Flamingo, have every reason to want to clear up this case."

Irina Flamingo neither denied nor confirmed this. She stared at Pedersen as if she could see right through his head and into the bookcase behind.

Pedersen squirmed. He sat drumming one paw against the floor and couldn't stop. The austerity of the consummate library and Irina Flamingo's condescending manner were endlessly provocative. Her perfume could only be described as vulgarly intrusive.

"Lamb says the reason he was late on Monday was that he was picking you up outside the Auction House," he said. "And that you, for some reason, wanted to keep that a secret."

"I see," said Flamingo.

But she appeared uncomfortable.

"Is that right?" asked Pedersen. "This is important, Mrs. Flamingo. If you can't verify Lamb's testimony, then we have to—"

"Yes, yes, that's right," said Flamingo with irritation.

"That's right?" Pedersen repeated.

"I don't intend to say what I was doing at the Auction House," Flamingo hissed, "because that has nothing to do with you."

Pedersen suppressed a desire to inform Irina Flamingo that, on the contrary, it did have to do with him.

"Thanks," he said, finally getting the paw to stop. "That was all I needed to know. For now."

He hoped that sounded sufficiently ominous, and he left the widow in the library.

"What do we do?" said Falcon.

The traffic was not letting up. They were still stuck in the middle of one of the five northbound lanes on North Avenue. It was more than three miles to the next exit. Stuffed animals caught in the middle of this mess had given up; not even the most hot-tempered was hoping for any quick improvement. Anna refrained from noting how many in the cars around them were picking their noses. Falcon drummed absently on the steering wheel. In the luggage compartment was a brand-new badminton racket, and even though it was expensive, it was worth the money. He'd decided to put his tennis racket on the shelf for good; he won no friends, or matches, at tennis. For that reason he had signed up for the Tourquai police's badminton series. He'd tried playing last winter, and he was at least no worse than at tennis.

"So what do we do now?" he asked.

"C'mon, what do you mean?" she asked.

"Well . . . should we confront her directly? When she talked with Bloodhound she maintained that she hardly knew who Vulture was. According to Cobra . . . it's not that way."

Falcon was holding both wings on the wheel and looking

straight ahead, out the windshield, as if any moment now it would be time to drive.

"And Cobra's telling the truth?" asked Anna, sounding more sarcastic than she intended. "What the beautiful Emanuelle Cobra said is the truth and nothing but?"

"Nothing is true until it can be proved," Falcon replied, sullen and surprised. "What do you mean? That Domaine d'Or isn't an escort service? That Jasmine Squirrel isn't involved?"

"I don't mean anything," said Anna. "C'mon, think about it. Assume that Jasmine Squirrel is running an escort service. According to Wasp, it's an extensive operation. Health insurance and pensions go out to a number of stuffed animals every year. We can only speculate about how much money Squirrel earns."

"That can probably be figured out—"

"That has nothing to do with this," Anna Lynx cut him off. "Squirrel is ingenious. It's not enough that she manages to move her own client over to Cobra and get him to buy escort services at the office five days a week. It also includes extortion, which means that Nova Park pays a long series of fees to Squirrel's company . . . it sounds like a perfect setup."

"You're right. Let's not underestimate Jasmine Squirrel," Falcon agreed.

"C'mon, the question," Anna concluded, "the whole point is this: Why should Jasmine Squirrel want to cut the head off of Oswald Vulture? On the contrary, wouldn't that be the stupidest thing she could do?"

And with these words the traffic jam broke up in the miraculous manner that is sometimes the case in Mollisan Town.

They agreed to take Jasmine Squirrel to rue de Cadix before they asked any questions. Rather than give her the upper hand in her own environment, they might gain an advantage simply thanks to the bare-bones, unpleasant interview room.

Rue d'Oran was the only known address they had. True to habit, Falcon parked around the corner, then they walked back. On the way they had called to get the entry code from the building superintendent, under the pretext that they wanted to check fire security in the attic after an alarm from a neighbor. Squirrel lived on the third floor, listed as Bordeauz on the directory in the entry. The police officers took the stairs, and rang the doorbell. The door opened almost instantly.

"I . . . we . . . we're looking for Jasmine Squirrel," the falcon stammered to the squirrel in the doorway.

"Yes?" said the squirrel.

Anna came to her uncertain colleague's rescue, holding out her ID.

"Police," she said. "We would like to ask a few questions . . ."

"The police were here yesterday and asked a few questions," Squirrel answered, but her tone of voice was light and not at all aggressive. "I think I've said all I—"

"Let's find that out down at the station," said Anna.

Jasmine Squirrel observed the lynx for a few intense moments, and then decided with a curt nod.

"Just let me get my purse," she said.

"Of course," Falcon Ècu nodded.

They both saw how Squirrel opened the door and vanished into a room to the right in the narrow hall corridor.

A moment later Anna Lynx ran into the apartment. Was there another exit? A kitchen entry? With her pulse pounding in her ears Anna threw open the door to what proved to be a kitchen. At the kitchen table sat a mouse in a white trench coat. He seemed familiar, but Anna couldn't place him. She assumed he was a "customer." Jasmine Squirrel stood facing the door, with a purse in her hand.

"Oy," she commented drily. "Goodness what a hurry you're in."

Anna was not embarrassed.

"We're leaving now," she said curtly. "After you."

6.5

A hem," Larry Bloodhound growled into the microphone on the table, "it's Saturday, the eighteenth of June, right after the Afternoon Rain, and we are beginning the interview with Jasmine Squirrel. Present are myself, Superintendent Larry Bloodhound, plus Inspector Field Mouse Pedersen. In addition Jasmine Squirrel and her legal counsel, Attorney . . . what was your name?"

"Flounder Finkenstein," the attorney added.

" . . . Attorney Flounder Finkenstein," Bloodhound concluded.

"My client still does not understand why she is sitting here," Finkenstein complained. "As far as we understand she's not accused of anything. I firmly demand that she be released immediately."

Bloodhound sighed. Later he would find out who had let Jasmine Squirrel call a lawyer, but now the damage was done. And this . . . Finkenstein . . . was the very worst type. Far too well dressed and well educated to be sitting in a little interview room at the police station on rue de Cadix.

"Besides," Attorney Finkenstein added, "I wish to convey a particular greeting from Judge Duchamp. He said he was astounded at this action, bringing stuffed animals in for questioning without informing them of their rights or obligations. He said that he would contact those responsible at the station later."

"I look forward to that," Bloodhound growled. "Now perhaps you can shut up, Attorney, so we can start this interview?"

Finkenstein leafed through some papers in order to avoid expressing an opinion on the insult.

They were in the north interview room. Jasmine Squirrel's perfume was discreet but still hard to ignore. The room was too small for that. It smelled of cinnamon and lavender.

Squirrel sat across from Bloodhound, and Finkenstein across from Pedersen.

"Name?" asked Pedersen.

"My name is Jasmine Squirrel," Jasmine answered obligingly.

She was dressed in unpretentious jeans, a black blouse, and a lovely white jacket that was certainly as expensive as it looked simple. Her lawyer was wearing a black suit, white shirt, and dark red tie. They were mirror images of each other.

"Age?"

"Age?" she repeated. "Exactly what does that have to do with this?"

"Date of delivery?" Pedersen clarified. "In order to eliminate any chance that we're talking to the wrong Jasmine Squirrel."

Squirrel gave him the information.

"Address?"

"I'm living on rue d'Oran for the time being," said Jasmine.

"But you're not registered there?" growled Bloodhound.

"No."

"Where are you registered?"

"That I don't really know," said Jasmine with the hint of a

smile on her lips. "I think maybe I'm still registered at home with my parents."

"We would like to talk with you a little about your company, Domaine d'Or Logistics," Bloodhound growled.

"Domaine d'Or," Squirrel repeated flatly.

"Now that's enough," Finkenstein broke in. "We're not saying anything more until you explain why we're sitting here."

"We're in the middle of a murder investigation," Pedersen replied. "This interview is meant to survey the circumstances surrounding Oswald Vulture's death."

"Domaine d'Or," Bloodhound continued, undisturbed. "Do you mean to deny that this is your company? Maybe you've forgotten it?"

Jasmine gave the lawyer a look. Finkenstein nodded.

"It's my company," Jasmine answered.

"Where you run an escort operation, prostitution?"

"Excuse me?"

Squirrel opened her eyes and looked so wronged that Pedersen was forced to hide a smile. Bloodhound was not amused.

"How dare you!" Finkenstein exclaimed. "Is this what you call a murder investigation? You are accusing my client of procuring? Is that why—"

"Yes, yes, Attorney," Bloodhound interrupted, turning again to Jasmine. "We'll forget about that. Tell us instead how you know Emanuelle Cobra."

Once again Squirrel looked at her attorney. This time he shook his head firmly.

"I don't know any Cobra," Squirrel replied.

"In the same way that you alleged you didn't know Vulture when we met the last time?" Bloodhound asked.

"I was mistaken."

"And perhaps you're mistaken now, too?"

"Maybe," said Jasmine. "But I don't think so."

"You called Emanuelle Cobra last Monday morning. You

called from your home telephone to her telephone at Nova Park," Bloodhound maintained.

Squirrel looked him right in the eyes.

"I don't know any Cobra," she repeated.

"I want to see documentation that someone used Jasmine Squirrel's telephone to make such a telephone call," the attorney interjected. "And I want to know why we are sitting here. Is Jasmine Squirrel suspected of the murder of Oswald Vulture? Is this an arrest?"

"Calm down, Attorney," said Pedersen.

"We haven't arrested anyone," Bloodhound growled. "We are just sitting here, talking. This is really enjoyable."

"This is a formal interview, Superintendent," Finkenstein protested, "and I wish to remind you that such interviews must be run in a formally—"

"Cobra, then," Bloodhound interrupted harshly. "That's not anyone you know, Squirrel? You realize that it's easy for us to produce papers on the health insurance payments from Domaine d'Or to Emanuelle Cobra?"

Jasmine turned toward Finkenstein. This was a question.

"We will comment on this matter when you present such documents," said the attorney.

But there was no worry in his voice. Bloodhound knew why. Proving the relationship between Squirrel and Cobra was one thing; proving that it was about prostitution was something completely different. And, besides, they were sitting here to talk about a murder. Finkenstein had no reason to be worried.

"You get one last chance," said Bloodhound. "You called Cobra last Monday morning and asked her to leave the office at Nova Park so that the murderer could slip out of the scene of the crime unobserved. Why?"

Jasmine still sat turned toward her attorney, and her facial expression remained unchanged.

"No comment? Oswald Vulture was on Domaine d'Or's list of customers," Bloodhound continued. "There was no reason for you to kill him. Yet you made that call. Was Vulture killed on your orders, or were you just carrying out an assignment for someone else?"

"Are you accusing—" Finkenstein began in a loud voice.

The superintendent got up unexpectedly. The attorney fell silent, and Jasmine Squirrel finally turned her head and looked at the police officer.

"Squirrel," Larry Bloodhound growled, "you're staying here overnight. And if your attorney is wondering on what grounds I'm holding you, it's because you're obstructing a murder investigation. And Mr. Attorney? Up yours."

And with these words he left the small interview room, the surprised attorney, and the taciturn squirrel.

6.6

It was the most expensive picture he'd ever bought; he couldn't afford it. And the seller, the walking stick, would find out. Not tomorrow, maybe, but on Monday, when the bank reported that the account the check was drawn on hadn't been used for years, and the account was closed.

The picture was in a yellowed plastic pocket placed in a brown envelope. It was a copy; he hadn't even been able to buy the original. A simple piece of paper, weighing an ounce or two, eight inches wide, a little more than half as high. The picture was full-bleed, a color picture that looked like it was black-and-white. No photographer had been behind the camera, no one had adjusted the focus. It was an automatically generated image in a long suite of images. The surveillance camera had no feeling for artistry, thus the many fuzzy objects.

This had nothing to do with VolgaBet or the organization behind the game. As the grandstands were being disassembled in the bottom level of the public garage, sometimes the surveillance cameras happened to get the players in focus. At a long distance from the garage a tired stuffed animal was sitting in a sterile office, staring at a dozen screens that changed images at regular intervals. The bridge abutment. Garage. Bus stops. Public environments that Mollisan Town had decided to monitor. Over the years some of these desk guards had learned the value of what these hundreds of surveillance cameras could provide in the form of extra income. So pictures that flickered past during the night's long, lonely hours were saved systematically; files were smuggled home toward dawn, when the shift ended.

The guards themselves seldom knew whether they had taken something of value; it was like a lottery. Intermediaries—in this case a walking stick—with intimate knowledge of the city's rich and powerful, inspected the images. Often they were duds. Sometimes there was a jackpot. And occasionally it happened like it happened yesterday: a buyer who knew what he wanted, and asked for enlargements.

He stroked the inside pocket of the jacket without thinking. The picture was there, inside the thin cloth. He was standing in an entryway across from the police station on rue de Cadix, and the weather had just changed to evening; the breeze had returned and the sun was going down.

It had been a long shot that hit the target. He'd done deals with the walking stick before, a hard-boiled fence whose business instincts were well developed. But today they had fooled each other.

He was certain that Superintendent Larry Bloodhound would soon show up in the entryway, en route to his obligatory beer at Chez Jacques after work. There was one possibility—slip into the restaurant cloakroom while the superintendent was in the bar and get at his briefcase.

Another alternative, of course, was to locate the superintendent's private residence and put the envelope with the picture in the mail slot. But that felt uncertain. There was no time for mistakes, and what did he know about how the superinten-

dent handled his personal mail? There were many who left
envelopes lying on the hall floor for days. Others who scooped
up the mail, assumed it was just advertising, and put it all
straight into the recycle bin.

He decided on a third alternative.

That was why he was waiting another half an hour until
Larry Bloodhound suddenly appeared on the stairs on the opposite side of the street. The worn-out, wrinkled dog looked
around, spit on the stairs, and then hurried along rue de Cadix
en route to Chez Jacques.

On the other side, the stuffed animal with the expensive
picture in an inside pocket stepped out of the darkness of the
entryway and crossed the street. He jogged up the steps to the
police station and opened the front door in a way that showed
he had done it many times before.

In the police station lobby there was a whirl of motion in
the transition between day and night personnel. The intensity
suited him perfectly, even if it was chance, not skill, that made
him choose just this point in time. With calm, slow steps he
went straight toward the elevators. He directed his gaze ahead
of him, not looking at anything or anyone, and pressed the
button. Waited. Fingered the lapel of his jacket, able to confirm
with a careful pressure that the envelope had not disappeared.

When the elevator doors glided open, there stood a panther
he had known a long time, an inspector at GL who was re-
nowned for his bad breath. He put on a relaxed smile, gave the
panther an easygoing nod, and stepped into the elevator. As
if he had an errand he didn't need to account for. He received
a curt nod back, then he was alone. The steel doors closed on
him, and he pressed the button with the numeral 3.

By riding the momentum of the moment he had made it
the whole way to WE on rue de Cadix. But during the short
trip up in the elevator there was time for reflection, and as he
exited at Superintendent Larry Bloodhound's department, his
self-assurance deserted him for a few moments.

He got out of the elevator, looked out over a hostile office, where he felt that everyone turned to eye him suspiciously. He remained standing, uncertain of direction, facial expression, posture.

Then he pulled himself together—what alternative was there?—and stretched. Put on a gloomy face, furrowed his eyebrows, and walked straight ahead instead of choosing the less conspicuous alternative along the outside wall.

The rash courage gave him renewed energy. He kept his gaze directed straight ahead, still just as resolute, and hurried through the shadows that made the massive office area black-and-white.

He opened the door and went into Bloodhound's office. He realized this was taking a step too far; no one could enter the superintendent's unoccupied office without a reason.

He took the envelope out of his inside pocket, pulled the photograph out of the plastic sleeve, and set it on top of the pile of papers on the superintendent's desk. So as not to leave any room for doubt, he had drawn a large red circle around Igor Panda's head, where the bear was sitting on the grandstand at VolgaBet. He also circled the date, automatically generated on images of this type.

It couldn't be more obvious.

He turned around and quickly left.

IGOR PANDA 6

The Dondau flows out of the underworld along mustard yellow Krönkenhagen, in the middle of central Lanceheim. The river is the only one in Mollisan Town, and its beautifully adorned bridges and restaurants with verandas overlooking the murmuring water are the pride of the district. After less than eight miles in a northerly direction, the Dondau disappears back down into the primeval crevices that finally unite it with the sea in the west.

Right before the Dondau's northern falls is a small industrial area, mostly warehouses. The river runs parallel to Krönkenhagen. This makes it cost-effective for producers of clothes and electronics to leave the goods in storage along the north Dondau and let the barges bring the containers along the river the last few miles, instead of driving trucks into the heart of the city. The warehouses are reminiscent of massive boathouses, in which piers run alongside each other like long tongues in a giant's wooden maw. There is room for two barges at each pier, and there are four piers in each boathouse. It feels like having the sea in the middle of the city, especially since the restaurateurs in the area set food out for the shrieking, red-billed gulls, who come back every day and contribute to the atmosphere that entices patrons to the restaurants.

Unloading was done at dawn, most of the loading and pickup happened in the afternoon and evening, and for Jake Golden Retriever the afternoon hours in Boathouse 3 were optimal. Whether the paintings were small or large was unimportant; no one raised an eyebrow as he carried packages between the cars. And even if anyone were to get a glimpse of the paintings, the risk of being discovered was minimal; the dockworkers were not art experts.

Now the Morning Weather had just cleared after the rain and Jake had plenty of time. He sat on one of the piers between the boathouses, smoking a cigarette and looking out over the calm, cold water. Right here the river was widest. On the dock on the other side a few houseboats were moored. They had been there as long as Jake could remember. Besides the barges with their loads, only the skiffs of the sailing school used the Dondau. But they stayed a little farther south.

Jake smoked in peace and quiet, then tossed the cigarette into the water. He was too well dressed to hang around the harbor, in a gray suit, white shirt, and light blue tie. While he walked back to Boathouse 3, he thought about Igor Panda. The lying, cheating, gambling art dealer was probably the worst possible partner Jake could imagine, but at the same time he was necessary for the sale of Esperanza-Santiagos.

Jake Golden Retriever had this same thought at least once a day.

He went into the massive boathouse. It was deserted. The river lapped quietly against the wooden piers. If Jake had understood correctly, it should be a large painting today. He sat down on a folding chair that one of the skippers had left behind in the morning's stress.

Igor Panda was standing inside the harbor captain's momentarily empty office, looking out through the wooden blinds. He saw Jake Golden Retriever set up a small folding chair and light a cigarette.

There was no doubt the dog was waiting for someone, waiting for the real forger.

Igor Panda had been extremely careful and not left any traces. Still the vipers had found him. And they would find him again. Time was about to run out.

Igor Panda had been following Jake Golden Retriever since the big loss last Thursday night. Getting hold of the source— the forger—through the retriever was the panda's only chance to acquire quick money. Besides, the pretentious dog was superfluous. He was a simple go-between who could be tolerated only if he added value and kept a reasonable margin. Golden Retriever fulfilled neither of those requirements. Panda put his paw in his jacket pocket. The box cutter was the only weapon he had found in the office.

Igor Panda peeked out through the blinds and saw Jake Golden Retriever toss his cigarette butt in the water and get up. The dog's body language said that someone was entering the boathouse. Through the thin window glass he could hear a conversation but could not make out any words.

Igor sneaked up to the door and opened it without a sound. Not because he could see better from there, on the contrary, but through the crack in the door he at least heard what they said.

"I only intend to give him until the Evening Weather," said Jake Golden Retriever.

"Can he manage it?"

"If it's a bluff it's best to find that out as soon as possible."

Jake lit another cigarette. He had a large, square lighter that looked like steel but was silver. It was the only luxury item Golden Retriever used. The dog's clothes, nice-looking but discreet, were from discount outlets.

"I have a large painting with me today," she said. "Four by six. It's out in the car. I don't even know if it will fit in your little sedan."

"I'll put down the backseat," said Golden Retriever. "It's worked before."

"This is an elaborate painting. Oil and acrylic. Maybe not the best I've given you, but significantly better than the last one."

"That makes me happy," Jake replied. "Around two million?"

"Maybe more," she said. "Let Panda judge that."

"Okay. We'll meet here tomorrow. Same time. Either I have the money with me, or you get the painting back. It's a matter of discipline."

Igor Panda felt the fury surging through his body. He had heard every word, and understood exactly what it was about. Jake Golden Retriever intended to give him a single day to sell the new painting, and if he failed he would not get another chance. Not for a while, in any event. Regardless of the circumstances, it irritated him to be at the mercy of the retriever's arbitrary ways.

He heard Golden Retriever and the forger walk away from the boathouse.

What should he do?

The harbor captain's office was almost all the way out on the northernmost pier. Igor stepped out and saw at a distance how the door slammed shut behind the dog. There was an odor of cold sea from the water lapping below, mixed with the smoke from the cigarettes. A gull sleeping on a post flapped in fear over to the next pier as the panda started walking quickly. He had to follow Jake Golden Retriever and the great forger.

He saw it after five seconds. It glistened in the rays of the sun that reached all the way to the pier.

Jake's lighter.

It was on the folding chair where the retriever had just

been sitting. Igor Panda continued walking, but the anxiety retreated through his body and was replaced by certainty.

Jake Golden Retriever would return.

It took five minutes.

Then Jake Golden Retriever came back into the boathouse. He was stressed, and immediately found the lighter on the chair.

Igor Panda was standing behind the door. In his left paw he held the box cutter. He walked soundlessly up to Jake from behind. With his right arm he locked the retriever's upper arms from behind, and with his left paw he cut along the dog's neck with the box cutter.

From one side to the other.

Jake did not have time to react. When he did, it was too late. He twirled around, but his head was already hanging to one side. Before he realized what had happened he was on his knees in front of the panda, gasping for air.

Panda screamed. Panic welled up out of his throat. He regretted what he had done even as he was doing it. And with a howl of desperation he severed what remained of the dog's neck.

With Jake Golden Retriever's head under his arm, Panda left the boathouse. Outside was Jake's car. The painting was already loaded, the car keys in the ignition.

Panda saw no trace of the forger.

He threw the head down on the passenger seat in Jake's car and turned the key.

Tomorrow at the same time Panda would return to Boathouse 3 and settle accounts with the forger, without Golden Retriever. And hopefully by then he would have already paid his debt to the vipers.

DAY SEVEN

7.1

The haze lay damp and heavy over the city. The sky was milky white and the sun still no more than a pale, yellowish ball of light just over the horizon.

Igor Panda was freezing. He was sleeping under the open sky, wrapped up in a dark blue wool blanket with yellow embroidery he had found in Golden Retriever's car. During the night, the blanket had absorbed the dampness of the forest and no longer provided any warmth. Panda shivered.

There was a simple explanation for why he had made his way to the narrow ravine in the mountain in the Bois de Dalida. As far as Panda knew, only he and Jake Golden Retriever knew about the ravine.

En route through the forest toward the mountain yesterday evening, Panda buried Golden Retriever's head in the soft earth next to a copse of wild raspberry. He had not chosen the place with any particular care; it was yet another of the impulsive decisions of the last few days. He had dug with only his paws, and despite his powerful claws the work had been hard.

This grave would not do in the long run; he would have to get rid of the head. But that was a problem for later.

Igor squirmed restlessly in his sleep. His arms hurt, his shoulders, his entire upper body. And at last it was sore muscles that caused him to waken.

He opened his eyes.

It was Sunday, the ninth of June, and he was alive.

That was his first thought.

The second thought was about the vipers. There had been occasions when Panda himself had been drawn into the vipers' surveillance work, when he had given them information in exchange for services; he knew how they functioned. His deadline had expired at midnight, now an example would have to be made; that was a prerequisite for VolgaBet's operation.

Igor sat up with a jerk. He threw off the blanket, feeling the outside of his jacket.

The bundle of currency was still in the inside pocket.

He breathed out, his shoulders lowered.

He had thought about asking his mom. When he left yesterday with the painting in the backseat and the dog's head on the floor on the passenger side, that had been his first thought.

Mom.

It was a lovely forgery. The painting was associated with Hummingbird Esperanza-Santiago's earliest period, which had been a surprise. The forgeries that Panda had sold during the past year had been more reminiscent of the artist's later works.

A canvas that size could mean a price tag of between three and four million. That would be enough to pay the gambling debt; it would go further than that. He was certain that Dad had money at home in the safe under the open fireplace in the bedroom.

With a gnawing feeling of doubt, Panda drove down toward Amberville. The thought of his parents had been instinctive.

The secure, prosperous parental home was imagination's natural refuge in a desperate situation like this. But the longer Panda drove, the more time he had to reflect.

With only a few miles left until he reached his childhood home in Le Vezinot, he changed his mind. He could not draw Mom and Dad into this. On the contrary, he had to keep them as far away as possible. There was a life on the other side of all this misery, and Panda had to try to preserve that, too.

He turned off of oxblood red Mina Road into the neighborhood by Swarwick Park, parked outside a café, and went in. He ordered a latte, asked them to sprinkle the milk with cardamom, and sat down on a high bar stool next to the window so that he could see the car—and the painting—from his seat.

There were a handful of buyers who would bite. But there were only one or two who had that kind of money available the same day.

Igor Panda finished his coffee and returned to the car. From there he called Rodrigo Buffalo.

"Rodrigo?" said Panda, trying to sound casual. "Am I calling at a bad time?"

"Not a problem," Buffalo sighed. "Not a problem."

Panda had been up in Buffalo's office six months earlier. Now he pictured the dark room with the gigantic plasma screen hanging on the wall across from the desk and showing sports around the clock. Rodrigo Buffalo's primary occupation was looking for investments for his family's money.

"I thought about making it into an auction," Panda said into the telephone. "But . . . the truth is I'm in a hurry. This is something outside the ordinary. It's an Esperanza-Santiago. It's been in private hands for over twenty years, and now it's on the market. You'll make at least ten percent on the investment in six months. At least."

Outside the car window in Swarwick Park, life went on as usual. The dark-tinted windows on Igor Panda's Volga Deluxe allowed him to sit in the midst of reality, but still screened off.

None of the stuffed animals walking past could imagine the circumstances around the negotiations going on in the black car.

"Ten percent in six months, you say," Buffalo repeated and Panda could hear how he took a gulp of something, maybe coffee. "And you can guarantee that?"

"We know each other," said Panda, impatient about having to listen to the rich buffalo's attempt to demand guarantees they both knew were impossible to give. "We know one another, you give me half now and half when you sell."

"How much is half?" asked Rodrigo Buffalo.

In the background the cheering of a wild sports crowd could clearly be heard. Buffalo was probably watching reruns of last year's championship matches. They always showed that kind of thing in the afternoon.

"One and a half million," said Panda, trying to make it sound like a trifle.

"Lot of money," Buffalo sighed. "Lot of money. And ten percent you say?"

"In six months," Panda repeated without conviction.

Involuntarily Panda's gaze fell on the plastic bag on the floor in front of the passenger seat. For a dizzying moment he imagined that what he'd done was not yet done.

The thought made him nauseous.

"When do you need the money?" Buffalo asked at last.

Igor Panda was hungry. His body heavy from dampness and aching, he slowly climbed up the edge of the low ravine and sat down to wait for the sun on the cliff. He did not recall when he'd last eaten, and now his belly was screaming. The haze was about to disperse, and morning would come, warm and clear as always. But Panda knew that for him the sun would never look the same again.

He weighed his options. Probably it was wisest to remain in Lancheim. In Yok he would attract attention and, besides,

that part of the city was full of the vipers' informers. In Tourquai everyone had a purpose, on their way to or from a meeting, and his lack of that would expose him. And in Amberville
he might very well run into an acquaintance or customer.

Yesterday he had been hiding from the police. Today he had
the vipers to think about as well. But he had the money. Even
if the deadline had passed, he had the money. It was a matter
of a few hours, no more; that ought to make a slight difference. If he only gave VolgaBet an opportunity to get out with
their honor intact, it would work out for him.

He decided to remain sitting on the cliff in Bois de Dalida
until the sun had dried him off. Slowly the haze dissolved
across the sky. Panda twisted his head and looked northward,
toward the forests that surrounded Mollisan Town. He was
sitting so high that he could see the massive crowns of the
trees disappear toward the horizon in what appeared to be an
immeasurable infinity.

A feeling of insignificance filled him, just as strong as it had
when he was little. Only the fact, he thought, that the short
life span of stuffed animals seemed to be measured out even
from the start, made all conflicts and intrigues ridiculous. It
was like living in a closed room where you run into the walls
over and over again while pretending not to. At the same time,
Panda thought, within the narrow framework of our lives,
freedom was endless. In the closed room you not only could—
you had to live. Igor Panda knew it was this freedom that had
finally crushed him.

He turned his head in the other direction and closed his
eyes. The sun warmed his face.

Life was best when it was simplest.

Panda had parked his black Volga Deluxe in an abandoned
stable in one of the least accessible areas in Bois de Dalida.
He didn't dare keep driving Jake's car; he had no idea whether

anyone missed the dog and was searching for him at this point. It took him almost half an hour to walk to the stable from the ravine, and during the last ten minutes the Morning Rain started to fall. In a trash can along the path he found an old newspaper that he folded and held over his head, but as he came to the stable he was just as damp as he'd been when he woke up an hour earlier.

During the walk there, he had made a plan. It made him feel stronger and better. First he would return to the pier and there expose the forger. An established art dealer and an ingenious forger could accomplish great things together. Whatever happened in the future, Panda knew this: his need for money would not diminish.

Only after that would he look up the animals behind VolgaBet and pay the loan. With interest.

Panda stepped into the decaying stable where the rain seeped down through the roofing. The chrome on the black car shone in the daylight; there was something inappropriate about the contrast between the luxurious vehicle and the simple building. Panda knew the car was conspicuous, and he hesitated: Should he leave it there? But to make it down to the boathouse by the Dondau in time he was more or less forced to drive. A taxi was not an option; the city's taxi drivers had always been the vipers' deepest, richest source of information.

Igor Panda turned the ignition key and backed out.

After ten minutes on a double-rutted forest path that tested the shock absorbers beyond any reasonable limit, he turned onto North Avenue. Panda saw a couple of police cars parked by the sidewalk in the crossing at gray Friedrichstrasse and he smiled to himself. The police were standing outside the refreshment stand at the corner. All on their own, the cops sustained the city's sales of pineapple flambé.

Panda accelerated. It would work out. He felt it.

7.2

The photograph was the first thing Larry Bloodhound saw when he opened the door to the office. Bloodhound always worked on a Sunday; he got more done on Sunday than during the rest of the week, and Cordelia had no objections. Every week built up toward the crescendo that was Saturday night, and then, the stillness of Sunday morning. The deserted department up on the fourth floor on rue de Cadix was never more grandly dramatic than in solitary semidarkness.

It might seem strange that he saw the photograph immediately; the piles of old junk scattered across the desk and on the shelves in Larry Bloodhound's office—both organic and electronic waste could be glimpsed between the drifts of binders and papers—were not comprehensible to just anyone. Nonetheless, the superintendent immediately discovered the photograph. It stuck out, like a grease stain on a wire-brushed drying cabinet or fridge. Someone had been in the office without his knowledge.

The superintendent remained standing, staring at his desk. Had anything else been moved? But no paper towers had toppled, no inability to let things alone had upset the disorder, and the pleasant odor of old bacon was intact.

Larry Bloodhound went up to the desk and picked up the picture. The black-and-white graininess immediately revealed that it was taken by a surveillance camera, and Bloodhound recognized the portable grandstand that had become something of a trademark for VolgaBet. On the other hand, he did not recognize the mournful bear that was circled with a marker. It took him a moment to turn the picture over, so that he discovered the text on the back: "Igor Panda at VolgaBet."

The superintendent's expression changed. It was difficult to say whether the grimace was an attempt at smiling.

"Up yours," he muttered to himself, picking up the phone.

He called in his team, even though it was Sunday.

Ècu and Lynx were on the scene thirty minutes later. While waiting for the inspectors, Larry had emptied the vending machine by the elevators of all the mint chocolate pigs by fiddling with the opening with a small chisel that by chance he had discovered worked as a skeleton key when he was trying to fix the vending machine six months ago.

With his mouth full of chocolate, he showed the police officers into his office, letting them sit down in front of the desk while he went to the other side.

"Here," he said, picking up the picture and letting it nonchalantly float through the air.

Anna still had her coat on. She had left Todd with Mom and taken the direct route to work without asking Larry for an explanation. She had heard it in his voice; it was urgent. The picture landed upside down on her lap, which is why she first read the text on the back and then turned to the picture. Ècu had also seen what it said.

"This is . . . the heir," Falcon observed.

He had been in the middle of cleaning the stove and oven, and his wings still smelled of the strong detergent.

"And the surveillance camera has dated the occasion for us," Anna observed.

In the top-right-hand corner of the picture was the date—a little more than a week ago—and the time: a couple of hours and some minutes after midnight.

"But," Ècu said excitedly, "this is . . . all we need, isn't it? The heir, the son: Igor Panda is the one who gains the most from his father's death. And he plays VolgaBet! This is too good! For heaven's sake, everyone who gambles is in debt to that organization. And if you're used to dealing with lots of money . . . his debts must be gigantic."

"The tipster strikes again," Anna muttered, moderately enthusiastic.

Falcon directed his wide-open gaze from the superintendent to Lynx and back to the superintendent again.

"But, this is just . . . too good to be true!" he said. "Do you want me to check on it? It's not hard to find out whether Panda is mired in debt."

Anna did not reply. She set the picture back on the superintendent's desk, almost putting her hand in a sticky stain she had discovered several days ago, which she believed was traces of an overturned chocolate milkshake.

"Tipster or not," Ècu continued, raising his voice in a way unusual for him, "this is a good deal better than Jasmine Squirrel! This is someone who actually gains from Vulture's death."

"Calm down, cloth-bird," Bloodhound growled. "To start with, I want you to find out who came into my office yesterday evening, or during the night," Bloodhound growled.

"The picture?" asked Anna.

"Didn't come in the mail," the superintendent confirmed. "It was lying here when I arrived this morning."

"And why take the risk of putting it in your office instead of sending it in a letter?"

"Haste," the superintendent answered with certainty.

"And what would be the cause of that?"

"Something that happened in the investigation. Something that happened yesterday or on Friday."

"Squirrel?" asked Lynx.

"Might be," said Bloodhound.

"So this is to save Squirrel?"

"Might be," Bloodhound growled again.

During this conversation, Falcon's grip on the armrest of the chair grew tighter and tighter, and now he shot up.

"But," he said. "Excuse me for saying this, but what are you talking about? We have to act. We have to arrest the panda. This is—"

"Sit down," Superintendent Bloodhound growled.

Falcon fell silent and stared at his superintendent. He sat down. He was quivering with frustration. After several days of mistakes and false leads, a clear, uncomplicated, and obvious suspect had been identified. What was there to talk about?

"And if it's a police officer?" asked Lynx, not concerned in the least about Falcon Ècu's outburst.

"What do you mean?" growled the superintendent.

"The only one who could make their way into your office without risk is a police officer," Anna continued. "And if the tipster has been a police officer all along, it would explain how he could call our direct lines last Monday. He knew he would get you to go to Nova Park by calling Falcon."

"He called our direct extensions?"

"According to Charlie."

Bloodhound suddenly remembered that the call last Monday did not go through the switchboard. And the suspicion he had was growing to a gnawing conviction.

"Hmm," he growled.

Falcon Ècu couldn't sit still any longer. He got up again.

"Please excuse me," he said. "For even though I think what you're saying is interesting, it has nothing to do with the case. We arrest Panda. I can get him to explain both the telephone calls and the mysterious pictures."

"You think that Panda put a picture of himself on Bloodhound's desk to draw attention to it?" Anna Lynx asked with surprise.

"With all due respect, Anna, I don't care who put the picture there. It's there. Look at it!"

Bloodhound dismissed Falcon's theatrical maneuvers as stupidity.

"Falcon, we're not going to do a damn thing. One day you'll grow up and get some common sense stuffed through your beak. We are absolutely not doing a damn thing. This picture," the superintendent growled, holding it up and shaking it in front of Ècu's eyes, "hints at desperation. Believe me. We forget about this, and worse crimes than breaking into my office are going to be committed."

"But you can't—" Falcon began with a raised voice.

"Shut up!" Bloodhound growled, holding up a threatening paw that pointed at Falcon. "You do as I say. Understood?"

Falcon summoned all the self-control of which he was capable and managed to remain quiet. Intellectually he knew that he ought to nod an "understood," but that was more than he could bear. His normally white cheeks shone as pink as his throat, and without a word or a gesture he left the superintendent's office.

"What was that all about?" Bloodhound asked when Ècu had closed the door.

"He didn't have time to finish scouring the oven before he came here," Anna replied to smooth things over. "He'll understand . . ."

But Inspector Lynx was wrong about that.

———

The fatal mistake of which Falcon Ècu was guilty immediately after the meeting with Superintendent Bloodhound on Sunday morning, the ninth of June, could not be excused. It was due not only—but partly—to the unfinished oven cleaning and the ignominy that the arrest of Earwig had entailed. It was due not only—but partly—to his constant feeling of isolation in combination with an improbably high level of ambition.

Falcon Ècu left Bloodhound and Lynx, went with determined steps over to the stairs, and continued two floors down to Captain Jan Buck's well-swept, light-filled office in the northwest corner of the police station. Without a thought that it was Sunday morning and that Captain Buck probably wasn't there, Ècu went straight into Buck's office and discovered his highest commander sitting in front of the computer, playing strategy games.

"What the—?" Buck exclaimed in irritation, failing in an attempt to click up another document in front of the game.

As Falcon Ècu told his story, however, Captain Buck's astonishment turned to readiness for action, and when the inspector was done, Buck had already put on his jacket and taken the pistol from the regulation drawer.

"Show me," he asked.

Ten minutes after Falcon Ècu had rushed out of Superintendent Larry Bloodhound's office, he returned. This time with Captain Jan Buck in tow.

Anna Lynx was again sitting at her workstation. From a distance she heard Falcon approach with his sententious steps breaking the silence of the office area. She immediately read the situation and understood that her colleague was beyond saving. In a way this mortified her; she had invested both time and concern to get him to fit in. But the matter was clearly hopeless, and the countdown of Falcon Ècu's days at rue de Cadix had begun. If he left tomorrow or in a week, it was impossible to guess, but once you stuck a knife in Larry Blood-hound's back you could count on being paid back in the same currency. At best Falcon Ècu would be offered a job as a traffic cop, but nothing else.

"Superintendent?" Ècu cleared his throat outside Blood-hound's door.

Captain Buck, however, did not intend to wait to be invited. He squeezed past the inspector, opened the door, and stepped into Bloodhound's burrow.

"Larry," Buck said, "I hear you've fished up a new prime suspect in the Vulture case."

Bloodhound looked up from his desk with surprise, flab-bergasted and wondering for a few seconds how Buck turned up in front of him, but then he caught sight of the falcon out-side the door and understood what had happened.

"Captain," he began, "I—"

"Do you have the picture here?"

"I have the picture here. But I don't think that—"

"May I see it?"

It was impossible to refuse him, so Bloodhound dug in his wastebasket and found the picture. He handed it over to Buck, who only gave it a confirming glance and nodded.

"Good," he said. "Let Squirrel go and issue an arrest war-rant for Panda. Search the whole city—I want him here no later than this afternoon."

"Captain," Bloodhound growled with restraint, "with all due respect and without trying to be an ass, I don't intend to do that. I'm rather certain. My suggestion is that we wait."

"Why?" asked Buck, without seeming interested.

"Because I believe that the pile of shit who put the picture on my desk has a few things to tell. And he's soon going to tell them."

"Really?" said Buck. "And what 'pile of shit' are you talk-ing about, Superintendent?"

"That . . . I'm not quite sure of yet," Bloodhound admitted.

"You're not sure?" Buck repeated derisively. "Well, I'm sure. Release Squirrel. I've already talked with the prosecutor. It's Panda we're going to bring in."

"You've talked with the prosecutor?"

"I gave you a chance, Bloodhound," Buck explained. "You didn't take it. You've despised me since the first day I installed myself here at rue de Cadix. You think you're better than everyone else. But I'm a professional. So I gave you a chance. You should view me as a role model. I'm taking over this investigation, Bloodhound. As of now. We'll have to figure all this out when Vulture's murderer is sitting behind lock and key."

And with these words Captain Buck turned his back on the superintendent and left him behind his desk.

Casino Biscaya in northwest Tourquai.

At the blackjack tables stands a dealer with wings crossed in front of his chest, waiting for the bouncers to do their job.

"Counting can't be prohibited," the young player at the table says. "Keeping track of the cards can't be prohibited. This is a game of skill. It's not roulette. You can't accuse me of anything."

The young animal does not understand that the owner of the casino can do whatever he wants. No evidence is required. Anyone who wins a suspiciously large amount during the evening is the object of extra attention. And if the player in question keeps winning, he gets thrown out. It's no more complicated than that. But the naïve mouse doesn't realize that.

"I haven't done anything wrong."

In the mouse's jacket sleeve are four aces of spades. Philip Mouse is twenty-five years younger than when he sits in the kitchen at Jasmine Squirrel's and sees her taken away by the police; he is naïve, but not so naïve that he doesn't understand that if the bouncer discovers the extra cards, it will no longer be a case of simply being thrown out. Philip stands at the center of the attention; the players around the table observe him tensely. It is impossible to get rid of the aces right now. It is impossible to explain that he needs the money he's bet, and that he's not going to use it for himself.

Casino Biscaya is not one of the larger gambling establishments. At Biscaya, drinking is just as important as betting, and the drinking is attended to with the same passion and consideration. Mouse has chosen this casino because he thought it would be easier to cheat at a place like this. It's dark in the room. In the background is the gurgle of elevator-music arrangements of classics by the old masters. At the bar a couple of guests are arguing about who has made the all-time most free laps on the Lanceheim Lasers, and around Philip Mouse there is a vacuum. The dark, varnished wood on the edges of the blackjack tables is sticky with old liquor.

"I haven't done anything," he repeats. "And I don't intend to leave. No farther than to the bar. You misunderstood."

But the dealer is already tired of the player, and finally the bouncer shows up. He's a big ape, as he should be, an orangutan with wild reddish hair sticking out in all directions. Without thinking, Philip raises his paw from the sticky table and puts it around his jacket sleeve. It is a guilt-laden gesture, and many of the surrounding players understand immediately what is about to happen.

The orangutan stops and stares. Not at Philip but at his jacket sleeve.

"Stand completely still," says the ape. "Completely, completely still."

Philip stands still while the orangutan slowly approaches.

When a yard or even less remains, something unexpected happens. Out of the clump of animals that has formed around Philip Mouse a squirrel separates herself. She is beautiful in a simple way and radiates a self-assurance that takes him by surprise. She places her paw behind his neck, draws his head next to hers, and kisses him right in front of all the stuffed animals.

"Darling," she says. "We're leaving now."

And naturally he follows her, so close that he can hear her whisper to the orangutan, "He's with me."

Philip Mouse had Jasmine Squirrel to thank for his life. Neither more nor less. They went home to her place that night so many years ago, and he realized in the dawn that he would never get a better answer to the question of "Why?" than what she had already given him.

He had looked so defenseless as he stood waiting to be unmasked. She had never experienced a stuffed animal so wide open to attack, so unaware of how he could fend off life.

That was her explanation. The words she used: fend off life.

That was something she herself was occupied with, day and night.

Back then Jasmine Squirrel lived in a two-room apartment: from the sidewalk you went down a short stairway to the outside door, and facing the courtyard you could open double doors onto a little garden. It was not unusual that basements were turned into apartments in the most densely built-up areas in south Lanceheim.

Jasmine Squirrel had so many pieces of furniture and colorful rugs and curtains and pillows that there was hardly room to move through the two rooms, but Philip was prepared to exchange his bachelor pad in a moment. He had celebrated his twentieth birthday with a big party a week earlier, and had still not cleaned up. Maybe that was why he didn't go home after that first night; maybe it was due to something else altogether.

Not once during all the years he had known Jasmine Squirrel had he dared ask her how old she was. But she was much older than him, especially then, at Casino Biscaya. He worshipped her from the very first moment. She was no teacher, however; she had no such ambitions. She didn't share her experiences, she didn't tell him about life; he had to draw his own conclusions.

And when he did, she shrugged her shoulders.

The same thing at night. She was no adolescent fantasy, not an older, experienced lover who instructed young adepts. She concentrated on herself and her own enjoyment, and Philip often felt expendable. Yet there was an intensity in her manner, a force in her pleasure that he would never experience with anyone else.

Many times he wondered whether it was the lack of demands she offered by being so strong, so willful and self-sufficient. She did not need him during the day or at night, thus freeing him from responsibility. In his twenties this was a major liberation. Perhaps for the first time in his life he experienced that there were no expectations, no one critically observing his way of being or thinking.

Is this what it's like to be an adult? he sometimes wondered at night.

And later, many years later, when he was an adult, he realized that it had never been about anything other than Jasmine Squirrel.

She became his first great love, from that first night in her two-room apartment.

After a few months she threw him out. It was a long time, for Jasmine Squirrel. Philip had not had any expectations; he was neither surprised nor bitter. He stuffed the few things he had smuggled into her apartment into a plastic bag and returned home to his own loathsome studio.

She gave him no reasons.

With a father who abandoned the family early on and a mother who was an alcoholic, Philip Mouse was deprived of his final sense of security in his teens when his big brother was sent to King's Cross after a failed postal robbery.

It was an old aunt who needed the money he tried to get through trickery at Casino Biscaya, an operation on a nasty tear she couldn't afford, and the young Philip had tried to help out. But there had been desperation in the act, as if the need to practice charity toward his aunt was a subconscious attempt to compensate for the whole family's dysfunctional history.

Even after Jasmine threw him out, his love still remained. During the year that followed, Philip Mouse made a courageous but clumsy attempt to find his way back to the squirrel's heart. It was doomed to fail. She was never cruel to him, she might even spend the occasional night with him, but she made it clear that it was no more than that.

He was so young.

When Philip Mouse started at the Police Academy, he realized it had to do with his upbringing, but he didn't know whether the Academy was a protest or a confirmation. He didn't care. Several years had passed since the night at Casino Biscaya, and his life was going nowhere. He was desperate, and the Police Academy seemed to provide a certain outlet for the fury he kept stored up inside himself.

Six months into training, he dropped out and decided to start working as a private detective instead. He pretended it had something to do with attracting females. Despite repeated attempts with Jasmine, he got nowhere. So he decided to forget her. He courted a number of young stuffed animals and was involved with several others. That was why he could state with such certainty that "private detective" had higher standing than "police officer," at least in the eyes of females. At one of his regular haunts he met a young, beautiful shrew with the longest eyelashes he had ever seen. She summarized the general perception.

"It's the uniform or the mystique," she said. "And I prefer the mystique."

Philip Mouse was not cut out to be a police officer. He didn't share the reverence for rules and hierarchies, he wasn't interested in power. The females were an excuse.

Along with his love relationships, Philip Mouse was slowly building a life for himself. It happened without his realizing it. He had luck with his assignments, soon he could provide references, and he could barely keep up with his intensive social life.

The years passed, and one day there were routines, and friends, and Daisy Hippopotamus. Daisy kept him on a short leash, and Philip came to feel a sense of responsibility for her, although it more likely appeared to be the other way around.

What built his reputation as a private detective was his ability to show discretion—to the border of disinterest—along with his well-developed contacts within the police. The insurance companies in Mollisan Town became repeat customers and were the main reason that, in time, Philip was able to move the office to baby blue Knackstrasse up in Lanceheim. He also was able to abandon his stuffy studio and buy a condo on Fischergrube, no more than ten minutes from the new office. The moving-in party coincided with his thirtieth birthday, and he could not refrain from inviting Jasmine Squirrel to the festivities. He hadn't seen her in over four years but still had a hard time not thinking about her.

When she showed up, late at night after most of the other guests had already gone home, the sudden reunion was so emotional that the mouse was forced to crouch down for a moment. It was not joy he felt, it was pain. His eyes were filled with tears, and he embraced her long and hard.

"Happy to see me?" she whispered in his ear. "Or are you trying to kill me?"

He could not reply. As he stood with Jasmine close to him, as he felt her sweet scent and warm body, he realized that nothing was worth anything without her; her presence was equally painful and tangible.

Jasmine Squirrel gave no explanations. That night she moved into his new apartment and they stayed there together for two weeks. The outside world faded away, work had to wait. Daisy, who had to explain Philip's absence to the clients, was furious of course, as was the current girlfriend, but by pulling out the phone jack, Philip elegantly resolved both conflicts in a single motion.

Days and nights flowed together into one moment. During those weeks she showed him her soul and her heart. And he showed her his.

One morning when he awoke she was sitting dressed on the edge of the bed. At the same moment he knew something was wrong. He was wide awake and sat up before she could say it.

"You can't go," he said.

She placed a finger against his lips. Her massive tail was standing straight up, swaying hypnotically behind her back.

"Shhh," she said. "Don't make a drama out of this. It's not dramatic. We're living in the same city. I'll call you."

She kept her finger there until she was sure he had understood. At the same moment she took it away, he repeated, "You can't go."

But she went. More surprisingly, she actually called the following week.

They met over dinner at a restaurant that was right next to Kleine Wallanlagen, and then went home separately. It was Jasmine's way of starting over. Philip quickly adapted to the change, but he did not accept it. He would never be able to play down his feelings.

He proposed twice. Once when they were celebrating the twentieth anniversary of their first encounter with a magnificent candlelit oyster buffet at home on Fischergrube. He got down on his knees in the dining room.

Afterward he did not hear from her for six months.

Despite that, Philip tried again, less than two years later, when her absence struck him with a feeling of emptiness so draining that he was physically incapable of getting out of bed. He called, pretending to be mortally ill, and she came over immediately. When she realized what it was about, she gave him a forceful slap to remind him of her wishes.

This time, too, she went underground.

It was not the usual fear of relationships that caused her reaction. It was pure rage. Jasmine Squirrel became equally angry and disappointed when she realized how Philip Mouse wanted to express his love. Marriage? To more easily keep an eye on, control, manage, or bind her? What did that have to do with love?

"But I only wanted to . . . only . . . I didn't want you to disappear from my life again," the miserable private detective whimpered.

"And you think that has anything to do with love?" she asked.

Jasmine Squirrel had moved to rue d'Oran a few months before Vulture's death. It was not a permanent address; during certain periods she moved often, and Philip didn't ask why. He didn't want to know. He didn't know what she did, how she supported herself, who she associated with. He sensed, but dismissed it. There were signs that indicated that sometimes she hid herself, fled; that her life was a tangle of secrets and lies. But who was he to judge? Her sort of uncompromising integrity would always guide her past shoals and reefs. The circumstances were, however, the least of his interests when they met.

He had called her yesterday evening, but it hadn't gone well.

"I'm so tired of this nagging," she hissed into the phone. "You have to stop it. This is not destiny, it's me."

The self-assured Philip Mouse felt miserable. He sat in the armchair in his living room without turning on any lamps.

"But there is no better word," he defended himself. "It's not Magnus. I don't believe in paradise, or in the underworld. When we're used up, then that's that. It doesn't need to be so terrifying. If it's over, then it's over."

"I've never believed in heaven," she said. "But I don't believe in anything else, either. There is nothing to blame. We have the responsibility. If all goes to hell, it's only our own fault."

"I agree," he said.

"You don't at all. That's exactly what you don't do. You believe in a context, a destiny, something bigger than yourself, something bigger than your life."

He could hear that she was standing up. Probably in the kitchen, where there was a telephone next to the refrigerator. She sounded restless.

"But of course there's something that—"

"And that's just cowardice," she spit out. "You take responsibility for your actions. It's only you, no one else, who decides what you should say, what you should do."

"I agree," he repeated. "I'm responsible. But I have my assumptions, my limitations. You know? You're the first to say how hopelessly romantic I am. That I always have been. Yes, but that's how I was delivered, and no one taught me anything else. I'm not making excuses. And why should I? That's what I mean by fate. I can't be something I'm not."

"But that's just bullshit," she interrupted. "Excuses. You have to take responsibility for your actions, Philip. Then you can be as 'romantic' as you want."

"I'm *taking* responsibility. It's not that. It's just that the factory made me a certain way, with a certain ability, and I grew up in an environment that marked me, then and forever," he continued, eager to make himself understood. "It's everything around me, too. You. This city. Whether I want to be or not, I'm part of a system, a collective. And we're all dependent on each other. When I turn a street corner, someone else goes in through a door. So we don't meet. If we had run into each other, both of our lives would have been changed. Maybe."

"And?"

"And . . . you don't need to call that 'fate.' You can call it what you want. I'm carrying my own assumptions around, and they collide with someone else's assumptions. Yours, for example. And together we create something new, we react to one another, and release an infinite sequence of reactions . . . which are not chance."

"Philip," said Jasmine into the phone, "I'm in kind of a rush, and I'm just on my way out . . . You can call it what you want, but the responsibility for your life is your own."

"I'm taking responsibility," he answered. "But I couldn't act in any other way."

He did not remember how they concluded the conversation.

7.4

Superintendent Larry Bloodhound was walking east on rue de Cadix. Perhaps he was catching a cold? A splitting headache was lurking right behind his right temple. Maybe it was just the detox? After stepping on the scale this morning, he realized it would never happen without the cocaine; he had gained a pound in just two days. He had taken out the equipment and found enough powder to be able to skip lunch and the cake with coffee. This was a defeat, of course, but Larry had decided to find someone besides Siamese to buy from. If nothing else, that was the lesson Anna had taught him.

At the corner of burgundy red rue des Écoles, an alarm vehicle caught up with the superintendent. Buck had called out all patrol cars and unmarked vehicles from rue de Cadix; sirens and screeching tires caused the stuffed animals on the sidewalks to turn and inquisitively watch this armada of power seep out across the streets of Tourquai. Bloodhound was certain that the citywide alarm had already gone out. With an effort of this level, it was only a matter of hours before Panda was brought in.

But Panda was not the guilty one.

Before Bloodhound managed to cross the street, an unmarked police car pulled up to the sidewalk with screeching tires and the front door on the passenger side was thrown open.

"Superintendent!" Anna Lynx called. "They've caught sight of the panda. He's driving south along the Dondau. Hop in and come along! We'll catch up with him before Haspelgasse."

But the superintendent shook his head so that his long ears started swinging.

"Just make sure Buck makes a big deal out of it," he growled, smiling shrewdly.

"Big deal of what?"

"Of arresting Panda."

The superintendent closed the car door. Falcon was sitting behind the wheel and accelerated. He did not want to miss out on the resolution of the drama at any price.

After twenty minutes Bloodhound had walked off the worst of his anger, and he hailed a taxi. He was still in Tourquai, but no more than a few minutes from North Avenue. The walk had been needed. What he had to do now was difficult enough as it was; he needed to put the irritation behind him.

The taxi reeked of garlic, but without thinking about food, Larry asked the driver to take him to baby blue Knackstrasse in Lanceheim, where private detective Philip Mouse's office had been for many years. Bloodhound had been there once before; all he remembered was the decrepit wooden ceiling fan.

He sank back in the backseat of the taxi, observing the clear blue sky through a darkening film that the taxi's owner had taped to the windows, and going through the evidence in his head. He could not know for certain, of course; you never did.

When had the suspicion first entered his mind? It was something Mouse had said, that Larry had committed to memory but not thought about very much.

It had been last Monday after work, when he went down to Chez Jacques after having discovered Vulture's body up at Nova Park in the morning. It was completely natural that Philip Mouse had already heard about Vulture and the investigation that had been started; the private detective knew about most things going on in the police station on rue de Cadix. And when Mouse made his comment about heirs that needed money, it had seemed reasonable. General. There were always heirs, and who didn't need money? It was only this morning, with the picture of Igor Panda in his paw, that the superintendent remembered Mouse's words. Had the private detective known about Panda already last Monday?

It could be chance.

But that wasn't likely.

"It's here," he said to the driver. "The green door, number 34."

The taxi stopped. Bloodhound paid and waited for the receipt, which he crumpled up and put in his jacket pocket. He stepped out onto the sidewalk and breathed in the air of Lanceheim: dusty cement, diesel fuel, and a tinge of metal, probably something the air was carrying from the cold spring-water flowing in the Dondau. Yet another reason never to move from Tourquai, the superintendent thought.

The outside door was open, and Bloodhound took the elevator the three floors up to Philip Mouse's office. He knocked on the door, and after a few moments, Daisy Hippopotamus opened. She recognized him immediately.

"Superintendent Bloodhound," she said. "But . . . he's not here."

"Mouse? He's not?"

"He hasn't been here since yesterday evening. I called him this morning, but he didn't answer."

She was dressed in a red sweater that flattered her buxom figure, and Bloodhound seemed to hear a measure of worry in her voice.

"If he shows up," said Bloodhound, "say that I was here looking for him. Ask him to call me."

"I'll do that," Daisy promised. "I'm sorry, Superintendent."

"Well," Bloodhound growled, "it was just a long shot. We hadn't arranged anything . . ."

Bloodhound left the private detective's office with unfinished business, but he had an idea. Over the years the two of them, the dog and the mouse, had, intentionally and unintentionally, revealed quite a bit to each other. Now the superintendent recalled that Mouse sometimes talked about a place where he went when he needed quiet and solitude. It was worth a try, thought Bloodhound; only Buck's circus waited for him at rue de Cadix.

It was Lynx who had said it: that the tipster, the one who phoned in the tip about Vulture that first day, must have been someone familiar with the police and the police station. Anna had drawn her conclusion because the tipster obviously wanted Bloodhound in particular at the scene of the crime, and calling Falcon was a way to lure his superintendent there.

Well, Bloodhound thought, Lynx was right. But he ought to have realized it himself. When the telephone jangled on the desk last Monday morning and his instinct had been not to pick up, it was because someone was calling his direct extension. He thought it was his mother calling, and he didn't have the energy for another guilt trip. The direct extension was not in any directory; only colleagues and his mother had it. He had been surprised at getting a "tipster" on the line; "tipsters" called in through the switchboard, even if they were often transferred. Why didn't he remember that before Lynx pointed it out this morning?

Because it had not seemed significant.

And the reason the tipster wanted Larry in particular to take on the case? The answer was simple. If the tipster was also the murderer, and had a close relationship to the investigating superintendent, he ensured getting himself a view into the investigation process. He could influence the investigation in the direction he found suitable, if that was necessary. Like when the tipster sneaked into Larry's office yesterday evening and placed the picture of Igor Panda on the desk.

Tour de la Liberté was one of the first skyscrapers built in what came to be Tourquai's city center, a forty-story-high cylinder-shaped construction sheathed in light, seamless marble. Around the tower, but at a respectful distance, one skyscraper after another shot up out of the asphalt. In later years the buildings became more and more spectacular, and together they finally formed the financial center of glittering shafts of prosperity that was Tourquai today. But through the years, Tour de la Liberté retained its dignity—an eternally modern work of architecture in an environment striving for effect.

After some mucking about in the lobby, Larry Bloodhound was able to get into the beautiful skyscraper's elevator and push the topmost button, the fortieth floor. The elevator was dark and gloomy; it creaked and complained. It was a slow ride up through the round body of the building, and Bloodhound had time to sigh once or twice. Over the years he had learned to keep reality at a distance. At work, sooner or later the greed of stuffed animals, their envy and madness, became unbearable to observe. Then distance was all-important. Together with Philip Mouse, he had always been able to reduce the oddities to patterns and archetypes. That was what the relationship between them was about. They reminded each other that not everyone was crazy, and that had made them the best of friends.

During the elevator ride Bloodhound mentally took a few steps back from the table near the window at Chez Jacques and without illusions observed the two figures who were sitting there. The one in good faith, the other with an insidious purpose.

There was nothing that hurt more than being betrayed by someone who was so close.

The elevator doors opened, and the superintendent went up the short stairway to the roof, opened an old sheet-metal door, and stepped out under the sky.

On the roof a running track in the form of a figure eight had been set up. The stuffed animals working in the tower could go up at lunch or after work and do a few laps. The narrow track was edged by tall Plexiglas, and running up there was dizzying, the view magnificent.

In the two "eyes" of the track the building manager at Tour de la Liberté had set up two oases: minimalistic but astoundingly magnificent gardens, explosions of green, red, and pink surrounding each elaborately carved piece of garden furniture. The view to the west hinted at the blue sea as a distinct line between sky and earth, the view east offered the urban jungle.

Mouse had confessed to Bloodhound that he sometimes made his way to this exclusive yet public place, and to the creaking, white-painted rib-backed settee. Here he could be in peace; except for the building manager, no one came up on the roof during business hours.

"Bloodhound?" Philip Mouse exclaimed with surprise.

Even though the garden had been described to the superintendent, reality exceeded his fantasy. He had not been prepared for the absurd dimensions: a magically pruned luxuriousness that seemed to hover freely high above the streets of Tourquai. I have to show this to Cordelia, he thought.

"Here you are," said the police officer, sitting down on one of the two rib-backed settees at the table.

Mouse was on the couch. He still looked surprised. Not, however, in a negative way, the superintendent was able to discern.

"It sure is magnificent," said the detective.

Bloodhound nodded and looked out over the edge of the tower. It was more than that. The aroma from the roses filled his nose.

"I was just thinking about you," Mouse continued. "I heard sirens. Lots of sirens. Has something happened?"

"That depends on how you look at it," Bloodhound growled. "But the fact that the infantile buck let himself be fooled isn't so strange, is it?"

Mouse smiled, but there was an uncertainty about his smile. "No . . ." he haltingly agreed.

"Besides, they've released Jasmine Squirrel. But maybe you already know that?"

"Squirrel?" asked Philip Mouse.

"That's how it started," said Bloodhound. "When I went up to Squirrel last Friday, your coat was hanging in her hall, Philip. I don't know if that was only a mistake, or if you actually thought I wouldn't see it. But that coat . . . it's you."

Mouse sat completely still on the uncomfortable wooden couch. He stared gloomily at Bloodhound and answered in a monotone, "I haven't had that coat tailored, if that's what you think. There are lots like it."

"I checked," Bloodhound sighed, turning his gaze across the city because it hurt less than looking at his former friend. "It wasn't particularly difficult. Squirrel has been careful about hiding her tracks backward in time, but you haven't been. Squirrel is the love of your life, isn't she, Philip? We've

talked about that, after all, that there has always been someone special—you've led me to understand that."

"You have no idea about that," said Mouse in a low voice.

"But I do," Bloodhound objected, displaying a certain irritation. "Hell, it's me you're talking to, Philip. It's me. When
I searched for Squirrel in your life, she showed up everywhere.
When you applied to the Police Academy a hundred years ago,
she was one of your references. There's a picture of you and
her when you were interviewed after the case with the buz-
zard. And Jasmine gave your telephone number as a 'close
relative' when she was admitted to the hospital ten years ago."

"She did?"

"She did."

"Okay," Philip sighed. "I actually had no idea about that."

"Can we get through this without losing our dignity?"
Bloodhound growled.

"Get through what?"

Mouse was squirming in his seat, staring straight into the
police superintendent's eyes.

"Get through what?" he repeated in a louder voice.

"Well . . . maybe you should tell me."

"I have nothing to tell, Larry. Absolutely nothing. I'm
happy that Jasmine Squirrel is no longer at rue de Cadix, but
I have nothing more to say."

Bloodhound looked out toward the horizon. He felt heavy,
tired, and downhearted; he had hoped for something else.
He had felt it, the reason he was sitting here was bits of evi-
dence, all of which pointed in the mouse's direction. But the
hope of being wrong had still been there. Well, no longer.
Superintendent Bloodhound felt a premonition of the Lunch
Breeze, which set his ear swinging, and he answered lightly,
"What were you doing at the police station yesterday evening,
Philip?"

"Huh?"

"You heard me."

"I—"

"You couldn't believe, after all the years at Chez Jacques, after having systematically gotten to know all the police officers in leading positions at rue de Cadix, that you could make your way into the building without anyone seeing you and recognizing you?"

Philip Mouse sat motionless, staring at his friend. He did not say a thing.

"What were you doing there? In my office?"

"You're bluffing," Mouse said at last. "You have no idea where I was yesterday evening."

"Shit into hell, Philip," the superintendent moaned. "Remember who you're talking to."

Bloodhound suddenly felt restless and stood up. He took a turn around an incomparably blossoming pink rhododendron, but Mouse remained sitting motionless on the couch.

"Bring out the head," Bloodhound growled, sitting down again.

"Don't know what you're talking about," Mouse replied.

"I can guarantee that I can . . . It doesn't need to be more than a few years," said Bloodhound. "Bring out the head, then we'll sew it back on and suddenly we're talking about malicious damage, not murder."

"I don't know what you're talking about," Mouse repeated.

As soon as Larry Bloodhound showed up on the roof, Philip Mouse had lost all energy; it was as if his capacity to think and speak had been sucked out of him. But now at last he got up from the couch and pointed at the police officer with a sharp claw.

"You have nothing," he said. "You have absolutely nothing. If you had anything, you wouldn't have come yourself."

"Philip, I—"

"Nothing," Mouse repeated. "What kind of craziness is this? You coming here and suggesting . . . coming and maintaining that I . . . no, the hell you will."

"Philip, there's no way out of this. I know. This requires more than just—"

"Bullshit," Mouse spit out. "Bullshit."

And he turned his back on the superintendent, going with determined steps away toward the door that led down to the elevators. Bloodhound let him go. The private detective was right. There was no evidence. But that was only because Bloodhound hadn't figured out how things hung together until this morning. Producing evidence was easier when you knew the answer to the riddle.

And Larry Bloodhound—who had been hopefully uncertain when he'd taken the elevator up through Tour de la Liberté—was now convinced.

7.5

No matter what time of day it was, the daylight never reached the corner next to the stove. That's why it was there Hummingbird Esperanza-Santiago would pray. The cramped space suited her religious temperament; it was as if she were standing in the corner for her faith.

She did not pray at fixed times, and she did not keep track, but she fell on her knees in the corner next to the stove at least four or five times every day. She performed these hours of prayer as a kind of meditation, letting her thoughts wander freely with a starting point in a text from the Proclamations. She would usually stick with the same text as long as she felt it engaged her, which might be for days or months.

Early in the morning on Sunday, the ninth of June, Hummingbird Esperanza-Santiago woke up in her bed, filled with energy and desire. During the night, dreams had tormented her, and she longed for her place by the stove. Since early in May, she had repeated the same piece from the First Proclamation in her prayer. The rhythm and sound of the words calmed her, the text helped her ease the night's anxiety.

She stumbled into the bathroom, pushing aside the piles of dirty laundry and heaps of old newspapers, and made her way to the toilet. Many years ago she had transformed the bathroom into a combination archive and closet. She did her business in the toilet, sometimes she stepped into the drying cabinet, but otherwise hygiene and cleanliness were not the sort of thing Hummingbird Esperanza-Santiago was interested in. She hadn't turned on the faucet for many years, and were she to make an attempt today, it was doubtful whether the pipes would function.

In the darkness in the bathroom she found a pair of underwear, a skirt, and a blouse. She dressed herself quickly in yesterday's clothes. She neither laundered nor bought new clothes; she wasn't vain, what she already had was just fine.

Out in the kitchen she made a fire in the stove with a couple of dry sticks of wood and set a saucepan with water on the large burner. Then she fell down on her knees in her customary corner. Half aloud, she mumbled the words of Noah Whale from the First Proclamation:

And Magnus heard the mighty sea, and understood its soul.
At water's edge he felt the ocean cold intense.
He opened wide his mouth, for questions crave defense.
But it was not their fault, the seaweed and algae scold.

Horizon melded sky and sea together as a whole.
Through the water came a golden fish swimming toward
*   the strand,*
a creature true, but one that could not thrive on land.
"A pitiful life," said Magnus, "but nonetheless a soul."

"He knows not where he is." Magnus looked into its eye.
"He only recalls the now, and of that but a moment,
his reasoning is stunted, his spirit is in torment,
and to pray for him and for his life is pure futility."

He spoke about Creation not as something to perfect;
he raised up the fish and cried, "Desire
that memory of the feeble-minded's life not expire,
a life in harmony has nought to do with intellect."

The more than three thousand verses in the First Proclamation followed the same patterns, simply rhymed and rhythmically wrought. After having mumbled four verses, Hummingbird Esperanza-Santiago proceeded to wordlessly sing the rhythm and melody as a kind of mantra.

Before her mind's eye one of her students appeared, the mournful Agnes Guinea Pig. Hummingbird was flooded with hatred, an unreasonable jealousy that stuck in her wings and cut in her chest.

The inward image became clearer. Hummingbird saw before her Agnes Guinea Pig standing by the easel out in the greenhouse. The building's white paint was flaking, the beautiful glass roof had fallen apart in several places, and ivy and weeds had moved in and taken possession of the building. Agnes Guinea Pig—Hummingbird's oldest pupil—stood in the midst of this green decay in a blue dress with white lace at the throat, as if she were younger than she was.

And Agnes took a step back to observe what she had achieved. She had spent six months in front of the same motif, and the last few weeks she had concentrated exclusively on the sky. Like all of Hummingbird's pupils, Guinea Pig worked to become just as technically proficient as her teacher. To imitate, to the slightest detail, was to conquer. Esperanza-Santiago's pupils ended every term by painting their own large, new canvases in the style of Hummingbird Esperanza-Santiago. It was these paintings—if they were sufficiently good—that Hummingbird signed and sold via Jake Golden Retriever and Igor Panda.

For Agnes Guinea Pig, however, examination day was far off. Her sky looked like a sea, her mixing of color lacked feeling, her technique was stiff and obvious.

———

Esperanza-Santiago is on her knees on the floor by the stove, praying. Before her she sees Agnes Guinea Pig, who observes her incomplete work, who squints and shuffles as if she were an artist, and who then exclaims, "I think I'm starting to understand."

A mockery.

It was nothing other than a mockery. Agnes Guinea Pig had not understood. Nothing in what she had accomplished, in her facial expressions, in her lack of development, suggested that she had understood.

Hummingbird saw before her how she slowly went up to the pupil, placed herself behind her, took her paw, and together they again approached the canvas. With a careful but determined wing, Hummingbird led the guinea pig's brush across what was supposed to depict a sky, and with all of her body the artist felt that Agnes Guinea Pig was, and remained, a lost cause.

Hummingbird Esperanza-Santiago again experienced, in the corner next to the stove, all of the painful stages of jealousy.

To be Agnes Guinea Pig.

To be so free from talent, from compulsion, from self-insight. Hummingbird sank her forehead deeper down toward the floor. She was filled with feelings that were not only shameful, they were indefensible. From Magnus she had received a gift, a favor, and here she was, fantasizing about escaping it. To awake one morning without demands, without expectations, to live a day as spiritually empty as Agnes Guinea Pig. To get to experience what was talked about in the First Proclamation as "the feeble-minded's fortune."

Hummingbird Esperanza-Santiago wept.

The tears were running down her cheeks, and she was overcome by shame.

"I'm weeping with happiness," she called to her Lord, but realized that He would hardly let Himself be fooled.

She painted for His sake. He had given her the gift, she was in eternal debt to Him. And the money Jake Golden Retriever earned on the pupils' paintings Esperanza-Santiago donated entirely to charity through the organization A Helping Hand. But however much she exerted herself, she could not free herself from this: the feeling of envy at stuffed animals like Agnes Guinea Pig, who lived without compulsion and without self-insight.

At last she calmed down. The spasms subsided, and her desperate prayers were transformed into quiet crying. Outside, the morning haze still lay heavy over her garden and greenhouse, and she had plenty of time.

A few hours later, Hummingbird Esperanza-Santiago parked a dark red Volga Minibus in the parking lot outside Boathouse 3. It was a rusty vehicle with dents on the front that belonged to the neighboring farmer.

The boathouse was silent and deserted. Hummingbird was early. There were thousands of places in Mollisan Town where she could have held her meetings with Jake Golden Retriever, but she had chosen this one. She liked the smell from the clear, cold Dondau, and the stillness of the river in the morning, when the surface of the water was smooth and mysterious.

Hummingbird went out on one of the piers and sat down on a bench. She knew how chaotic it had been here only a few hours ago. She knew how the dockworkers loaded and unloaded, swore and shouted, ran and carried as the captains worriedly glanced at the horizon to determine how little time they had and how mean they needed to be. And now: silence.

Hummingbird was lost in thought.

A few minutes later the silence was broken when the door

to the boathouse opened with an ominous creaking. Hummingbird gave a start and got up. She immediately discovered that the figure walking up the wharf was not Jake Golden Retriever.

At about the same time Igor Panda recognized his artist.

He stopped. He turned pale, and the panic showed in his eyes.

"Hum—Hummingbird," he stammered to himself.

In patrol car 767-600 sat three police officers, each eating a pineapple flambé. The car was more than twenty years old, the stuffing was poking out of the seats, and a little samba band was stuck to the instrument panel. It couldn't be removed; they had tried for several years. The windows of the police car were fogging over from the hot fruit; empty, trampled plastic water bottles were on the floor, both front and back. The aroma of coconut and cinnamon inside the car was overwhelming, and the kangaroo behind the wheel complained as usual, "It would have been better if we'd eaten before we got in the car. I knew it would smell like this. I'll just have to throw this uniform in the wash!"

"Stop whining," answered a leopard from the backseat. "We all have households to run."

"And there are worse smells," said the beetle sitting next to the leopard. "Hell, when I come home and smell like coconut and pineapple, the cubs are always happy."

"Listen, we're tired of your cubs," the leopard snapped. "We hear about your cubs from the minute we sit in the car until we get out of it. It's starting to feel like they're my cubs."

"That's easy for you to say," the kangaroo complained to the leopard. "You have a washing machine. If you had to reserve the laundry room, you probably wouldn't think this smell was so—"

"*Your* cubs?" said the beetle to the leopard. "Listen, watch yourself, Leopard. Badmouth my cubs again and you'll have to ride in another car."

"Promises are all you give me," the leopard sighed.

The kangaroo, finishing first, opened the glove compartment and took out a roll of paper towels to clean up with. It was then he saw the black Volga Deluxe drive past.

"Listen up," he said, pointing. "Wasn't that the car they just put a search warrant out for?"

The beetle and the leopard turned around, but the windows were fogged over and they saw nothing.

"Yes, yes, I'm sure," the kangaroo maintained.

He started the car and made a U-turn to follow the black Volga.

"I'm sure," he repeated. "I remember the registration number. It's almost like mine. I have PK 444 JK7. Igor Panda's car had PK 444 something else."

"We have to call this in," said the leopard in the backseat.

"This'll be something to tell the cubs," the beetle chuckled. "That it was Dad who arrested Igor Panda."

Igor walked quickly over to the bench and sat down, careful to accommodate the artist. He could not for his life understand what was going on. Where was the forger? Why was Hummingbird here? Had she uncovered everything?

"Well," said Hummingbird Esperanza-Santiago as Panda sat down. "Tell me, now, what are you doing here?"

She had known this moment would come, ever since she and Golden Retriever had started the collaboration. Sooner or later Panda would have to discover them; it had taken an unexpectedly long time.

"I . . ." Panda replied, desperately seeking a way to continue the sentence, "I . . . agreed to a meeting here. Now."

"A meeting," Hummingbird nodded encouragingly. "Good. A meeting. With whom?"

"With . . ." Panda began, "with . . . a dog."

"With a dog," Hummingbird repeated. "Good, a dog, then. I was supposed to meet a dog, too. Can it be the same dog?"

"A golden retriever?" he asked.

"That's right," Hummingbird answered. "Jake."

Igor Panda tried feverishly to understand what was going on. If Jake Golden Retriever arranged a meeting with Hummingbird, must he have been planning to become Hummingbird's dealer himself?

"Jake, yes, that's right," said Igor Panda.

Should I cut off her head?

The thought came to him without Igor Panda having been prepared for it. Yesterday he had taken a life only twenty-some yards from where he now sat. With a deceased hummingbird, the value of her paintings would increase dramatically. Which made it even more critical to find out who the forger was.

"But there doesn't seem to be any Jake Golden Retriever here, does there?" said Hummingbird.

There was something that puzzled her. That Panda was here was one thing, but where was Jake? A significant reason that she had chosen him as an intermediary was his reliability. She had gotten to know him when he worked as a janitor at the College of Art, many years ago.

"No," Panda agreed.

"And you can't have been mistaken?" Hummingbird asked. "About the day? Or the time?"

"Maybe," said Panda.

He could not let go of the thought he had just had. He squirmed in his seat. He hardly knew what he had said. From the well of memory the golden retriever's eyes showed up, as they looked when he buried the dog's head yesterday evening. Could he bury the hummingbird's head in the same place? He saw before him the little beak sticking up from the loose soil. The image made him dizzy. He felt nauseous. He turned around. Did he hear the vipers creeping outside the walls of the boathouse? No, it must be his imagination. The weight of the money in his inside pocket made him nervous.

He got up. Where was the forger? He was no longer interested in the neurotic artist; she didn't supply him with anything he could sell. It was the forger he wanted to meet. Had Hummingbird scared him away? Igor Panda put his paw in his pocket. The box cutter from yesterday was still there.

"When you came," he asked, "was there anyone here then?"

"No," she answered. "No one was here."

"That's not possible," said Panda, without concealing the fury in his voice. "There had to be someone here. You must have seen someone?"

"No one," Hummingbird promised. "There was no one here."

But she felt afraid. She got up. The panda came slowly toward her, and she started to back away. Suddenly there was something threatening about the scene. They noticed the change at the same time. Panda grasped the box cutter, which was still in his jacket pocket.

He wants to hurt me, thought Hummingbird. He wants to hurt me.

The next moment she turned and ran.

Outside Boathouse 3 the police had not left anything to chance. Ten police cars stood arranged like a convex wall fifteen feet from the one door, and more than thirty police officers had taken their positions with drawn weapons. Captain Jan Buck had given strict orders. Before he got to the scene himself, no one could so much as sneeze. Igor Panda would be Buck's trophy, and no one else's. Now the captain stood with a megaphone in hand, at a safe distance from the door of the boathouse, and raised his arm just as the door was thrown open and Hummingbird Esperanza-Santiago came running out.

Nervous police officers' trigger fingers twitched, but the

artist was so tangibly small and thin that not even the most psychotic police officer—and there were a few of those standing with their rifles steadied on the hoods of the cars—could perceive Hummingbird as a threat.

The next moment Igor Panda came out through the door.

If the situation had not been so intense, it would have been a parody. Panda came rushing out of the boathouse but refused to understand the obvious. He didn't seem to see the police officers, the cars, the drawn weapons, or hear Captain Buck screaming in his megaphone, either. Igor Panda ran after Esperanza-Santiago: he was chasing his salvation and his dream, he was chasing his last hope.

"STOP, OTHERWISE WE'LL SHOOT!" Buck screamed again.

But Panda continued running inside his own destiny.

7.6

Jasmine Squirrel hadn't taken the bus for years. Now she was sitting on the Route 3, which went between Rosdahl in Lanceheim and Parc Clemeaux in Tourquai. She observed that they had taken away the little buttons you pressed for the next stop; these were replaced with a strip that ran along the windows. She did not recall the turquoise tint of the seats, the gravel on the floor, or the advertising messages on the ceiling, but, as always, she felt nauseous from all the braking and accelerating. Outside, the breeze had just set in and the Evening Weather colored the sky a gentle red. Except for a few bears sitting in front, she was alone on board.

She was still furious.

Monday morning, when Mouse called, her first reaction had been suspicion. What he'd said was impossible to understand, impossible to accept; it was the sort of thing that happened only in melodramatic novels sold at Monomart.

"I've cut the head off Oswald Vulture," he had said. "Jasmine, my darling, I have cut the head off Oswald."

She'd been sitting on the couch in her cozy living room and

didn't move from the spot. She breathed into the telephone receiver and listened to his breath on the other side. It was not fear or anxiety that made the words get stuck and refuse to cross her lips; when she realized that he was telling the truth, surprise was replaced by fury. She went crazy.

"Where are you?" she finally forced out.

"I'm still here," he answered. "At Nova Park."

"Where?"

"Inside Vulture's office."

The image immediately entered her mind: the impersonal, lavish, and dark office where Philip Mouse stood perplexed by the desk, where the headless Vulture sat in his pin-striped suit.

It was heinous. It was incomprehensible. It was her fault.

"Mouse, you are one hell of an idiot," she whispered.

She didn't know why she lowered her voice.

"Darling, I . . . did it," he whispered back.

He sounded like a lunatic. He was in a state of shock. But before she let the madness get the upper hand she concentrated on the practical.

"You are one silly, silly idiot," she repeated slowly. "Listen to me now. When we're through talking, you put down the receiver, Philip. Go over to the door, peek out through the keyhole, and wait until Cobra leaves her seat. Then you open it and leave."

He had not answered a word; there was only his breathing on the phone.

"Philip, did you hear what I said?"

With a grunt he confirmed it at last.

Squirrel hung up, picked up the receiver again, and dialed Emanuelle Cobra's direct extension.

"Emanuelle, it's me. Don't ask. Leave there. Leave the office. Take a smoke break. I'll explain later."

Without surprise or making any objections, Emanuelle Cobra did as Squirrel said. She got up and left the office. It was not the first time she had obeyed orders, and it would be far from the last. On her way out, in the corridor, she also realized that Squirrel would never explain what was behind the request; their relationship was not like that.

Outside the windows of the bus, evening was settling carefully over Mollisan Town. It was the street lighting that revealed the darkness: from one moment to the next, Jasmine Squirrel noticed that the neon signs above the display windows demanded attention and the light that fell across the sidewalks from inside the shops suddenly seemed warm and inviting.

The bears sitting at the front of the bus got off at North Avenue, and a hyena with a dark green hoodie got on and took one of their seats. In the large rearview mirror Jasmine caught a glimpse of the bus driver's stern visage. With the regulation cap pulled down over his forehead, he sat staring straight ahead. He couldn't be bothered to give her a glance.

Philip Mouse got on at orange-colored rue Leblanc. Jasmine shut her eyes. It pained her to see him. The wrinkled white trench coat, the narrow face, the curious gaze. In conflict with her nature, she felt endlessly sorry for him.

Philip had always chosen not to understand. He had chosen not to see and hear. It was pathetic, but it was his own choice.

Jasmine had already started Domaine d'Or Logistics when she met Philip Mouse the first time. Even if she seldom talked about work, he must have understood. She assumed that; anything else seemed unreasonable.

The main reason the escort operation could go on year after year without involvement from the police or Mafia was because Jasmine never got greedy. She maintained a small stable of clients; she tied her females close to her. Emanuelle Cobra was a perfect example. Cobra had been around a long time, and the last few years she had only a single customer. Oswald Vulture. It was Vulture himself who suggested that Cobra should become his secretary, something that gave Domaine d'Or many advantages. For one thing, Jasmine was paid for Cobra's services, and besides she could simply blackmail Vulture for extra money when such tactics were required. What she didn't know today about his business deals wasn't worth knowing. But she never pushed too much, never too hard. She had a long-term perspective on her operation.

Her telling Philip Mouse about Oswald Vulture a week ago had been a mistake. A gigantic mistake. She had done it without thinking about it; in the context, Vulture had been a natural association, a cheap shot. And when she realized what she'd done . . . it was too late. For the first time Philip had not been content with evasion.

Jasmine had finally told about her life in a way that was close to the truth. A truth that she knew Philip could accept. She depicted herself as a victim, and Vulture as a sadistic lunatic.

But it had been a fatal mistake.

The bus accelerated and Philip went carefully back and sat in the row ahead of Jasmine.

"He guessed it," was the first thing Mouse said.

"Who?"

"Bloodhound. He knows. Or, he doesn't know, but he senses. He knows about you and me."

"That's not my fault," she answered quickly.

Mouse thought about disputing this, but realized that it would only lead to meaningless bickering.

"Bring out his head," whispered Jasmine. "Philip, for the last time, I'm begging you. Don't be such a fool."

"Don't start—" he begged.

"This is ridiculous!" she burst out. "I spent the night in jail at rue de Cadix. You're asking me to sit on this damn bus and—"

"I don't dare see you anywhere else," he interrupted. "I don't know what Larry is thinking. Maybe he's already put out a search for me. I want to stay mobile."

"The last thing I want to be doing tonight is sitting here," she repeated. "And the only reason I'm doing it is to convince you. Bring out the head, Philip. I know an ape who can sew on the head without the stitches showing. We can—"

"It can never be undone," he replied.

The bus careened around a curve, and they were both forced to take hold of the seats to counter the movement.

"I promise," she whispered loudly as the driver turned and stopped at the bus stop at the corner, "I can convince Vulture not to file charges. I can get him to do anything at all."

Philip was about to answer when an elderly couple, an ostrich and a llama, got on and sat down a few rows ahead.

"And then everything goes back to how it was," he whispered.

The bitterness in his voice was not to be mistaken.

"Yes, and is that so bad?" she hissed.

He didn't answer. They had had this conversation earlier in the week.

"You're not my guardian angel," she said.

She was talking too loud. Mouse was certain that the couple sitting ahead of them could hear what she said. With a gesture he tried to quiet her.

"It's my life you're destroying," she said. "My life. Who gave you the right to do that? Who gave you the right to interfere in things that have nothing to do with you?"

He wanted to answer but didn't dare. She got up and pressed the strip under the window. The bus driver reacted immediately and slowed down. They were already at the next stop.

"Bring out the head, Philip," she said, and he saw the llama and ostrich turn around. "Until you do, I don't want to see you again. I mean it. Either you bring out the head or else this is the last time."

And with these words she left him on the bus, which drove farther into Tourquai's ever-darker heart.

If Philip Mouse knew that the Route 3 bus to Parc Clemeaux went via oil black Boulevard de la Villette, he'd forgotten it that evening. He sat staring out through the window as if paralyzed in the vacuum Jasmine created by leaving. When he saw the dark silhouette of Bourg de la Villette towering up against the dramatic twilight sky a few minutes later, it was a surprise.

He decided immediately.

He had to remove the remaining evidence; anything else was impossible.

Nova Park might of course have changed all the codes after everything that had happened, but they might just as well have forgotten to do so for the same reason.

That was why Philip Mouse relived his Sunday night exactly one week later. Many times he had laughed at the assertion that a criminal always returns to the scene of the crime: Who could be so stupid?

Now he had the answer.

He went into Bourg de la Villette's massive lobby without hesitating, and raised his paw in greeting to the bored guard in reception. The guard hardly looked up from his book. After office hours the elevators, stairwells, and doors were locked and alarmed; only the authorized could make their way into the building.

Philip went up to the elevators and punched in the code. It worked. The doors glided apart and Philip stepped into the elegant, mirrored metal box.

The office was empty and dark, just as empty and dark as a week ago, and just like then Philip punched in the security code on the little box that sat hidden behind the computer in reception.

The black night sky outside generously reflected the illuminated city and, thanks to the large windows, he avoided turning on lights as he went down the corridor toward Cobra's and Vulture's offices.

Oswald Vulture's office had been locked last Sunday, but the lock was an ordinary one and for an experienced private detective with a set of skeleton keys it was no challenge. This evening the door was unlocked. When he opened it and looked over toward the desk, the image of the headless Vulture appeared in his memory. Confused, Philip took a few steps into the room and sat down on the armchair by the sofa, as far from the desk as possible.

What is freedom?

Is it moving through a room unhindered, in any direction you want, fast or slow? Or is it being able to think any thought whatsoever, high or low, without shame or fear? Is freedom being able to openly express your convictions, and then trying to influence others to think the same thing? Or is freedom having the possibility to choose, being able to say no to what you don't want?

But Mouse, who had been able to and still could do all this, did not think any of these words described what he defined as freedom.

During his entire life he had felt bound by external circumstances. Expectations and obligations. How this mental yoke had developed—and whether it was self-assumed—was the therapist's business to decide. Mouse experienced what he experienced. Often it felt as if he were behind a wall of compulsion, unable to make his way out to reality.

It was suffocating to carry the hope of being able to reach further, and achieve more, but never finding the way out of the labyrinth of life. Sometimes the frustration created an aggressive energy, which could be positive, but more often over the years he felt a disillusioned melancholy.

Freedom, thought Philip Mouse, would be to outwit the limitations fate had once given him. To break out of the social, intellectual, and emotional framework that the factory and his youth had defined.

Freedom, thought Mouse, was to surprise life by placing yourself above your fate.

What he felt was not regret. He could not feel regret. He had tried, but it wasn't possible.

Deep inside he had always known how Jasmine Squirrel lived. But with the years he had begun to doubt. He had established a charade that felt most comfortable. He stopped asking himself where the money came from. He made sure not to surprise her, never demanding details about who she met or what she had done; he pretended he was showing trust.

Why had he forced a confession from her last Sunday? Why hadn't he—like so many times before—simply let it go? Talked about something else?

He didn't know.

When she confessed, his anger mostly consisted of shame. Not disappointment, not judgment, only a glowing hatred that he chose to direct at Oswald Vulture, even if it might just as well have been directed inward, toward himself.

When he forced her to give him the codes to the elevator and office, he had not had a plan. He found himself in an almost hallucinatory state; all the years of insinuations and half-truths came rushing toward him, and he understood how easy it would have been to expose her secret earlier. If he had only wanted to.

When he stepped into Oswald Vulture's office late Sunday night, or rather early Monday morning, he still had no plan. En route from Squirrel to Bourg de la Villette, he had stopped at a number of late-night bars and drank himself into courage and confusion.

He had walked around in Vulture's large office, looked

through the contents of the bookshelves, investigated the globe, started the computer on the desk and turned it off again. Time had passed, faster than he thought, and suddenly he'd heard sounds outside the office. He felt panic—he'd almost forgotten why he was there—and he threw himself behind one of the curtains hanging from ceiling to floor.

There he remained standing while Oswald Vulture took possession of his office.

If nothing more had happened after that, maybe everything would be different today. But as Mouse stood sweating behind the curtain for half an hour and almost decided to swallow his pride and leave the vulture to a different fate, Emanuelle Cobra stepped into the room. The private detective didn't know who Cobra was, he had never met her and did not see her now, either. At a distance of a few feet, though, he heard a scene play out, a scene so perverse, so obscene, that the emotions from the night returned with full force.

He heard Cobra flatter and entice, moan and sigh, and he knew that this might just as well have been Jasmine.

That was when he saw the sword. Only a few inches away. That was how he got the idea.

After fifteen minutes Cobra and Vulture were interrupted by Leonard Earthworm.

Earthworm stepped into the office, and their meeting lasted about an hour. When the earthworm finally left and Philip Mouse was about to part the curtain to seize the knight's sword, a furious Oleg Earwig made an entrance. For forty minutes the inventor told off the incessantly patronizing and unmoved Vulture.

Mouse stood steadfastly behind his curtain and listened without hearing. The alcohol from the night left his body, he quivered, his head ached, and his anxiety increased. The sounds from the morning's perverse exercise echoed in his head, but it was his own, beloved squirrel he heard. He imagined her pleading for help, for rehabilitation, for a way out.

Philip Mouse does not remember what happened next. He has no memory of how he takes the sword, how he goes up behind Vulture and, in a single massive stroke, separates the head from the body.

When his memory functions again, he is sitting on the sofa where he now sits, with Vulture's head in his hands and a sudden, ice-cold clarity about what has happened, what he has done. He realizes that on the other side of the closed door, scarcely two yards away, is the secretary who just opened the door and showed the inventor the way out.

Mouse also realizes that the secretary might be on her way in at any moment with the next visitor.

The idea of getting rid of the head is instinctive. If he doesn't get rid of the head, all has been in vain. If he takes the head with him, the risk of being found out increases. Philip Mouse is a private detective, he's seen that sort of carelessness many times; it is suddenly clear that he has to get rid of the head as soon as possible.

It's like a nightmare, a trapdoor that opens under him and he is falling down into a black hole that seems to have no bottom. His body is starting to shake, he understands that he has to collect himself, but fails. He goes up to the desk, picks up the telephone receiver, and calls Jasmine. There is no intention behind this: he simply needs to hear her voice. When she talks to him, the effect is sobering. She gives him instructions, and he nods and understands.

Philip sneaks up to the door and peeks out through the keyhole in time to see the cobra outside pick up the phone, listen, and then get up and go. Mouse waits a minute or two and then leaves Vulture's office. He doesn't know whether anyone sees him on his way out to the street; he never raises his gaze from the ground.

He seems to be functioning again; logical thinking replaces the terror and confusion.

An alibi. This is what he's concentrating on. He has to give himself an alibi.

How the trains of association interlock with each other is impossible to understand, but Mouse is thinking about Samson Zebra, the old tailor.

Out on the sidewalk Mouse is moving at top speed, running through Tourquai's business district toward Zebra's studio. As he crosses blue rue de Montyon he sees the phone booth, and decides not to take any chances. He calls Bloodhound, twice, without getting the superintendent to act. Falcon Ècu on the other hand reacts as expected. By phoning in the tip, Mouse knows that the police will find the vulture at a time when he can document that he's been in a different place.

Zebra has his boutique around the corner from rue de Montyon, and as usual the old tailor is napping behind the counter. Mouse writes his name on the tailor's calendar and then goes into one of the fitting rooms. He takes off his trousers and coughs loudly. Zebra wakes up, excuses himself because it has taken so long, and asks what Philip wants. The detective sighs, maintains that they've been trying samples and fabrics for over an hour, and Zebra does not protest. It might very well be so. Mouse's alibi is thereby arranged.

Philip got up from the armchair. The office was in darkness, but he thought he heard something. A throat clearing? A chair against the floor? Was there someone outside in Cobra's office?

It was late in the evening, and no one ought to be here. Mouse held his breath. He had to destroy the evidence, he had to burn up the head.

Then he heard it again.

There was someone outside there.

He had to hurry.

EPILOGUE

What this city really needs is a thorough reorganization of the taxi business. I'm not talking about under-the-table money, cars that lack proper inspection, or the hygiene in the backseat. No, my proposal is that we jointly decide to send the taxi drivers off to some sort of school where they'll learn some good manners and common sense.

"Rat, stop here up at the corner, please?" I asked amiably.

"I'm a hamster," my taxi driver answered bitterly. "Not a damn rat."

As if a taxi driver can take that tone.

"Listen, for me you are and you will remain a little rat," I pointed out.

The customer is always right. It may take effort, it demands character, but it is a rule that leads to success. I know. Success is something I'm familiar with. I was so bold as to point this out to the taxi driver; it was like taking a tone-deaf animal to the Conservatory of Music.

"Little rat," I said, "if you ever want to get anywhere, and not spend the rest of your life sitting behind the wheel and driving in circles night after night after night, you might start with your attitude. The customer, you know, is always right."

"You're completely off your nut," the rat/hamster replied.

"I see," I pointed out nicely. "Yes, then perhaps you can explain why you're sitting in the front seat in a shabby flannel shirt and driving me around for peanuts, while I'm sitting here in the backseat in a tuxedo, wondering whether I should give you a tip or not?"

"We should have ridden with the gnu," my wife complained. "It's always like this when we take a taxi."

"Do you want to get sick?" I asked. "Well, maybe it doesn't matter to you, you don't have anywhere to go during the day. But I don't have time to lie in bed with a thermometer in my beak for a week. Kai has to get healthy before I get in the car with him."

"Hypochondriac," my wife hissed.

I chose not to hear this. Once again—character. In what other way could this miserable marriage have survived? But my wife's influential family has still not played out its role in my professional life, and therefore I'm going to put up with her damn whining for a few more years. I have character.

"All right, so stop already," I said sharply. "We're here!"

Circus Balthazar had put up its octagonal tent on one of the many fields in Bois de Dalida. This evening, for the great premiere, a forty-stuffed-animal-strong orchestra played outside the entry, searchlights big as wine casks drew patterns straight up against the black sky, and champagne was served on silver trays. Long gowns, real jewelry, white shirt fronts, and expectant giggling. The odor of cigars, butter-drizzled popcorn, and spun sugar. My wife and I walked along the circus wagons where the artists lived, and I nodded graciously at stuffed animals I encountered.

As usual I didn't recognize anyone, but everyone knew me.

That's the way it should be. Nova Park had been one of the first companies that dared invest in Circus Balthazar; I don't even need to point out how profitable that investment proved to be. These trapeze artists, clowns, and animal trainers were all in debt to me, and they knew it. The circus director himself was conspicuous in his absence, but I suspect he was running around inside the tent, preparing for the performance. He was an unusually nervous spider of a sort I couldn't name, and I never thought he had any style. He fits the circus, though.

We took our seats a moment later, and I managed to stay awake for at least twenty minutes. Seeing stuffed animals stumble in shoes that are too big or climb on each other's shoulders is not really what I understand as culture.

At the intermission I left my wife's side to go out and buy refreshments. In the long line to the wagon where wine and beer were sold—here the quantity was more important than the quality; personally I was looking for mineral water—I ran into Superintendent Larry Bloodhound. Unfortunately I discovered him too late and was forced to say hello.

"Superintendent," I nodded.

"Vulture! Up yours," the yokel exhorted me elatedly. "You look just like new!"

"I wish I could say the same," I replied, leading him to the side, away from the beer wagon and all the stuffed animals who stood there listening.

The police superintendent is one of the most slovenly stuffed animals I've ever met. He looks like a fat scarecrow, and could very easily have appeared together with the clowns inside.

"I guess it suits you to get the most out of living," he said.

That was so stupid an observation that I could not even comment on it. Beer foam was stuck in his whiskers.

"It's appropriate, I'd say," he continued, "that we should meet here."

"Perhaps that has something to do with the fact that you received an invitation to the premiere from me?" I pointed out.

"You know what I mean," he said.

I knew it. He had told the story twice, and I had not been impressed even the first time. The alarm had gone off at Nova Park late on Sunday evening. Someone had used the old security code, just as Bloodhound had thought. The police had arrived on the scene in a few minutes and caught the pitiful private detective inside my office. But my head was still missing. It was Bloodhound who found it on Monday morning. And that was thanks to the posters that Circus Balthazar had put up all over the city. The clown that walked on his hands. With his feet up in the air and his head down toward the ground. Bloodhound boasted about his flash of insight. When he saw the clown on the poster, he remembered the globe that was on the bookshelf in my office. The globe was upside down, with Mollisan Town on the upper half and the forest on the lower. Bloodhound had rushed up to Nova Park and found my head in the globe, which the private detective in his confusion had put together incorrectly. That was, of course, why the pitiful mouse had returned on Sunday evening, to finally get rid of the head. But he ran out of time.

"Truly grand of you not to press charges," said Bloodhound.

Was he being impudent?

"Time is money," I answered. "And there's no money in sitting in court, listening to tiresome pleadings. The pitiful mouse will have to live with what he's done."

"That's big of you," said Bloodhound.

But I thought I saw a grimace on his lips, a hint of a smile. Was the fat bloodhound having a laugh at my expense?

"I've never been much for looking back," I replied. "Excuse me, you're spilling—"

Without thinking about it, Bloodhound had turned the mug, and beer was running over his pants. It was not only unpleasant, it was pitiful, to put it bluntly.

"Crapola," he answered, but didn't seem to care about it.

I did not file charges against the mouse because Jasmine asked me not to. I am a gentleman. If a beautiful female asks me for something, it's a matter of honor to fulfill her wish.

I had nothing more to say to the police officer.

"Well, then, perhaps it's time to return to the tent?"

The superintendent nodded. I made sure to take a different way; he reeked of beer.

I was sitting in my seat again well before the intermission was over. My wife asked about the mineral water, but I had forgotten it.

"Oswald," she said, "I think you've become more absent-minded after that incident with your head."

That was nonsense, of course; everything was exactly as before, but I nodded compliantly. The lights were dimmed, the orchestra began to play, and it was time for another hour of ridiculous acrobat numbers and droll stumbling.